FIERCE

CreateSpace ISBN: 14-8116-471-6

www.bluespikepublishing.com

Printed in the United States of America

To My Old Men—
Literal, Figurative & Matrimonial

OTHER BOOKS FROM DAVID LENNON

The Quarter Boys

Echoes

Second Chance

Blue's Bayou

Reckoning

Author's Notes

As I've mentioned before, I never planned to write a series. It was only a few weeks after I finished *The Quarter Boys* that it occurred to me I could build a series around some of the characters. Of course, I wasn't sure I had even a second book in me at that point, but as I mulled the possibility, I decided it would have to be a limited series. I didn't want to risk getting to a point where I was just carting out the same characters year after year, sticking them in increasingly uninspired mysteries. I liked the idea of a short series of discrete mysteries, linked together by a larger story arc.

The original plan was to end the series with the fifth book, and even as I worked on *Reckoning*, I thought it would be the end. And after he read it, Brian agreed it was a good place to stop...until the next morning. Then, as I sat sipping my coffee and enjoying my first morning without writing in a very long time, he walked out to the patio and said, "I think you need to write one more. You left things in a really ambiguous place."

After I stopped pouting, I began to consider it. I already had another plot I'd been kicking around for a few months (because you never know when you might need one), so it was just a question of how to extend the overall arc without it feeling contrived. I hope I've managed it. Whether I have or not, *Fierce* is the end of the journey. Absolutely. Positively. Probably.

I'm grateful to all of the readers who embraced Michel, Sassy, Joel, Chance, etc...even if a few were very vocal in their disagreement with some of my choices (you know who you are). Thanks to the folks at Lambda Literary Foundation for shining a light on my work, and for the nifty crystal book. Thanks to Amos Lassen for your kind reviews and support. No thanks to *Bay Windows* and *The Newton Tab*.

They say it takes a village to raise a child. I've learned it takes almost as many to proofread my work. Thanks to my "village"—Bob Mitchell, Esme McTighe, and Vion DeCew—for your friendship, support, and keen eyes.

Thanks to my friends Ernie Gaudreau, Ed Makuta, Drewey Wayne Gunn, Kim and Ken Dixon, Leslie Ellis, Paul Saltzman, Michelle McCarthy, Caron LeBrun, Pauline Dowell, Joel Fortner, and Randy Stephens for your thoughtful comments and enthusiastic cheerleading, and to my family—blood, step, faux, in-laws and outlaws—for your encouragement and for making sure I sell at least ten copies of each book.

And, of course, my love and gratitude to Brian and Blue for putting up with me when I'm playing with the imaginary friends in my head, and for giving me a wonderful life to return to when I'm done. Being able to share this adventure with you has made the sometimes painful work worthwhile.

D.L.

FIERCE

A Novel

DAVID LENNON

Prologue

September 1996

The boy was still except for his thumbs, which bounced around the controller like a pair of hyperactive toddlers on sugar highs. The only sounds in the room were the hard tapping of the buttons, and the muted cries of the two warriors on the TV screen.

A sudden motion to his left caught the boy's eye, and he looked down for a split second. The white kitten gave a feeble, high-pitched meow. The boy looked back at the screen and kept playing. The kitten continued staring at him for a moment, then walked to the foot of the bed and lay down.

The boy executed a series of roundhouse kicks on screen, then moved in for the kill. As his opponent swayed back and forth, the boy quickly punched in an eleven-button sequence, his heart racing with excitement. His opponent exploded, leaving behind only a pile of bloody bones.

"Yes!" the boy shouted, jerking up into a sitting position.

Suddenly he felt tiny needles in his left foot, and looked down. The kitten had wrapped herself around his sock and was trying to gnaw at his big toe.

"Leave me alone, you little shit," the boy said.

He swept his leg sideways over the edge of the bed and shook his foot. The kitten dropped to the floor. She looked around in a daze for a moment, then scrambled clumsily out of the room.

The boy rested the controller in his lap and looked at the clock. It was nearly 5 PM. His parents would be home soon. He grabbed a chocolate chip cookie from the plate on the nightstand and took a bite, then washed it down with some milk. Out of the corner of his eye, he saw the kitten peering at him around the door frame.

He finished the cookie, put the half-empty glass beside the plate, and lay down. The TV screen was prompting him to start a new game, but he ignored it. Instead he grabbed the bed spread with his left half and lifted it a few inches. He shook it back and forth. The kitten immediately slipped into the room and dropped into a crouch. She began slowly moving forward as she stalked the dancing fabric.

The boy waited until he felt the kitten tugging on the spread, then ripped it upward. The kitten tumbled halfway across the room, and ran toward the door. The boy let out a squeal of laughter, and began to bounce the spread again. The kitten stopped and turned back. She watched curiously for a moment, then crouched again.

The boy closed his eyes and tried to visualize the kitten's approach. He held his breath, and was sure he could hear velvet footsteps. He shook the spread more vigorously, feeling the excitement building inside him again.

Then suddenly he sat up and swung his legs over the side of the bed. He brought his feet down hard, and heard a satisfying cry of pain. He leaned forward and lifted his feet.

"I think you're dying, kitty," he said, as he watched the kitten's body spasm.

He got down on his knees to watch more closely, and considered crushing the animal's skull, but knew that would be too hard to explain. Instead he lifted the tiny body and placed it on his pillow. He watched it for a few minutes, waiting for it to stop convulsing, and for its spirit to rise into the air.

Finally it stopped breathing and he placed it on the floor. He sat back on the bed and finished his milk.

*****

October 2007

"Did you ever have nightmares when you were a kid?"

"Sure."

"About what?"

"Being ordinary."

A laugh in response.

"I'm serious, but I don't have to worry about that anymore."

"Why not?"

"Because I did something amazing."

"What?"

"I killed someone."

"Yeah, right."

"I wouldn't joke about something like that."

A nervous pause, then, "Why did you do it?"

"To see what it was like."

"And?"

"It made me feel poweful."

A much longer silence.

"So what did *you* have nightmares about as a kid?"

"Dying. I still do."

"I can help you get rid of them."

"How?"

"By teaching you to control death."

Chapter 1

June 2008

Michel Doucette opened the front door and flipped on the hall light. He hadn't planned on being out so late, but he'd started chatting with a cute redhead, and before he knew it, one drink had led to three, and it was dark. As usual, Blue was standing at the end of the hallway, waiting. After a moment's hesitation to be sure it was him, she skittered forward excitedly.

"Hey, girl," Michel said. "Did you miss me?"

Blue bowed her head, ears back but tail bouncing. It was the same each time he came home. First caution, then excitement, then shyness, as though she needed assurance he still loved her. He rubbed her neck and kissed the top of her head.

"I'm sorry I left you alone for so long," he said.

Blue gave him a quick nibble on the nose. Michel turned to the redhead standing just inside the door.

"Blue, this is..." he scrunched his face with embarrassment.

"Harlan," the redhead responded.

Of course you are, Michel thought with a mental eye roll.

"This is Harlan," he said, "and this is Blue."

Harlan squatted down, and Blue walked cautiously toward him. When she was two feet away, she stopped. Harlan held out his right hand, and Blue sniffed his fingers. She quickly backed away. Michel sighed silently.

"I'm sorry," he said, standing up, "but this isn't going to work out. I can call you a cab, if you want."

Harlan stood slowly, disbelief on his face.

"Are you serious?"

"Yeah," Michel replied flatly.

Harlan began to smirk. He suddenly looked much older and a lot less cute.

"A friend of mine told me you brought him home, then kicked him out because your dog didn't like him," he said, his tone ripe with ridicule. "I figured that was just an excuse when you saw what he looked like with the lights on, but I guess not."

He stared at Michel as though expecting a response. Michel just shrugged.

"And what if I don't want to leave?" Harlan asked.

Michel wasn't sure if it was meant to be playful or a threat. He decided it didn't matter. He wanted Harlan gone. He squared his body to the door and looked down at the floor for a long moment. In the past, he'd often felt his attempts at intimidation had been unconvincing, even silly. Since his boyfriend Joel had been murdered two years earlier, however, that hadn't been a problem. Now, even when he tried to be friendly, people sometimes reacted as though there were something unsettling about him. Apparently whatever small charm he might once have possessed had curdled.

He lifted his eyes and fixed Harlan with a cold stare.

"Do you really think that's an option?" he asked.

Though he'd kept his tone neutral, Harlan's head still jerked back involuntarily.

"Fuck you, freak," he stammered, then turned and hurried out the door.

"That went well," Michel said, watching him fade into the darkness. He knelt and hugged Blue's neck. "You know, one of these days you're going to have to let Daddy get some."

Blue rested her head on his right knee and looked up at him with her soft brown eyes. Michel let out a resigned sigh.

"Or not," he said.

Chapter 2

"So how can I help you?" Michel asked, studying the well-groomed couple on the other side of his desk. He'd been intrigued when he'd received the call from the Taylors' assistant, particularly by the prospect of meeting Patricia "Trish" Campbell Rhodes Taylor.

Trish Taylor—then Trish Rhodes—had entered the national spotlight during her first husband's run for the 1996 Republican Presidential nomination. Smart, outspoken, and sometimes outrageous, she'd provided some of the campaign's most memorable sound bites. As the campaign had gone on, however, she'd begun to lash out at the media with increasing ferocity, and rumors had swirled that she was drinking heavily and addicted to prescription pain killers. Finally, six weeks before the convention, she'd checked herself into rehab.

When she'd re-emerged, she'd been serene and gracious, and her husband, Steven, a senator from New York, had swept to the nomination. When he'd died of a stroke a month before the election, Trish had ascended to that most sainted of public positions, the grieving political widow.

She'd used her new position to advocate on behalf of several worthy causes, but had stayed away from politics, despite rumored entreaties from both parties to endorse candidates or run for office herself. In 2000, she'd quietly married Scott Taylor, and essentially retired from public life.

Scott Taylor had been considered a legitimate Heisman Trophy candidate during his senior year, playing quarterback at

Harvard. Rather than enter the NFL draft, however, he'd gone on to get an MBA, then into a successful career in investment banking. Though he'd never shown any apparent political ambitions before, in the past few months he'd inexplicably emerged as a front-runner for the U.S. Senate after the death of a beloved Massachusetts Democrat who'd held the seat for five terms. Michel had seen Scott Taylor on television a few times, and had considered him to be a well-coached suit with better-than-average hair and no discernible ideas of his own.

Both Taylors appeared to be in their late forties, though Michel knew that Trish was at least ten years her husband's senior. Aside from the telltale "turkey neck" below her taut jawline, however, she could easily pass for his contemporary. Her cosmetic surgery had been excellent, and she now looked better than she had during her first husband's campaign twelve years earlier.

"Our son, Campbell, is missing," Scott Taylor replied gravely.

"Missing, as in you think he may have been kidnapped, or as in you think he's run away?" Michel replied.

The Taylors exchanged concerned looks for a moment.

"We're not sure," Scott Taylor said with a weary sigh. "That's what we're hoping you can find out."

It was a stock response right out of a bad movie, and the delivery had been unnaturally stiff, as though he were reading from a teleprompter. Michel immediately sensed that something wasn't right, but decided to play along for the moment. He sat forward, crossing his forearms on the edge of his desk, and furrowed his eyebrows.

"How long has he been missing?" he asked.

"For three weeks," Trish Taylor replied, echoing her husband's earlier sigh, but adding a not-very-subtle note of despair for dramatic effect.

"And you think he's somewhere in New Orleans?"

The Taylors nodded simultaneously.

7

"He was a student at Tulane," Scott Taylor replied.

"Was?"

"He dropped out a month ago," Trish replied.

"And I take it that wasn't something he discussed with you in advance?" Michel asked.

"We didn't find out until we received a letter from the school," Scott Taylor replied. "We called his apartment and his roommate said he'd moved out a few days earlier. We've left dozens of messages on his cell phone, but he hasn't returned any of them."

Michel was amused by the way the Taylors were alternating responses in a clumsy imitation of natural conversation.

"And when was the last time you spoke to him?" he asked.

For the first time, there was a break in the rhythm. It was obviously Trish Taylor's turn to speak, but she hesitated for a moment. Michel thought he saw uncertainty in her eyes.

"The beginning of March," she replied finally.

Michel ticked off the time in his head.

"So roughly 12 weeks?" he asked.

Trish nodded.

"Is that unusual?" Michel asked, keeping his eyes locked on her.

Trish held his gaze without flinching.

"No, it's not unusual," she replied.

Michel sat back in his chair.

"And how would you characterize your last conversation?"

The Taylors exchanged another quick glance.

"Tense," Trish replied, looking back at Michel.

"In what sense?"

"We'd gotten a letter from the dean of students telling us Cam was failing three of his classes," Scott Taylor replied, "and we'd gotten the bill for his credit card. He'd been taking large cash draws."

"And you confronted him about that?"

Taylor nodded.

"Did he have an explanation for the money?" Michel asked.

"He said it was for an art project," Taylor replied, without conviction.

Michel nodded deliberately, then frowned.

"So he was failing school, taking out a lot of cash on his credit card, and now he's dropped out and disappeared somewhere in New Orleans?" he summarized.

The Taylors nodded in seemingly rehearsed unison again. Michel pretended to give the situation careful consideration for a moment, then shrugged casually.

"I have to say, I'm not hearing anything that sounds like a cause for concern," he said.

Trish Taylor's eyes widened.

"You don't think the fact that he's been missing for three weeks is a cause for concern?" she replied indignantly.

Michel shook his head.

"No, and obviously you don't either, or you'd be talking to the police," he said, "and you wouldn't have waited so long. So why don't you tell me what this is really about?"

Trish Taylor glared at him coldly for a moment, then her eyes softened and she let out a smoky chuckle. It was the laugh Michel remembered from her many television appearances. It was rich and earthy.

"You're quite clever, aren't you?" she said.

"Not particularly," Michel replied, with a thin smile, "but I've been around the block enough times to know when someone's blowing smoke up my ass."

Trish studied him for a moment, then nodded.

"We think that Cam is hiding," she said.

"From?"

"Us."

Michel raised his eyebrows. He wasn't sure what he'd been expecting, but it certainly hadn't been that.

"Why didn't you just tell me that in the first place?" he asked. "Why the charade?"

"Because it's embarrasing to admit that your own child is hiding from you," Trish replied, looking down.

Michel suspected it was the first completely honest response she'd given him. He offered a sympathetic smile.

"I can understand that. So why do you want to find him?"

Trish blinked in confusion for a moment.

"Because he's my son, of course," she replied.

Michel noticed her tone was oddly dispassionate.

"Yes, but it seems that he doesn't want to be found," he said.

"That's not really your concern," Trish replied with sudden sharpness.

"I'm afraid it is," Michel replied, refusing to back down. "Your son is over 18. He's an adult. If he doesn't want to see you, he has that right."

"And we have a right to look for him," Trish replied.

Michel cut a quick look at Scott Taylor, whose blank expression made it clear his role was complete. Michel looked back at Trish.

"That's true," he said, "but if you want me to do the leg work, you're going to have to give me a reason."

Trish's intense green eyes tried to burn a hole through Michel's face, but he didn't react. Finally she blinked, and looked down at the small black purse in her lap. Michel guessed that she was stalling while she assessed her options.

"Do you mind if I smoke?" she asked abruptly.

Before Michel could reply, she had a Marlboro 100 clenched between her teeth and was lighting it with a thin silver lighter. She took a long drag and held it for a moment. As she exhaled, her body visibly relaxed.

"That's better," she said. "It's the only vice I have left."

Michel gave an automatic smile.

"So why is it so important to find your son?" he asked.

"Because that's what he wants," Trish replied bluntly. She blew a thick plume of smoke at the ceiling. "That's what he *always* wants."

"He's done this before?" Michel asked.

Trish shook her head. "Never *this*, but things *like* this, and every time, it's for the same reason. To provoke a reaction from me. And if he doesn't get the reaction he wants, then he'll just do something more extreme. Unfortunately, Mr. Doucette, my son is a drama queen."

"Excuse me?" Michel replied with a laugh, certain he'd misheard her.

"He's a drama queen," Trish repeated.

Scott Taylor shifted uncomfortably in his chair.

"Do you know what happened when he came out to us?" Trish asked. "We hugged him, and told him we loved him."

Michel nodded slowly, wondering where she was headed.

"But apparently that wasn't the reaction he wanted," Trish continued. "Apparently he'd been hoping for anger and screaming and tears, so a few days later, when we got home from playing golf, we found him getting gangbanged by a half-dozen Mexican landscapers down by the pool."

Michel studied her for a moment, trying to decide whether she was exaggerating. He decided she wasn't.

"So you think he wants you to look for him, and if you don't, he'll up the ante?" he asked.

Trish nodded.

"And do you think the timing has anything to do with his father's Senate campaign?" Michel asked.

"Stepfather," Trish said in a tone that made it clear she wanted to distance her husband from her son's actions, "and yes, probably. Cam's always had a knack for knowing the absolute worst time to manufacture a crisis."

Michel was surprised by her damning assessment.

"Do you think he's trying to sabotage it?" he asked.

Trish leaned back and ran fingers through her long auburn hair, pulling it back from her face. Michel realized she had a very masculine energy. It was something she'd clearly learned to temper in front of the cameras. It was also clear she was stalling.

"That would require planning," she replied finally, with a too-casual laugh. "Cam is bright, but forethought has never been one of his great strengths. He reacts in the moment."

Michel noticed that she'd avoided a direct yes-or-no answer. He also noticed she'd contradicted herself given the obvious planning behind Cam Rhodes's poolside gangbang.

"So what's he reacting to now?" he asked.

An involuntary blink told him Trish hadn't been expecting the question. She took a long, meditative drag on her cigarette.

"I imagine he's probably feeling neglected because of the time Scott and I have been spending on the campaign," she replied after a moment.

Michel tried to keep the surprise from his face. Though it sounded reasonable, again it didn't fit with what she'd already told him. It was clear she was improvising now, and not very well. He decided to push for an unfiltered reaction.

"But you just said it wasn't unusual to go months without speaking to him," he said, "so why would he suddenly feel neglected *now*?"

Though he'd expected anger, the whiplash change in Trish Taylor's demeanor still startled him.

"This is a simple *fucking* job," she spat, her eyes glittering furiously. "I don't need some half-assed family therapist. All I need is someone to find my son before he does something stupid, and to do it discreetly. If you can't handle that, then I'll find someone else who can. Is that clear?"

Perfectly, Michel thought. You want your drama queen son under your thumb where he can't cause any embarrassment for your husband's campaign. He suddenly wanted to find Cam Rhodes, if only to tell him to stay away from his mother.

"That won't be necessary," was all he said, "but you haven't given me much to go on."

The anger in Trish's eyes diminished only slightly. She reached into her purse and pulled out an envelope, tossing it on the desk directly in front of Michel.

"There's a picture of Cam in there, and his former roommate's phone number," she said. "There's also a check for $2,500. I believe that's your retainer fee."

Michel didn't bother picking the envelope up.

"How do I reach you if I find anything?" he asked.

"You have our assistant's number," Trish replied curtly.

Michel looked at her curiously.

"You don't want me to call you at your hotel?" he asked.

"We won't be staying," Trish replied with a look of distaste. "We just came down for a dinner party. We'll be going back to Boston in the morning."

Wow, and I thought my mother was cold, Michel thought.

Chapter 3

Michel walked up the narrow staircase to the empty apartment above the office, and opened the door. Blue was waiting just inside, her tail wagging vigorously. Michel leaned down and let her take a quick nibble on his nose.

"Sorry about that," he said. "There was only room in the office for one bitch at a time, and Mrs. Taylor has much sharper teeth than you do."

He kissed the top of Blue's head and rubbed her neck for a moment, then stepped to the side. She shot past him and scampered down the stairs. "I'll be down in a second," he called to her tail as it disappeared into the office.

He walked into the apartment and quickly scanned the floor for any accidents. In the two-plus years he'd had Blue, it had happened only a few times, in the weeks immediately following Joel's death, but it had still become habit to check whenever he left her alone. The only wetness he could see were a dozen or so drops of varying size and shape spattered around her water bowl. He pulled a paper towel from the roll on the kitchen counter and wiped them up. The bottom of the paper towel came up a medium gray.

"Definitely time to vacuum," he muttered, then frowned, realizing there was no reason.

When they'd first opened the office, Michel and his partner, Alexandra "Sassy" Jones, had planned to use the second floor for storage and a conference room. But a few weeks later, Joel's best friend, Chance, had bought the building and converted the space into an apartment for himself. Now Chance was attending Loyola University New Orleans and living closer to campus, and the apartment had been empty for the last year and a half. It had become a tangible reminder for Michel of how much his life had changed since Joel's death. Though it was something he tried not to dwell on, occasionally self-pity crept up on him.

He took a deep breath and shook his head to clear it, then took another quick look around, absently registering the rain-streaked film of dirt on the windows. He picked up Blue's water bowl and walked out.

*****

Blue was standing in the middle of the office, furiously sniffing the air. She stopped and looked at Michel. He was certain he could see reproach in her eyes.

"It wasn't me," he said defensively. "It was Mrs. Taylor."

He crossed to the desk and picked up the butt of the cigarette Trish Taylor had unceremoniously ground out on the scarred oak top.

"See." He held it out. "Not my shade of lipstick."

Blue tilted her head and stared at him for a moment, then seemed to lose interest and walked to her usual spot by the window. She turned in a tight circle a few times before settling down with a groan.

Michel walked around to the other side of the desk, and dropped the butt into the wastebasket. He settled into his chair and opened the envelope Trish Taylor had given him. Inside were a folded piece of paper and a four-by-six photograph.

"Striking," he said, looking at the photo.

It was a moody black-and-white head shot. Cam Rhodes's face was tilted down and to the right, but his heavily-mascaraed eyes stared intensely into the camera. Though his expression was neutral, his lips were pushed out into a seductive pout. It was the sort of shot a model would have had in his portfolio in the late eighties, but which now seemed either dated or intentionally ironic. Michel guessed it was the former.

He studied the face, trying to imagine it without the makeup and exaggerated lips. Rhodes had his mother's eyes and nose, but his face was narrower, and his chin softer. If anything, he actually appeared more feminine than Trish Taylor.

Michel laid the photo on the desk and covered the right half with his right hand. The expression on Rhodes's face remained the same. He switched hands and covered the left side. Rhodes suddenly appeared sad. It was unmistakable in his eyes, and the down-turned corner of his mouth.

Michel frowned and flipped the photo over. It was dated June 25, 2005, almost three years earlier.

"Gee, Trish, you didn't have anything more recent and a bit less stylized?" he wondered aloud.

He put the photo to the side and unfolded the sheet of paper. The retainer check was nestled in the middle, and the name Skylar Ellis and a local phone number had been handwritten across the top.

"Skylar Ellis?" Michel said to himself, grimacing. "Sounds like a douche bag."

He checked his watch, then picked up the phone and dialed the number. An answering machine came on after the third ring.

"Hey, this is Sky. You know what to do." The voice was singsongy, and annoyingly cheerful.

"Hi, *Sky*, my name is Michel Doucette," Michel said. "I'm a private investigator, and I've been hired to look for Campbell Rhodes. Please give me a call."

He left his number, then hung up. Before he could pull his hand back, the phone rang and he gave a small start.

"Jones and Doucette Investigations," he answered curiously, wondering if Ellis had been monitoring his calls.

"So what are you going to do about Sassy?" a familiar voice started in immediately.

Michel hesitated for a moment, trying to get his bearings. "Pearl?" he asked finally.

"Of course it's Pearl," Pearl Cousins replied. "Who else would be calling you up and harassing you about Sassy without even saying hello?"

Michel smiled. He'd met Sassy's cousin a few years earlier while investigating a murder involving his cousin, Verle. They'd bonded instantly, and had stayed in touch since.

"So what are you going to do about Sassy?" Pearl repeated.

"What do you mean?" Michel asked.

"I just called the house and Russ said she was sleeping," Pearl replied impatiently. "It's 11 o'clock on a Monday morning. She should *not* still be in bed."

"Pearl, she just finished her treatments last week," Michel replied. "She's probably..."

"Michel, don't be telling me about any treatments," Pearl cut him off. "I've been there, done that, and got the pretty pink ribbon to prove it."

"I'm sorry," Michel replied awkwardly. "I didn't know."

"And there's no reason why you should have," Pearl replied. "It wasn't the defining event in my life."

Michel smiled appreciatively, certain that was true.

"And you know what I did a week after I had my mastectomy?" Pearl continued. "I went back to work. And that's what Sassy needs to do. She needs to get back to work and start living her life again."

The final words had a declarative emphasis that suggested she was done with her speech.

"But she's been more or less retired since she married Russ," Michel replied.

"And that's another thing I don't understand," Pearl began again immediately. "You're the one with all the money. If anyone should be retired, it's you. Why's she spending so much time at home? If anything's going to kill the romance, it's spending too much time together, and once the romance is gone, the marriage will follow. Believe me, I know. She needs to get out of the house."

"Okay," Michel replied, "but why are you putting this on me? You're her cousin, and Russ is her husband."

"And you're her best friend," Pearl replied. "I can't do it because I'm not there, and as good a man as Russ is, he and Sassy have only known one another for a few years. He doesn't know her the way you do. Besides, you're also her business partner. *Make* her go back to work."

Michel wasn't sure what to say. Four months earlier he would have thought Pearl was right, that he was the man for the job, despite the fact that he and Sassy weren't as close as they'd once been. Since she'd been diagnosed with cervical cancer, though, Sassy had shut him out of her life almost completely.

"Look, she's been pushing me away, too," Pearl said, seemingly reading the reason for his silence. "She barely returns my calls. She won't let me come visit. I was willing to put up with it while she was getting the treatments, but now that they're done, she needs to be dragged back into the world, even if she's kicking and screaming the whole way."

"You're right," Michel replied, sighing with resignation, "but what am I supposed to say? 'Gee, I know you feel like crap, but let's go to lunch or solve a mystery'?"

"If that's what it takes," Pearl replied, "though you might try something that makes you sound a little less simple first."

Michel let out a small, dry laugh. "Thanks."

"Look, Michel," Pearl said, her tone more serious, "I know you think Sassy's tough, and you're right. She's dealt with a lot in her life, but I guarantee you that right now she's scared. All the we-caught-it-earlies and the-prognosis-is-goods don't mean a thing when you're the one with the cancer. But sitting at home isn't going to make it any less scary. If anything, it's going to make it worse, because it's all she's going to think about. You need to keep her busy, remind her that there's more to her life than the damn cancer."

18

Michel suddenly flashed on his mother. Though she'd never been prone to share her feelings, in the months before she died, she'd been even more reticent than usual. Michel felt a sharp pang of guilt, wondering whether she'd had anything or anyone to take her mind off the fact that she was dying.

"And remember, Sassy's not just dealing with the cancer," Pearl continued. "She's also dealing with the hysterectomy."

Still lost in his own thoughts, it took Michel a moment to register what she'd said.

"But she's already gone through menopause," he said finally.

Pearl unleashed a dramatically exasperated sigh.

"And if your equipment stopped working, would you mind if they just cut it off?"

Michel's whole body shuddered involuntarily.

"I can't believe you even said that," he replied.

"Then don't expect Sassy to be giving up her uterus like it's an old pair of shoes for the Goodwill," Pearl replied.

"Sorry," Michel replied quickly. "That was pretty stupid."

"Yes, it was," Pearl agreed. "So you're going to go see her?"

Michel imagined her staring him down expectantly, and smiled. The truth was that he wanted to see Sassy, and even if she refused to take the bait, telling her about the Rhodes case would give him an excuse. And if she did agree to help, it might be a chance for a fresh start in their relationship.

"Yes, ma'am," he said obediently. "I'll see what I can do."

*****

He walked outside and lit a cigarette. He was excited by the prospect of seeing Sassy, but also nervous. He and Sassy had been part of one another's lives since he'd gotten his detective's shield with the New Orleans Police Department eight years earlier, and for most of that time they'd been both partners and best friends. Other than Joel during the months before he was killed, there was no one with whom he'd ever been closer.

But even before Sassy got sick, their relationship had changed, though he was never able to pinpoint exactly how or when it started. It was almost as if he'd just woken up one day to find things different. Logically he knew that couldn't have been the case, that he must have missed the incremental shifts, but that was how it had felt.

Looking back, he knew that part of it was simply that they'd stopped sharing the same daily experiences, but a larger part was that he'd suddenly stopped feeling like part of Sassy's family. Though she'd still called almost daily and regularly invited him over for dinner—even after her marriage to Russ Turner—the connection they'd shared for so many years had faded. He knew that Sassy still loved and cared about him, but his position in her life had been usurped.

He shook his head and let out a bitter laugh.

"You're pathetic," he said aloud.

Regardless of what had happened to their relationship, he knew that Sassy needed him now. He also knew that if the situation had been reversed, she wouldn't have allowed him to push her away.

He dropped the cigarette and crushed it out, then pulled his cell phone from his jacket pocket and hit speed dial.

"Hey, Russ, it's me. Listen, I was thinking about stopping by in a little while."

Chapter 4

"So how's the patient?" Michel asked.

"On a scale of one to ten," Russ Turner whispered, "I'd say somewhere around a complete pain in my ass."

"So back to normal," Michel whispered back, with a conspiratorial smile.

"I heard that," a voice called from the back of the house. "I heard *both* of you."

Michel gave Turner a faux-frightened look, and Turner rolled his eyes in response.

"I swear to God the chemo gave her supersonic hearing or something," he said. "I can't even sneak a cookie without her knowing it."

"I heard that, too," Sassy yelled, "and you're not supposed to be eating cookies with your cholesterol levels."

Turner chuckled softly and shook his head.

"So are you going to come back here and see me, or just stand in the hallway flapping your gums all day?" Sassy yelled.

Turner made a sweeping gesture down the hall.

"After you."

*****

The last time Michel had seen her, just before her hysterectomy, the only telltale sign that Sassy was sick had been a slight bloating from a cycle of chemotherapy. The woman staring at him now could almost have been a stranger.

Michel guessed that she had lost at least twenty pounds. Though she was still far from waifish, her collarbones were clearly visible through her plum silk robe, and the cords along the sides of her neck stood out in bold relief, making her appear frail and vulnerable. Her once-firm skin had sagged into small jowls along her jawline, and what little was left of her hair was gray and matted. Only her eyes were completely unchanged, and Michel could see them studying him closely, watching for a reaction.

"What? You couldn't be bothered to comb your hair for me?" he asked.

Turner gasped audibly beside him, but Sassy just stared back placidly for a few seconds, then a slight smile curled the right corner of her lips.

"I *did* comb it," she replied. "I even braided it. You can see for yourself. It's over there in the wastebasket."

Michel smiled.

"You look like shit," he said.

"I could say the same," Sassy replied, making a show of looking him up and down. "Obviously you're still on the Jack-and-cigarettes diet."

"I haven't quite hit my goal weight yet," Michel replied with a casual shrug.

Sassy gave him a disapproving look, then shook her head.

"Get over here and give my old bones a hug," she said.

Michel walked to the bed and wrapped his arms around her. He was immediately aware of how much less space she occupied. He kissed her on the cheek, and felt her kiss him in return, then straightened up as her arms loosened around him.

"Obviously weight loss hasn't been a problem for you," he said. "I thought people on chemo gained weight."

"Some do, some don't," Sassy replied breezily, though her expression said the subject was closed.

"So how are you feeling?" Michel asked.

"Okay," Sassy replied flatly.

Again her expression made it clear it was something she didn't want to discuss. Michel struggled with what to say next.

"So what the hell do you want?" Sassy asked, breaking the momentary silence.

Though the question was blunt, her tone was more playful than accusatory.

"I can't just come by for a visit?" Michel replied.

Sassy lowered her head and stared at him over the top of her reading glasses.

"Uninvited? No."

"If I waited for an invitation, I'd still..." Michel started, then stopped as he saw a range of feelings flicker across Sassy's face. He knew at some point they'd have to discuss what had been happening in their relationship, but now wasn't the time.

"You still haven't answered my question," Sassy said, apparently deciding to throw him a lifeline.

"I need you to come back to work," Michel replied.

"What?" Sassy arched nonexistent eyebrows.

"You heard me," Michel replied.

"Yeah, I heard you," Sassy replied. "I just can't believe I heard you right."

"Why not?" Michel asked.

"Because I just finished getting blasted with radiation and pumped full of toxic chemicals last week."

"Right, you're finished," Michel replied. "So now what? Sit around watching your hair grow back?"

Michel could see her calculating a response, and wondered what tack she'd take to put him off. Her eyes suddenly narrowed with mock suspicion.

"Is this one of those Make-A-Wish things?" she asked. "Like, 'Surprise, little Sassy, you get a chance to play detective one more time before you die!' Because I don't remember making that wish."

"You're not dying," Michel replied flatly, refusing to play along. "It was stage 1."

"Stage 1 *B*, and we don't know that yet," Sassy replied with sudden seriousness.

"*I* know it," Michel replied, "but what are you going to do? Lie in bed for the next four months until the doctors give you a clean bill of health? Hate to tell you, but that's going to keep happening on every six months for the next five years. That's a long time to wait before you start living again."

Sassy's expression remained neutral, but Michel could see a sudden intensity in her eyes. She looked at Russ Turner.

"Would you mind giving us a few minutes, honey?" she asked softly but forcefully.

Turner looked back uncertainly for a moment, then nodded. "I'll be in the kitchen if you need anything."

"You've been talking to Pearl," Sassy said as soon as the door was closed. She didn't bother waiting for Michel to confirm it. "Look, I appreciate it, but she doesn't always know what's best. I'm not ready to go back to work yet."

"Why not?" Michel asked.

Sassy looked down at her hands for a moment, then patted the bed beside her. Michel sat and she took his left hand.

"Because I feel like hell," she said.

"And you're not going to feel any better whether you're here or working," Michel replied. "At least if you're working you'll have something to take your mind off it. And by the time we finish the case, you'll be feeling better, and then you can go back to nagging Russ at full strength."

Sassy gave a thin smile, but shook her head.

"The timing's not right," she said. "I've put Russ through hell the past few months. It's time for me to start pulling my own weight and taking care of him."

"By lying in bed all day while he waits on you?" Michel replied. He immediately felt Sassy's grip tighten, and saw the warning in her eyes.

"You've got one foot on the line right now, and you're about to cross over it," she said.

"I'm sorry," Michel replied. "It's just that..."

"I know," Sassy cut him off. "You're worried about me, and like I said, I appreciate it, but I'm not ready, and you're just going to have to respect that."

Michel studied her eyes, looking for any hint of wavering.

"Don't you even want to know about the case before you decide?" he asked.

Sassy shook her head resolutely.

"Thanks, but I'm going to sit this one out."

Michel sighed with grudging resignation, then nodded.

"Okay, but how about at least having lunch with me? Tomorrow. Just the two of us. My treat. I'll pick you up and drive you home."

Sassy looked down at their intertwined hands and nodded.

"That would be nice."

Chapter 5

"Thanks for agreeing to see me so soon," Michel said as he settled onto a sleek, red-leather club chair opposite Skylar Ellis.

"No problem," Ellis replied with a sunny smile, pulling his bare feet under him on the matching couch. "Classes are over for the semester, and I don't work until four today."

He was taller and more wholesome-looking than Michel had expected based on his voice. In fact, Michel thought he looked like a sandy-haired, midwestern farm boy, albeit from a farm with styling gel, located near a trendy men's clothing store.

"What do you do?" Michel asked.

He didn't really care, but hoped to put Ellis at ease.

"I'm a waiter," Ellis replied, wrinkling his lightly freckled nose. "At Jacques-Imo's over on Oak Street. You ever been?"

Michel shook his head. "No, but I've heard of it."

"It's actually a really good place," Ellis replied. "The food is great, and the owners are really nice."

"But you don't like being a waiter?" Michel asked.

"I don't mind it," Ellis replied, "but it's just such a cliche. A gay theater major working as a waiter."

He rolled his eyes dramatically, then stared at Michel as though waiting for a reaction. Michel gave just a reflexive smile and looked around the room.

"I have to say, I'm kind of surprised you have to work," he said. "This place wasn't furnished on a waiter's salary."

"Oh please," Ellis replied elaborately. "I'm a total charity case. Cam bought all this stuff and paid two-thirds of the rent."

"But you're able to afford it on your own now that he's gone?" Michel asked.

"Only because he paid his rent through the end of the summer," Ellis replied. "Then I'm either going to have to move or find another rich roommate." He looked around the room and sighed loudly, then looked back at Michel. "But until then, I've got the place all to myself."

The look in his eyes made it clear he'd added the last part very deliberately. Michel decided to ignore the invitation.

"That was very generous of him," he said instead. "I take it you were close friends."

Ellis studied Michel a moment longer, then seemed to accept that their interaction would remain purely professional. He gave a boyish grin.

"Well, not close like *that*, if that's what you mean," he said. "We were just good friends."

"'Good friends,' but you haven't heard from him since he moved out?" Michel asked, arching his eyebrows.

Ellis seemed to weigh his response for a moment, then nodded. "Yeah, I've heard from him."

"When?"

"A few days after he left, and then again last week."

"And he's okay?" Michel asked.

Ellis shrugged. "He seemed to be. I mean, I didn't get the sense he was trying to send me coded messages that he'd been kidnapped or anything like that."

Michel smiled and nodded.

"And do you know where he is?"

"Maybe," Ellis replied.

Michel tried to read whether he was being coy or genuinely wasn't certain.

"Do you care to elaborate on that?" he asked.

"He didn't say," Ellis replied, "but when he called the second time, I heard a lot of noise in the background. Like voices and music."

"He was at a club?" Michel asked.

"I don't think so," Ellis replied. "It wasn't dance music. Or at least not anything I'd want to dance to. It was that industrial-metal stuff."

"Okay," Michel replied uncertainly. "So then, where do you *think* he was?"

"Probably with Fierce and the Lost Boys," Ellis replied.

"Is that a band?" Michel asked.

Ellis laughed. "No, that's just what I call them. Well, not the Fierce part, because everyone calls *him* that, but the Lost Boys part is mine. Like from the movie. They're just a bunch of goth kids."

"Goth?"

"You know, the pale freaks who hang around coffee shops and look like they've read too many Anne Rice novels?"

"Thanks for the sociology lesson," Michel replied more harshly than he'd intended. "I know what goth means. I meant I didn't know Cam was into that scene. His parents didn't mention it."

Ellis's eyes showed momentary hurt, then it was gone. Michel suspected he didn't hold onto hurt—or anger, or any negative feelings—for long. Skylar Ellis seemed preternaturally inclined to cheerful enthusiasm.

"They probably don't even know," he said. "It's not like they saw him or talked to him very often, and he didn't really get into it until last semester when he met Fierce."

"So who's this *Fierce*?" Michel asked.

"He's like the leader," Ellis replied. "He has a place in the Bywater where they all party."

Michel sat back in the chair. "Any idea where, exactly?"

"I don't remember the address," Ellis replied, "but it's on Burgundy. I remember the cross streets were Piety and Desire, because I thought that was kind of funny."

"You've been there?" Michel asked with surprise.

Ellis gave a self-deprecating smile.

"Yeah, I know, right?" he said, looking down at his artfully distressed plaid shirt. "Obviously not my thing, but Cam brought me to a party once."

"What did the building look like?" Michel asked.

"Brick, I think," Ellis replied. "Or maybe stucco. It was dark, so it was hard to tell. There were three doors, I remember that much. And it looked kind of industrial."

Michel nodded. At least he had a starting point.

"So, tell me about Cam," he said.

"What do you want to know?" Ellis replied.

"Well, what's he like?"

Ellis gave him a slightly dazed look, as though he didn't quite understand the question.

"Okay," Michel said slowly, "for example, most kids into that scene are kind of dark and brooding, or at least that's the image they try to portray. Does Cam fit that description?"

Ellis frowned in concentration for a moment. Even his frown seemed improbably optimistic.

"Well, he definitely wasn't Sally Sunshine," he said finally, "but I don't know that I'd say dark and brooding either. Most of the time he was just kind of quiet. Like he was thinking about things. You know?"

Michel gave a quick nod, realizing he wasn't going to get any useful insight from Ellis.

"Did he tell you why he was leaving school so close to the end of the semester?" he asked. "Did something happen?"

"He just said that he had something important to do," Ellis replied, his eyes becoming troubled for the first time.

"Any guesses what that might have been?"

"I'm sure it has something to do with Fierce," Ellis replied. "I think Cam is kind of obsessed with him."

"Do you think they have a relationship?" Michel asked.

"I don't know," Cam replied. "Maybe, but I didn't see anything between them at the party. Cam kept watching Fierce, but Fierce hardly seemed to notice him back."

29

Michel nodded again. It was actually a good observation.

"This has been really helpful," he said abruptly. "I just have one more question for you."

Ellis nodded eagerly, though he looked mildly disappointed.

"Why didn't you tell the Taylors what you've told me?" Michel asked.

"They didn't ask," Ellis replied with a casual shrug. "Mrs. Taylor just called and told me a private investigator would be getting in touch with me."

"You didn't think that was odd?" Michel asked.

"For normal people, yeah, but not for her," Ellis replied. "At least not based on the stories Cam told me. I was actually surprised she called herself instead of having an assistant do it."

"I take it he told you she wasn't a very hands-on mother?" Michel asked.

Ellis laughed.

"He said she hired someone else to breastfeed him."

Michel returned the laugh, though he wasn't entirely sure Rhodes had been joking. He stood and took out his wallet.

"Thanks for your time," he said, pulling out a card. "If you hear from Cam, or think of anything else that might be helpful, please don't hesitate to give me a call."

Ellis unfolded his long body and stood up.

"Sure," he said, taking the card and flashing a sweet smile.

"Oh, and one other thing," Michel said. "Do you have a picture of Cam? The one Mrs. Taylor gave me was a few years old. Preferably something without makeup."

*****

Michel opened the truck door. Blue was sprawled across the bench seat, her head in the sun by the passenger door.

"How about making some room for me?" he asked.

Blue lazily lifted her head to look at him, then rolled to her belly and sat up.

"Thank you," Michel said as he slid into the truck.

Blue immediately turned her back to him.

"Look, we've talked about this before," Michel said. "I can't take you everywhere with me."

Blue twisted her head to look at him for a second, then turned back to the side window.

Michel checked his watch.

"I'll tell you what," he said, his voice rising enticingly. "I think we have just enough time for someone to go for a walk in Audubon Park before I have to meet Aunt Sassy for lunch."

At the word "park," Blue jumped up and spun around, her whole body vibrating with excitement. Michel raised his eyebrows, and she darted forward and licked his nose, then quickly sat back down. Michel laughed.

"If only it were that easy to make everyone happy," he said.

Chapter 6

Their conversation in the crowded cafe had been pleasant but innocuous, the kind of small talk usually shared by casual acquaintances. For the first half hour, Sassy had at least been animated, but as time passed, her energy had clearly flagged, so Michel had been surprised when she suggested taking a walk to Jackson Square.

"Have you talked to Chance lately?" she asked, slowly lowering herself onto a bench facing the park in front of the Presbytère.

"It's been a while," Michel replied.

"Any reason?" Sassy asked.

"I didn't want to bother him," Michel replied. "He's probably been busy with school."

Sassy fixed him with a curious look.

"Since when is calling a friend to say hello bothering them?"

You tell me, Michel thought. "It's not, I guess," he replied. He reached into his jacket pocket and pulled out a pack of American Spirit Lights. "Do you mind?"

"Would it stop you if I did?" Sassy replied. "Just blow it over there." She waved in the general direction of the park.

"I'll do my best," Michel replied. He lit a cigarette and settled back against the bench.

"So seriously, why haven't you called Chance?" Sassy asked. "Is there a problem between you two?"

Michel considered how to answer. The last few times he'd taken Chance to dinner, he'd had the sense that Chance was there more out of obligation than choice. After the last time, he'd decided to let Chance initiate their next get-together. It had been three months and Chance hadn't called yet.

"The last few times we got together, he just seemed distracted," he said finally. "I had the sense he'd rather have been elsewhere. No big deal."

"I'm sure he was just thinking about school," Sassy replied. "You shouldn't take it personally. I think you should give him a call. He must be on summer break by now."

Michel gave a noncommittal shrug. Sassy decided to let it go.

They were both quiet for a few minutes, taking in the scene around them: artists and artisans hawking their wares from folding chairs along the fence; men and women in business attire striding purposefully across the gray flagstones, clutching paper bags with takeout lunches; chubby tourists in shorts and hideous print shirts, so intent on capturing every moment of their vacations for digital posterity that they were missing out on the actual moments.

"I've missed this," Sassy said, with a contented sigh.

"*Which* this?" Michel asked.

"All of it," Sassy replied. "The sights, the sounds, the smells. Sitting in the sunshine."

"That's a lot of sibilance," Michel replied. "Are you sure you're not a gay man?" He paused to puff on his cigarette, then cut Sassy a sideways glance. "So, anything *else* you've missed?"

"And spending time with you," Sassy replied, rolling her eyes. "Now stop fishing for compliments."

"Me, too," Michel replied. "Maybe now that you're done with your treatments, we can do it more often. Maybe make it a regular thing."

"Oh sure," Sassy replied. "First it's lunch, then an occasional dinner, and the next thing I know you've got me working full-time and taken over my whole life again. I see your game."

She broke into a playful smile, but faltered when she saw the hurt in Michel's eyes.

"It was just a joke," she said.

"You sure about that?" Michel asked, looking down.

"Of course, I'm sure," Sassy replied. "I never felt like you were taking over my life. The job, yes, but not you."

Michel felt a rush of conflicting emotions, but pushed them back. He felt connected with Sassy for the first time in months, and didn't want to ruin the moment.

"Okay, just checking," he said with a crooked grin.

Sassy watched as he hunched forward and tapped ash onto the pavement, trying to gauge whether he was being honest.

"So how are you doing?" he asked before she could decide.

Sassy was taken aback by both the abruptness of the question and the shift into uncomfortable territory.

"It is what it is, and it's gonna be what it's gonna be," she replied with exaggerated nonchalance.

"I'm serious, Sas," Michel said. "Are you okay?"

Sassy knew from his tone that he wasn't going to be put off.

"Yeah," she said. "I'm okay. Physically, I'm still feeling beat to shit, but it gets a little bit better every day."

"And emotionally?"

"Let me get back to you on that," Sassy replied reflectively, then turned toward a burst of raucous laughter to their left.

Michel sensed she wasn't being evasive. He decided that was enough for the moment.

"Well, if there's anything I can..."

"Motherfucker!" Sassy exclaimed suddenly, jumping to her feet.

Michel looked up at her, startled, but her eyes were fixed on the corner of Chartres and St. Ann streets. Michel followed her gaze. A group of teenage boys was walking toward the square in the shadows of the balconies along the right side of Chartres. Their movements and voices were ostentatiously boisterous, encouraging anyone in their path out into the street. Michel studied them curiously for a moment, then realized Sassy's stepson, Corey, was in the middle of the group.

Sassy took a step forward. Michel reached out and gently grabbed her right wrist.

"Maybe you should wait and talk to him at home," he said.

Sassy's arm drifted back, then pulled free as she started for the corner. Michel hesitated a second, then followed.

"Corey!" Sassy yelled sharply from thirty feet away, as the boys turned toward the river.

All five boys and several dozen tourists stopped dead in their tracks. Michel was aware of heads turning, and a sudden lull in nearby conversation.

For a moment, the boys stood frozen, spread out in a line along the outer edge of the sidewalk. Then Corey's friends drifted back into the shadows, leaving him alone. It reminded Michel of a scene from a western, where the townsfolk move out of the line of fire before the climactic gunfight. Michel saw Corey's right hand twitch slightly, as though he were going for a gun, then realized he'd discreetly flicked a cigarette onto the ground behind him.

"Hey, Sassy," he said, all practiced casualness.

Sassy stopped six feet away.

"Why aren't you in school?" she asked.

To Michel's surprise, her tone was calm and reasonable.

"I have a free period," Corey replied.

Michel had expected him to be nervous, or possibly even scared, but his voice and expression were defiant.

"I thought you weren't allowed to leave school grounds until the end of the day?" Sassy replied evenly.

Corey eyed her for a moment, then shook his head.

"Nah, that's like just a suggestion," he said more loudly than necessary, obviously playing to the cheap seats.

His friends burst into laughter behind him, which seemed to encourage him more. He crossed his arms over his narrow chest and cocked his head to the left. The challenge in his eyes was clear. Michel couldn't believe it was the same shy, sweet kid he'd met two years earlier.

Sassy didn't reply for a moment. Michel could see her chest rising and falling quickly, then she took a long, slow breath, and lifted her chin slightly.

"Well, then I'd *suggest* you get back," she said, "because if you get caught, you won't be playing basketball next year."

Though there'd been no threat in her voice, Corey's bravado immediately faltered, and his gaze dropped to the pavement. Michel could see him calculating his next move.

"Yeah, all right," he said quietly, without looking up.

He shifted uncomfortably from one foot to the other for a few seconds, then turned around.

"I'm-a go on back," he said to his friends.

There was an awkward pause while the other boys decided how to react, then one of them raised his right fist and held it out. Corey walked over and bumped it with his own fist.

"Later, man," he said.

The rest of the group offered fists, shoulder slaps, and muttered condolences. Corey cast a last sullen look at Sassy, then skulked off around the corner. Sassy and Michel stood there for a few seconds more, then turned away.

"Nice hair," a voice said behind them, followed by a chorus of giggles.

They turned to face the boys again. A tall, skinny kid with close-cropped platinum hair was standing slightly apart from the others. From his smirk, it was obvious he was the one who'd spoken. Sassy walked up to him.

"What did you say?" she asked in a measured tone.

The boy stared her down, unblinking.

"I said..."

Sassy's right hand came up fast. Though her slap wasn't as hard as it would have been twenty pounds earlier, it still knocked the boy back two steps.

"Look, you little bleach-blond bitch," she said, jabbing her index finger at his face, "I may only have a few months left, and believe me, I'd have no qualms about taking you with me."

36

The boy took an involuntary step back, then seemed to realize that his friends were watching. He squared his shoulders and tugged at the bottom of his blue Pistons jersey.

"Ain't no thing," he said to no one in particular, then turned to the others. "Let's get out of here."

He walked past the rest of the group, and they fell in behind him, ambling slowly toward the river.

"You don't think that was maybe a tad extreme?" Michel asked, as they watched them go.

"No, actually I think it was just extreme enough," Sassy replied. "I should have started slapping people a long time ago. That felt good."

A smattering of applause broke out around them as they started back toward the truck.

*****

Sassy had been quiet while they walked. Michel had stolen an occasional look at her, and she'd been lost in thought. Her mood seemed to have darkened.

"Anything you want to talk about?" he asked as soon as they were back in the truck.

Sassy was silent for a moment, then her body began to tremble, and she banged her fists hard on the dashboard.

"God damn it!" she said, as tears rolled down her cheeks.

"Come on," Michel said, putting his hand on her shoulder. "You're not going to let some little 'bleach-blond bitch' get to you like that, are you?"

Sassy took a few wet breaths.

"I don't give a fuck about that kid," she said. "It's Corey."

"Oh," Michel replied, suddenly feeling stupid. "I'm sorry."

"For what?" Sassy asked, wiping her eyes with the back of her right hand.

"I just didn't know you were having problems," Michel replied, then immediately hoped Sassy wouldn't interpret it as an accusation that she'd excluded him from that part of her life. "That didn't sound like you back there," he said quickly. "I was expecting you to bite his head off. And why didn't you say anything about the cigarette?"

Sassy shook her head miserably.

"I don't know. I've tried being strict. I've tried being his friend. I'm not sure what to do or say anymore. All I know is that I just don't have the energy to keep fighting him."

Michel felt a pang of guilt. In his self-pitying fantasies, he'd imagined Sassy basking in the love of her husband and stepson, while he'd been cast aside. Now he realized that she'd been dealing with issues beyond the cancer.

"Ever since I got sick, he's been acting out," Sassy continued. "It's like he's turned against me."

Michel was reminded of what Trish Taylor had said about Cam Rhodes manufacturing crises to get attention.

"Do you think he might be mad at you?" he asked.

"Mad? Why would he be mad?" Sassy replied.

"Because you got sick."

"Like that was my fault?"

"No, but think about it from his perspective," Michel replied. "Corey lost his mother when he was a baby, then suddenly he gets a new mother, then you get sick. He's probably afraid he's going to lose you, too, and he's pissed off about it."

Sassy considered it for a moment.

"You think?"

"You're the one with the psychology degree," Michel replied, "but yeah, I do."

He suddenly realized that he'd been angry at Sassy for getting sick, too.

"So what am I supposed to do about it?" Sassy asked.

Michel shrugged.

"Not my area of expertise, but it might help if he saw you doing things again. It can't help that you're just lying in bed like you're waiting to die."

"I'm not waiting to die," Sassy replied in a clipped cadence. "I just don't feel well."

"I know that," Michel replied, "but for Corey's sake, it might help if you tried to move on with your life as though nothing happened."

"Oh, here we go," Sassy said, rolling her eyes. "I know where this is leading."

"I'm serious," Michel said. "You know why you got sick in the first place, don't you?"

Sassy fixed him with a hooded stare.

"Please, illuminate me."

"Because you quit working," Michel replied. "It's a proven fact. People who stay busy are far less likely to get sick."

"Or maybe I got it from inhaling your second-hand smoke for years," Sassy replied sharply.

Michel gave her an impish pout.

"Well, yeah, maybe that too."

"You're not even a little cute," Sassy said, "and when you're hooked up to an oxygen tank, don't expect sympathy from me."

"Oh, please," Michel replied. "You'll be pushing me and my tank around the neighborhood, feeding me soup, and wiping the drool from my chin."

He saw a sudden flash of anxiety in Sassy's eyes, and wondered if he'd struck too close to her own morbid fantasies. They were both quiet for a few moments.

"Just think about it, okay?" Michel said finally.

Sassy gave him a sideways glance.

"Fine," she said grudgingly. "I'll think about it."

"Good," Michel replied. "So you ready to go home?"

Sassy stared out the window for a moment, then shook her head.

"Not yet. I need to stop and get some clippers."

Chapter 7

Blue took her regular spot by the fountain, while Michel settled into his usual chair and put his drink on the side table. He lit a cigarette and checked the time on his cell phone: 10:15 PM. He wavered for a moment, then hit the speed dial.

"Hey!" Chance answered with unexpected enthusiasm after the second ring.

"Hey. I didn't wake you, did I?" Michel asked.

"No, I was reading," Chance replied through a loud yawn.

"I thought classes would be done by now," Michel replied.

He could hear Chance lighting his own cigarette.

"They are," Chance replied after a few seconds, "but believe it or not, I *do* actually read for fun sometimes."

Michel smiled. "Anything interesting?"

"Yeah, it's about the socio-economic impact of the collapse of the Soviet empire," Chance replied.

"Really?" Michel asked.

Chance began laughing. "You're so gullible. It's just some cheesy romance about gay rodeo cowboys, called *Roped and Hog-Tied.*"

"A romance?" Michel replied skeptically. "It sounds more like porn."

"Well, I didn't say I was reading with both hands," Chance shot back.

Michel felt his face grow hot. "So anyway," he said quickly, "I was wondering if you wanted to get together for dinner one night this week? It's been a while."

There was a long pause, and Michel suddenly wished he hadn't called.

"Ummm...what would you think about maybe doing something...*fun?*" Chance replied finally. "Like going to a club? I need to blow off some steam."

Michel felt both embarrassed and slightly hurt. It hadn't occurred to him that Chance might have considered their dinners boring.

"Yeah, clubbing is fine," he replied. "When?"

"How about tomorrow?"

"That'll work. Bourbon Pub at nine?"

"Cool," Chance replied. "Now if you'll excuse me, I have to get back to my book. Cowboy Kyle is about to 'brand' hot circuit newbie, Troy."

"Wow, that sounds..."

The line went dead before he could finish.

Chapter 8

The alarm was already off when Michel arrived at the office the next morning. He stared at the control pad for a few seconds, wondering if he'd forgotten to set it, then tried the door. It was unlocked.

He looked down at Blue. She was sniffing around the base of the door, her tail wagging excitedly.

"So does that mean it's safe?" Michel asked.

He opened the door, and Blue immediately ran inside and disappeared into the office.

"Hello, sweetheart!" Sassy's voice carried into the hall.

Michel walked to the office doorway. Sassy was sitting sideways behind his desk, leaning forward to let Blue enthusiastically cover her nose and lips with wet kisses. Her head was wrapped in a pale violet scarf.

"How've you been, baby girl?" she cooed. "Yes, Aunt Sassy's missed you, too."

She looked up at Michel, then down at her watch.

"9:36?" she said. "Seems like things have gotten a little lax around here since I left."

"Sorry, boss," Michel replied. "Traffic."

"Mmm hmmm," Sassy replied, with a mock scowl. "Traffic in the 10 blocks from your house to here?"

"I took the scenic route," Michel replied.

He walked to the other side of his desk and took the chair where Trish Taylor had sat two days earlier. "If I'd known you were coming, I would have brought you coffee," he said.

"I brought my own," Sassy replied, nodding at the tall paper cup on the desk.

She rubbed Blue's neck for another few seconds, then sat up. Blue took it as a cue and walked to her spot by the window. She sprawled out in the morning sun. Michel and Sassy stared at one another awkwardly for a moment.

"I have something to show you," Sassy said finally.

Michel nodded, his curiosity piqued. Sassy hesitated a split second, then pulled off the scarf. Her hair had been trimmed to an even gray stubble all the way around.

"What do you think?" she asked nervously, turning her head from side to side.

"Honestly?" Michel replied. "I think you look pretty bad-ass. What did Russ think?"

Michel could have sworn that Sassy's skin reddened slightly.

"Let's just say he liked it," she replied demurely.

Michel smiled and took a sip of his coffee.

"So, to what do I owe the honor?" he asked.

"I work here, remember?" Sassy replied.

Michel squinted in concentration for a few seconds, then shook his head.

"No, not really."

"Don't be giving me your nonsense," Sassy replied, "and don't start feeling all smug because I'm here, either. I thought about it last night, and either the cancer's gone or it's not, and sitting around waiting to see which it's going to be isn't going to change the outcome."

"So you're back to work?" Michel asked, surprised.

Sassy nodded.

"Just like that?" Michel asked.

"Just like that."

"Okay," Michel said.

He suspected there was more to the decision than she was letting on, but decided not to press. For the moment, he was happy just to have her there.

"So tell me about this big important case," Sassy said.

"Do you remember Trish Rhodes?" Michel asked.

"You mean Trish Carrington Colby Dexter Rhodes?" Michel smiled appreciatively. "One and the same."

"What about her?"

"Her son, Campbell, is missing."

"How old are we talking?" Sassy asked.

"He was just finishing his sophomore year at Tulane," Michel replied.

"But he didn't?"

Michel shook his head. "He dropped out and disappeared."

"How long ago?"

"Three weeks."

"So we've got a 19- or 20-year-old rich dropout who's probably been on a bender for three weeks. Doesn't sound like much of a mystery to me."

She gave Michel a look that clearly added, "and certainly not anything that requires my help."

"Wait, it gets better," Michel replied. "Trish thinks he's hiding. Primarily from her."

Sassy cocked her head curiously.

"Any particular reason?"

"She thinks he's trying to get her attention. That he's feeling neglected because she and her husband have been spending so much time working on the husband's Senate campaign."

"But you don't buy it?"

"Yes and no," Michel replied. "I buy that the kid might be trying to get attention, but I don't buy that he's suddenly feeling neglected. At least not any more than usual."

"I take it the family's not close?" Sassy asked.

Michel shook his head.

"They haven't seen the kid since January, or spoken to him since the beginning of March. Oh, and Trish called him a 'drama queen.'"

Sassy looked at him incredulously.

"Oh yeah," Michel replied. "She's a charmer. Like Angela Lansbury in *The Manchurian Candidate*, but without the maternal instincts."

"So then why does she want to find him?"

"She gave me the concerned mother routine," Michel replied, "but I think she's just afraid he's going to do something that'll create a shit storm for the campaign, and wants him where she can control him."

"So he's just another inconvenient detail that needs to be managed," Sassy summarized.

Michel nodded.

"Interesting," Sassy replied. "And interesting that you'd take the case."

Michel nodded.

"I haven't figured out what I'm going to do if I actually find the kid yet. Maybe just convince him not to do anything stupid unless he wants to spend the next decade in a psych ward."

"Since when do we have our own agenda?" Sassy asked.

"Since I'm no longer dependent on clients to pay my bills," Michel replied. "It's one of the fringe benefits of being rich."

Sassy shook her head reproachfully.

"So did Trish give you any leads?"

Michel pointed to a folder on the corner of his desk. Sassy opened it and saw two photos and the sheet of paper with Skylar Ellis's name and phone number.

"That's it?" she asked, giving the photos a cursory look. "Who's this Skylar Ellis?"

"Rhode's former roommate. I met with him yesterday before you and I had lunch."

"Did he give you anything?"

Michel nodded.

"Rhodes has been hanging out with a group of goth kids for the past few months. Ellis thinks he's obsessed with the leader, a guy who calls himself Fierce."

Sassy made a face.

"Any idea where to find them?"

"Rhodes took Ellis to a party in the Bywater, on Burgundy," Michel replied.

"Address?"

"No, but he said it was between Piety and Desire. An industrial-looking building with three doors."

"Sounds like it shouldn't be too hard to find," Sassy replied.

"That's what I was thinking," Michel replied.

"So what are we waiting for?"

"It's morning," Michel replied.

Sassy stared back at him blankly.

"They're goths," Michel said with an elaborate sigh. "They only come out at night."

"So then what the hell are we supposed to do all day?"

Michel shrugged.

"Get breakfast. Take Blue for a walk. Have lunch. Take Blue for another walk..."

"Wow, this is really just a hobby for you, isn't it?" Sassy interrupted.

"What can I say?" Michel replied. "They kicked me out of the canasta club."

Chapter 9

They'd done a quick drive-by just after lunch, and found a likely match to Skylar Ellis's description: a two-story brick building with boarded-up windows and three green doors. The street had been deserted, so they'd returned to the office to kill time until late afternoon. While Michel walked Blue and played solitaire on his computer, Sassy had gone up to Chance's old apartment to nap.

Now, as they approached again on foot, they could see two dozen people in the lengthening shadows in front of the building. Most sat on the edge of the sidewalk, or leaned against the building in a ragged approximation of a line to the still-closed doors. They were predominantly younger—late teens or early twenties—and uniformly smoking with practiced ennui.

Most had dark hair and heavily shadowed eyes, though from a distance it was impossible to tell if the shadows were the result of cosmetics or lack of sleep. Their clothing ranged from waistcoats and lace-trimmed shirts to torn jeans and Doc Martens, but with a definite skew toward the Victorian end of the spectrum. While they gave an immediate impression of being unwashed, it seemed to be a cultivated look, the result of hours spent trying to achieve just the right level of faux decay.

Two men and three women stood apart from the rest, not just physically, but in appearance and demeanor, as well. The women were slouched against a cracked, coral stucco wall on the opposite side of the street. Two appeared to be in their late-forties, though their hard eyes and weathered cheeks made it clear those years had been rough. Both had pale narrow faces framed by lank brown hair, and were dressed in baggy white t-shirts knotted at the waist and too-short jean shorts that emphasized the spindliness of their legs. The third looked to be much younger, though there were no traces of youthful enthusiasm left on her face. Despite the heat, she wore threadbare jeans and a long-sleeved sweatshirt with a faded Florida Gators logo on the front.

The two men had taken up position almost in the center of the street. Both had tangled shoulder-length hair, one brunette and the other dirty blond, and full but matted beards. They wore only ragged jeans, and though their faces were heavily lined, their bodies were surprisingly smooth and taut. They paced restlessly, their eyes constantly darting around, though coming back to rest on the doors every few seconds.

"Think they're trying to score?" Sassy asked.

"Or hungry and hoping one of the minnows will break away from rest of the school," Michel replied.

They'd stopped on the far corner of Piety. No one seemed to have noticed them yet.

"So, how should we approach this?" Michel asked.

Sassy studied the two groups for a moment, then shrugged. "Blend in?"

"Funny," Michel replied, cutting her a sideways look. "See anyone who looks like Rhodes?"

"No, but if he's crashing here, he might be inside," Sassy replied. "It looks like the rest of them are waiting for the party to begin. So what's the plan?"

Michel considered it for a moment.

"How about I take the ones with the sullen expressions on the left, and you take the ones with the crazy eyes on the right?"

Sassy blinked at him.

"And why do *I* get the Mansons?"

"Because you're a woman. They won't hurt you."

Sassy scowled back.

"Yeah, tell that to Sharon Tate," she said.

At that moment, the man with the darker hair suddenly turned and locked eyes with her.

"You think he heard me?" Sassy whispered as a chill worked its way slowly up her spine.

The man continued staring for a few seconds more, then said something to his friend. The other man looked over. The intensity in both their eyes suggested a confrontation was imminent, but then they seemed to think better of it. The first man turned to the women and barked something unintelligible. The women rolled off the wall in unison and began moving away down the block. The men glared at Michel and Sassy one last time, then followed.

"They must think we're cops," Michel said.

"You think?" Sassy replied sarcastically. "So I guess that means we'll both take the sullen ones on the left."

*****

"That was a waste of time," Michel said, as they waited for a slow-moving car to pass through the intersection.

"Maybe, maybe not," Sassy replied.

Michel raised his eyebrows as he lit a cigarette.

"Did you see the girl in the dominatrix outfit?" Sassy asked.

"The black one?" Michel replied.

"Really? That's all you noticed?" Sassy asked, narrowing her eyes. "Not the one with the piercing green eyes? Or the one who carried herself with poised elegance? Just *the black one?*"

"I was talking about her outfit," Michel replied defensively. "There were two girls...and one guy...in dominatrix gear. I assumed you meant the one in black *because* she was so striking." He almost added, "She was black?" but decided it would strain credulity.

"Oh," Sassy replied, then fought the urge to look back over her shoulder.

"So, what about her?" Michel asked quickly. "I didn't even see you talk with her."

"I didn't," Sassy replied. "And you're full of shit."

She left Michel standing on the curb as she crossed the intersection and started up the block. She was suddenly annoyed, though more by Michel's keeping a watchful eye on her than by his unconscious racism. She felt a dull throbbing in her temples, and took a few calming breaths.

"I *didn't* talk to her," she said, as Michel caught up with her, "but I got the sense she wanted to talk to me. Just not there. Not in front of everyone else."

"Did you give her a card?" Michel asked.

"No, but I made sure she saw me give them to a few of the others," Sassy replied. "If she wants to contact us, she will."

They walked a half block in silence, then Michel stopped.

"Are you all right?" he asked.

Sassy took another few steps, then stopped and turned to face him. For a moment, her expression was closed and unyielding, then it softened and she smiled tiredly.

"Yeah, I'm just not used to all this walking," she said.

Michel suspected it was at least a partial truth, and nodded.

"You want to wait here while I get the truck?" he asked.

"No, it's only another few blocks," Sassy replied. "I think I can make it. And if I can't, you can give me a piggyback ride."

Michel nodded, then a smile spread across his face.

"Hop on," he said, turning around and squatting down.

Sassy stared at him with disbelief.

"You've got to be kidding."

Michel looked over his left shoulder and shook his head.

"Come on."

Sassy stared at him warily for a moment, then took a tentative step forward.

"I don't even know how to do this anymore," she said.

"Just put your arms around my neck and jump up," Michel replied. "I'll catch your legs."

Sassy took another step, then stopped.

"This is silly," she protested, though she couldn't suppress a girlish giggle.

"So what?" Michel replied. "Think of it as my penance for centuries of slavery."

"Well, in that case, let me get my riding crop and some spurs," Sassy replied.

Michel smiled and squatted lower, patting his lower back with both hands.

"Come on," he coaxed.

Sassy hesitated a moment longer, then took two quick steps and hopped up as she threw her arms around Michel's neck. Michel let out an exaggerated grunt, then bounced up and down up a few times until he had a good grip on Sassy's legs.

"If you drop me, you're in big trouble," Sassy said, laughing.

"And if you pee on me, you're in bigger trouble," Michel replied.

He turned and slowly started up the block. Sassy let out a contented sigh and relaxed against his back.

"So any big plans for the night?" she asked.

"Yeah, actually I'm going out with Chance," Michel replied.

Sassy smiled to herself.

"Dinner?"

"No, he wants to go clubbing," Michel replied with theatrical dread. "We're meeting at Bourbon Pub."

"Good," Sassy replied. "Just remember it's a work night. I don't want you waltzing in at ten o'clock again tomorrow morning."

"It was only nine-thirty," Michel replied, "and don't worry, I'll behave myself."

Chapter 10

They pushed their way through the crowd ringing the bar and ordered more drinks, then moved out onto the balcony overlooking Bourbon Street. They both lit cigarettes, and settled against the railing. Michel had to check the impulse to look back at the doorway to the spot where he and Joel had first spoken. Instead, he forced himself to keep his eyes on the comings and goings in the street below.

"Thanks," Chance said after a few seconds. "I really needed this, and I don't really like going out by myself anymore."

Michel smiled, in part at how much Chance had changed from the scene-trawling hustler he'd been four years earlier.

"You're welcome," he said, "and I'm sorry about the dinners. I didn't realize you didn't like them."

Chance took a long drag on his cigarette, then slowly blew smoke into the night sky.

"It wasn't that I didn't *like* them," he said with an apologetic wince. "I mean, the food was great. It was just that they were kind of...awkward. It's like we were stuck at a table for two hours, but didn't have anything to say to one other." He looked down for a moment, then quietly added, "I guess it's been that way for a while."

Michel hadn't been expecting a serious conversation, and felt his stomach clench.

"Why do you suppose that is?" he asked cautiously.

"Why do you think, dumb ass?" Chance shot back.

Michel was suddenly aware of buzzing in his ears, the

echoing rasp of his own breathing, a drop of sweat rolling slowly down the center of his back. Chance looked at him with a mixture of sadness and what seemed to be hope for a few seconds, then turned back to the street.

"Probably because we were both too chicken shit or emotionally retarded to talk about Joel," he said. He wiped his eyes with the back of his left hand.

Michel felt relief, then immediate guilt. Chance sighed and gave an embarrassed smile.

"We probably should have locked ourselves in a room, gotten trashed, and had a good cry two years ago," he said. "At least we would have gotten it out of our systems." He paused, then turned to face Michel. "Instead we just kind of danced around each other. I kept thinking that one day we'd be ready to talk, but that day never came, and things just got weird."

"Yeah," Michel nodded.

"It was like, I wanted to hang out," Chance said, "but at the same time I didn't because it was too hard. There was just this shit between us that neither one of us was willing to talk about, or knew how to talk about, and it just built up. It was a total avoidance thing."

Michel gave him a teasing smile.

"I thought you were studying business," he said, hoping to lighten the mood.

"Well, I might have taken one or two psychology courses, too," Chance replied.

"Okay, doctor," Michel replied. "So how do we get past it?"

Chance shrugged.

"I guess we just have to start being honest with one other, and stop being afraid to talk about Joel anymore."

Michel took a deep breath. His pulse was beating faster.

"Do you want to do it?" he asked abruptly.

Chance gave him a bemused look.

"Do what?"

"Buy a bottle, go back to my place, and have a good cry?"

"Seriously?" Chance asked.

"Yeah, why not?" Michel replied with more certainty than he felt. "Neither one of us has school in the morning."

Chance considered it for a long moment, then shrugged. "Okay."

*****

Michel opened his eyes. Chance was lying beside him on the bed. His eyes were closed, and his breathing regular and slow. Michel wanted to reach out and brush his bangs away from his eyes, but didn't. He rolled carefully onto his back, then sat up and swung his legs over the edge of the bed. His clothes were in a pile near the foot, too far away to reach with his toes.

He looked at the open doorway. Blue was lying in the hall, just outside. She raised her head a few inches and gazed at him disinterestedly for a moment, then lowered it back to the floor.

"Well, at least *you* don't seem too traumatized," Michel thought. He edged forward and pressed his hands down on the mattress to keep it from moving, then stood up.

"Nice ass," Chance said softly behind him.

Michel jumped a little. He slowly turned and attempted a smile, though it felt unnatural and wrong-shaped. Chance lay in the same position, but now his deep blue eyes were watching Michel intently. Michel couldn't read his expression.

"How'd you sleep?" Michel asked reflexively.

He was suddenly acutely aware of his nakedness.

"Fine, I think," Chance replied, pushing up into a sitting position, "though I'm not sure if I slept or just passed out."

He stretched his arms over his head and yawned, then reached back to prop pillows against the headboard. As he scooted backward, the sheet slid down to reveal the line of black hair leading from his naval. The night before had been heated, almost desperate, and Michel hadn't taken the time to actually look at Chance's body. Now that he did, he felt himself flush. He quickly grabbed his boxer shorts from the floor and held them in front of him.

"Listen, Chance," he said, "I'm..."

"Don't fucking say it!" Chance cut him off, his eyes darkening.

"But..."

"Don't fucking say it!" Chance repeated angrily. "I'm already feeling weird enough about this, and if you tell me you're sorry, it's going to push me over the edge."

Michel stared at him for a moment, unsure how to respond. His own emotions were raw and confused, but oddly, he didn't feel guilty.

"I wasn't going to tell you I was sorry," he said, almost sure he meant it. "I was going to say that I'm out of coffee, and I'm going to the corner to get some. I was wondering if you want me to get you anything while I'm there."

Chance stared at him warily.

"Seriously?"

"Seriously," Michel replied. "I'm not sure exactly what I feel, but I'm not sorry about what happened. I think it was something we both needed to do."

Chance stared at him for another few seconds, then an impish smile crossed his lips. He pushed the sheet to his thighs.

"Do you think we need to do it again?" he asked.

Michel looked down and felt his mouth go dry.

"Maybe...just to be safe," he managed.

Chapter 11

"You and Chance did what?" Sassy asked with disbelief.

It was almost noon, and Michel had arrived at the office just a few minutes earlier.

"You heard me," Michel replied.

"And hell didn't freeze over?" Sassy asked.

"Not that I'm aware," Michel replied.

"Okay, I need to wrap my head around this for a second," Sassy said. She made a show of slowly rolling her head in a circle, then shook it vigorously. "You and Chance?"

Michel nodded.

"But how?" Sassy asked.

Michel dropped into his chair, stretched, and yawned.

"We were upstairs at Parade and started talking about the weirdness between us," he said. "We decided to go back to my place, get drunk, and finally talk about Joel. So first there were drinks, then tears and hugging, then suddenly kissing and clothes flying all over the place."

"Wow," Sassy replied. "I didn't see that one coming."

"Me neither," Michel replied with a laugh.

"Though maybe I should have," Sassy said.

"What's that supposed to mean?"

"Just that there's always been a little tension between you two," Sassy replied. "I just didn't realize what it was about."

"The *tension* was about Joel," Michel replied stiffly. "We were both jealous of one another's relationship with him."

"If you say so," Sassy replied breezily.

Michel gave her a mock scowl.

"So do I even want to know how it was?" Sassy asked doubtfully.

"Honestly? Pretty fucking amazing," Michel replied.

"Really?"

Michel nodded enthusiastically.

"Maybe you're right. Maybe there always was sexual tension. Whatever, it was great." He seemed to get lost in the memory for a moment, then his eyes focused and he blinked. "And that's as much as I'm going to say, so don't even try prying any details out of me."

"I wasn't planning on it," Sassy replied dryly. "So now what?"

"We haven't gotten that far," Michel shrugged.

"Well, it certainly seems to have put you in a good mood," Sassy said, "though I'm sure a big part of that is just relief that you finally talked about Joel."

Michel's smile froze.

"Sort of," he said sheepishly. "We *started* talking about him, but I'm not sure we got very far before the kissing started."

Sassy frowned disapprovingly.

"What?" Michel asked.

"Don't you think you should do that?" Sassy replied.

"Yeah, of course," Michel replied, "We will. We just got a little...sidetracked."

"Just don't wait too long, okay?" Sassy said sternly.

"Why? What's the big deal?" Michel asked.

"You've been avoiding talking for two years," Sassy replied. "It's time to stop."

"What? You think I had sex with him just so we wouldn't have to talk?" Michel asked.

"I didn't say 'just'," Sassy replied, "and I hope not." She shook her head. "I just don't want to see either of you get hurt."

Michel suddenly wanted a cigarette. "Yeah, I guess you're right," he said, hoping to end the conversation. "Then we'll just have to deal with the whole sleeping-together thing."

"But at least that's something you both have a lot of experience with," Sassy replied with exaggerated sweetness.

Michel opened his mouth to reply, then stopped as he sensed they were no longer alone. He turned and saw a young woman watching them intently from the doorway.

"I'm sorry," she said in a smooth, assured voice. "I can come back later, if you like."

"No, that's all right," Sassy replied, trying to place the vaguely familiar face. "Have we met?"

The woman took a step into the room.

"No, but we saw one another yesterday evening," she replied. "In the Bywater?"

"You were in the black leather dominatrix gear," Michel said, swivelling to face her.

The girl gave an amused but unembarrassed smile.

"That was me. Rachel Davis by day, Mistress Nightshade by dark," she said with a small bow.

Suddenly Sassy could see it. Though the girl had tied her hair back in a ponytail and was dressed casually in jeans and a simple white cotton blouse, the poise and confidence from the previous afternoon were still there. Sassy thought she was even more striking without the elaborate make-up.

Davis took another few steps into the room. Blue, who had been watching her from the corner, got up and walked over.

"Hey, girl," Davis said, kneeling. She held out her right hand, and after a cursory sniff, Blue moved closer and rested her head on the young woman's left thigh. "So you're trying to find Cam Rhodes," Davis said without looking up, as she began stroking Blue's neck.

"Yes. Do you know where he is?" Sassy replied.

Davis raised her pale green eyes and shook her head. It was clearly meant as a rebuke, rather than a response.

"Before we go there, I need to know why," she said, the warmth suddenly gone from her voice. She kissed the top of Blue's head, then stood.

"Because his parents are worried about him," Michel replied, though it sounded more like a question. "He moved out of his apartment three weeks ago, and hasn't been seen or heard from since."

"Try again," Davis commanded with unexpected force.

Sassy almost laughed at the shock on Michel's face. She turned to Davis and smiled calmly.

"So I take it you must know him..." she started, her tone friendly and relaxed.

"Don't even try that shit with me, sister," Davis cut her off. She put her hands on her slim hips and looked from Sassy to Michel, then back. "I'm the one asking the questions. At least until I hear something I like."

She tried to stare Sassy down, and Sassy felt a flash of anger. She studied the girl for a moment, then made a show of looking around the room. Finally she looked back at Davis.

"Does this look like a dungeon to you, *sister?*" she asked, leaning forward in her chair.

For the first time, Davis's self-assurance faltered, and Sassy saw a tremor of doubt in her eyes.

"Because this looks like an office to me," she continued in a controlled, but steely voice. "*My* office, which means I'm in charge around here. You have something to say, then sit your bony ass down and say it. Otherwise, get the fuck out."

The two women's eyes remained locked for another few seconds, and Michel imagined he could hear electricity crackling in the air between them. Then Davis lowered her eyes. She remained completely still for several seconds, then nodded and looked back up at Sassy.

"I'm sorry," she said softly, offering a contrite smile. "Bad approach. Let's try this again."

She walked to the desk and held out her right hand.

"Rachel Davis."

Sassy took her hand tentatively, wondering what had just happened, then Davis looked at the chair next to Michel.

"May I?"

Michel nodded. She sat down.

"So what was that all about, Miss Davis?" Sassy asked.

Davis sighed.

"Please, call me Rachel. And I was just being an idiot."

She looked from Sassy to Michel, then shrugged.

"Okay," Sassy replied, giving Michel a quick, puzzled look. "So *do* you know where Rhodes is?"

Davis shook her head, this time in reply.

"I haven't seen him for at least a month, but I wasn't around because I was busy with finals. I just started hanging out again last week. But I heard that he and Fierce had a falling out, and Rhodes left. No one's seen him since."

"How long ago was that?" Michel asked.

"About 10 days."

"Any idea what it was about?" Sassy asked.

"No," Davis replied. "Apparently, no one actually saw or heard the fight. Rhodes just stormed out in the middle of a party, and Fierce wouldn't talk to anyone afterward."

"Do you know Rhodes well?" Michel asked.

"Not really," Davis replied. "We've talked a few times, but just small talk."

"But you knew him well enough that you didn't buy that his parents were concerned about him," Sassy said.

Davis nodded.

"I heard him going on about his mother more than a few times. She sounds like a bitch."

Michel smiled, but didn't say anything.

"So if you don't mind my asking, why *are* you trying to find him?" Davis asked. "Is he in some kind of trouble?"

"The truth is that his stepfather is running for the Senate, and the 'bitch' is worried Rhodes might do something to embarrass the family and hurt the campaign," Sassy replied.

"I figured it was something like that," Davis replied, without judgment.

"Rhodes moved out of his apartment three weeks ago, but you said the fight was about 10 days ago," Sassy said. "Do you know if he was living on Burgundy during the gap?"

"I don't think so," Davis replied. "At least not that anyone's mentioned. Maybe he moved in with his boyfriend."

"Boyfriend?" Michel replied. "We didn't know he had one."

"Maybe he doesn't anymore," Davis replied, "but he did. He brought him to a couple of parties. Sweet kid, a little ditzy. Sandy hair, wholesome looking. And he had one of those cheesy gay porn star names."

"Skylar?" Michel ventured.

"That's it," Davis replied.

"Skylar was just his roommate," Michel replied.

"Then they were extremely close roommates," Davis replied with a small laugh. "I saw them going at it one night in the play room at Fierce's place."

Sassy shot Michel a quick look, lifting her bald brow almost imperceptibly. He gave her an equally discreet nod.

"You two have been working together for a while, huh?" Davis said, smiling.

"What makes you say that?" Sassy replied noncommittally.

"Mainly because you were talking about his sex life when I came in," Davis replied, "but you also have the whole unspoken communication thing going on."

Michel feigned a long-suffering expression. Sassy smiled.

"And I'm guessing you're either a phony psychic or a psychology student," she said. "I'm going with the latter."

Davis looked mildly surprised. "What gave it away?"

"You've obviously spent some time learning to read people," Sassy replied, "but fake psychics don't take finals. I also recognize the breed. I got my Masters in criminal psych."

"Figures," Davis said.

"So where are you studying?" Sassy asked.

"Tulane," Davis replied.

"My alma mater," Sassy replied approvingly.

"Did you know Rhodes from school?" Michel asked.

"No," Davis replied. "I saw him around campus a few times, but he didn't recognize me without the costume."

Michel cocked his head.

"I thought that calling it a 'costume' was kind of a no-no, because it breaks the illusion," he said

Davis playfully mirrored the tilt of his head.

"Oh, do you have much experience with the dominance scene?" she asked, then broke into a smile as the color rose in his cheeks. "You're right," she said, "but for me it *is* just a costume. It's all part of the research I'm doing for my thesis."

"You're doing your thesis on sexual dominance?" Sassy asked. "Wow, things have changed since my day."

"Cult behavior," Davis replied. "I chose the Nightshade persona because it allows me to get close but also maintain a comfortable distance. That's basically what I tried to do with you earlier. Assert control to create a safe zone for myself."

She gave another apologetic smile.

"Wait, so then Rhodes is involved in a cult?" Michel asked.

"A cult of personality, maybe," Davis replied, "but not technically a cult. There's no organized belief system or common ideology, or anything like that. They mostly just share the same taste in music, drugs, clothes, and sex. But some of the group dynamics are still similar."

"How so?" Sassy asked.

"Primarily that there's a charismatic central figure, and a definite power structure," Davis replied. "Fierce is at the top, then he's got a small inner circle around him."

"Have you seen any evidence of behaviorial control or brainwashing?" Sassy asked.

"Definitely behavioral control in the sense that if someone pisses Fierce off, they're gone, but everyone's free to do whatever they want when they're not at the building. It's not like anyone's being forced to turn over their life's savings or sleep with goats."

"And brainwashing?" Sassy asked.

"Not that I've seen, though it would be pretty easy," Davis replied with a dark laugh. "Most of those kids are dropping acid or mescaline two or three times a week."

Sassy nodded, knowing that LSD had been used in mind-control experiments during the early 1950s.

"So the group out front yesterday," Michel said. "We assumed they don't live there?"

Davis shook her head.

"No, they only come to party. There are a few genuine freaks, but a lot of them are just bored kids who like to play dress up. The ones who live there really buy into the lifestyle, and most of them have serious mommy-daddy issues. They're looking for a substitute family to make them feel whole."

"And Fierce is their father figure?" Sassy asked.

Davis furrowed her brow for a moment.

"More like a cool, emotionally-detached, older brother," she replied finally. "A father...at least ideally...would become emotionally invested. I don't see that with Fierce. He just breezes in when he's in the mood, laps up the attention for a while, then leaves when he gets bored. He doesn't seem to have any genuine ongoing interest in anyone's lives."

She considered what she'd said for a moment, then nodded.

"Breezes in?" Michel replied. "He doesn't live there?"

"I meant figuratively," Davis replied. "The building is attached to the old grocery store on the corner. He lives on the second floor there, though sometimes you wouldn't know it because he doesn't come out for days."

"So which group did Rhodes fall into?" Sassy asked.

"Good question," Davis replied. "He started out in the party group, but then he moved into the inner circle."

"Is that unusual?" Sassy asked.

Davis nodded.

"Everyone else in the circle lives there." She paused for a moment, staring into the middle distance. "Actually, now that I think about it," she continued, "that's not really accurate. He wasn't really part of the inner circle. He was something else. If anything, he was closer with Fierce."

She seemed surprised at her own observation.

"Do you think they were sleeping together?" Michel asked.

"No," Davis replied, shaking her head emphatically. "I wouldn't be surprised if Fierce is still a virgin."

Sassy and Michel exchanged surprised looks.

"That's part of what makes him attractive," Davis said. "The fact that he seems unattainable. He thrives on adoration, but he keeps an emotional and physical distance. I think he's actually afraid of intimacy."

"Sounds like a strange character," Sassy replied.

"He is," Davis replied, "but he's also definitely got something. Some kind of...aura, I guess, is a good word. He's very calm and sure of himself, and when you're talking with him, you feel like the most important person in the world. The way he looks at you, it's like he's really seeing into your soul."

"It sounds like maybe you have a bit of a crush on him," Sassy said.

"I wouldn't go that far," Davis replied with a tiny, embarrassed smile, "but like I said, he's got something, and it encourages people to open up to him. But about five minutes later, the spell wears off and you just feel kind of...empty...or lonely, maybe. It's weird."

"You think he's using hypnosis?" Sassy asked.

Davis shrugged. "Maybe." She shook her head as though trying to throw off sleep, then smiled self-consciously.

"I'm confused," Michel said. "You just said that he's able to get people to open up, but you also said he doesn't really show much interest in anyone's lives. So what does he get them to open up about?"

"Their fears," Davis replied. "He may not give a shit about hopes and dreams or the mundane details of daily life, but he's pretty damned interested in what makes people wake up in a cold sweat in the middle of the night."

"You think it's just part of the whole goth persona?" Sassy asked. "A fascination with the morbid?"

"I think it goes beyond that," Davis replied. "The first time I talked with him, I figured he was either trying to put me in an emotionally vulnerable position to manipulate me, or just getting his jollies, but I don't think it was either. I definitely didn't have the sense he was feeding on it. In fact, he was almost clinical. It was more like a science experiment where I was the test subject."

Michel grunted intrigued interest, but Sassy's attention had temporarily wandered.

"What do you suppose Rhodes told him that they suddenly grew so close?" she asked suddenly.

"Interesting question," Michel replied, "though I'm not sure it matters since they're on the outs now."

"Probably not," Sassy admitted, "but I'm definitely curious."

She pursed her lips for a moment, then looked at Davis.

"Is there anyone else from the group we should talk to? Anyone Rhodes was close with?"

"There was," Davis replied, "but I haven't seen him since just before Christmas. He said he was going home to visit his family. Maybe he decided to stay."

"What's his name?" Michel asked.

"Sparkle," Davis replied.

"Sparkle?" Michel and Sassy repeated in unison.

Davis laughed and nodded.

"I'm assuming that's not the name on his birth certificate," Michel said.

"Probably not," Davis agreed, "but it's all I've got."

"Let me guess," Sassy said. "A black drag queen with a thing for Curtis Mayfield tunes?"

"Actually, no," Davis replied. "A little half-Latino boy with a thing for glitter."

"The Mariah Carey movie?" Michel asked, wrinkling his nose with distaste.

Both women gave him deadpan looks.

"He always had it all over his body and in his hair," Davis said. "There was a trail everywhere he went."

"Any idea where his family lives?" Sassy asked.

Davis shook her head.

"Based on his accent, I'd guess northern Kentucky or southern Ohio, but I don't know for sure."

"Well, it's a possible lead if Rhodes doesn't just show up," Sassy said, then looked at Michel. "Anything else?"

He considered it for a moment.

"Just out of curiosity," he asked, "what was with the trailer trash out front yesterday?"

"You mean the Helter Skelters?" Davis replied.

Michel was struck that she and Sassy had both used a Manson reference to describe the group. He nodded.

"They showed up a few days ago," Davis replied. "And you were right about the trailer. Rumor is they were running a meth lab out of one in Florida. The police busted it two weeks ago, but they managed to get away."

"So what are they doing at Fierce's?" Michel asked. "They don't exactly fit in."

"It happens all the time," Davis replied. "There are always addicts, criminals, and crazies on the fringes. They're drawn by the free booze and drugs."

"That sounds like a dangerous combination," Sassy said.

"It is," Davis agreed, "but they never stick around for very long. After a few days, they tend to disappear."

"Disappear?" Sassy replied.

Davis gave an easy laugh. "Nothing permanent, at least so far as I know. He just has friends who encourage them to leave."

"You mean like hired muscle?" Michel asked.

"More like friends with badges," Davis replied. "The police presence on the street tends to go up when the scary quota gets too high, then drops to almost nothing. I assume Fierce is paying them."

"But it hasn't gone up since the Helter Skelters arrived?" Michel asked.

"Not yet," Davis replied.

Sassy and Michel exchanged a quick look.

"Any idea where they're staying?" Sassy asked.

"I heard they're camping out in an abandoned building somewhere close by," Davis replied. "Across from a park."

"Probably Markey Playground," Michel replied.

He gave Sassy a questioning look.

"Just one last thing," she said, turning to Davis. "You wouldn't happen to know Fierce's real name, would you?"

"Franklin Gaudreau," Davis replied.

"How much do you want to bet his middle name is Pierce?" Michel asked.

Sassy thought about it for a moment, then nodded.

"Franklin Pierce. Fierce. Clever," she said, as though it were anything but.

*****

While Sassy walked Davis to her car, Michel dialed homicide detective Al Ribodeau, a friend and former colleague with the New Orleans Police Department.

"Ribodeau," he answered on the first ring.

"Hey Al," Michel replied. "How's business?"

"Fortunately, a little slow at the moment," Ribodeau replied. "You're not going to fuck that up, are you?"

"No," Michel replied. "I've just got some information. Seems some folks who are wanted for running a meth lab in Florida have been holing up in an abandoned building near Markey Playground."

"That describes two-thirds of that neighborhood," Ribodeau replied. "Can you narrow it down a little?"

"Sorry," Michel replied.

Ribodeau gave a mildly annoyed grunt.

"Not your typical turf," he said. "Nor mine."

"I just happened to come across them, and figured I'd pass it along," Michel replied. "Do with it as you please."

"And in return for this valuable information?"

Michel smiled to himself.

"Well, we're working a missing person. An adult kid who's most likely just hiding from his parents. We got a lead that until recently he'd been partying with a group of other arrested development types in a building on Burgundy, between Piety and Desire. The leader of the group is a guy named Franklin Gaudreau. He calls himself Fierce. Ever hear of him?"

"Sounds like a wack job. Any reason I should have?"

"Not that I know of, but our source thinks he may have some connections on the force."

"What kind of connections?"

"Just badges to scare away undesirables," Michel replied. "Nothing serious."

There was a brief pause.

"I've got some contacts at the Fifth. I'll ask around and see if anyone knows anything about him," Ribodeau replied finally, though he didn't sound overly thrilled by the prospect.

"Great," Michel replied.

There was a longer pause, then Ribodeau chuckled.

"That's it?" he asked. "Nothing that's going to compromise my professional integrity?"

"Not at the moment, but I'll call if I think of anything that will," Michel replied brightly. "And thanks."

He hung up as Sassy came back into the office. He noticed that she was moving slowly, carefully.

"You okay?" he asked, though he knew it would probably earn him an irritated glare.

Instead Sassy gave him a small, diffident smile.

"Just some cramping," she replied, easing gingerly into her chair. "Residual effect of the chemo."

"Oh," Michel replied, surprised by her candor.

"So what did you think of Miss Davis?" Sassy asked quickly.

"I liked her," Michel replied. "She needs to work on her first impression, but I thought she was smart, insightful. What about you?"

"Same," Sassy replied, "though I think she may be a tad too sure of herself."

Michel smiled.

"That's funny. I was going to say she's exactly how I've always imagined you at that age."

Sassy narrowed her eyes at him.

"I had every reason to be that sure," she replied.

Michel laughed, then his expression grew serious.

"So do you think we can trust her?"

"Why wouldn't we be able to?"

"No particular reason, but it wouldn't be the first time we got played," Michel said. "Ellis already lied to me about his relationship with Rhodes."

"True," Sassy replied, "but what would be her angle?"

"Maybe she's a closer friend than she let on," Michel replied. "She sends us back to Ellis, he conveniently avoids us for a few days, and Rhodes has time to relocate."

"I guess it's possible," Sassy replied, "but if he's just playing hide-and-seek with mommy, why go through the effort?"

Michel considered it, then nodded.

"True. It's not like we can force him to go home, even if we find him."

"So now what?" Sassy asked.

"I'm thinking lunch first, then maybe an unannounced visit to Ellis to see who answers the door."

Chapter 12

"Nice place," Sassy said as they rolled to a stop outside the neat, two-story stucco building.

"Mostly on Rhodes's dime," Michel replied. "At least according to Ellis."

They got out of the truck and walked down a narrow brick walkway to the side door. Michel hit the buzzer.

"You planning to see Chance again tonight?" Sassy asked.

"I was thinking about it," Michel replied.

"So you can talk?" Sassy pressed.

"Don't you have a husband to nag somewhere?" Michel replied. He frowned and hit the buzzer again.

"Maybe he's at work," Sassy said.

"I don't think they're open for lunch," Michel replied.

He took out his cell phone and scrolled through the list of recent calls until he found Ellis's number, then hit REDIAL. The chipper greeting came on after three rings.

"Hey, this is Sky. You know what to do."

"Hi, Skylar. This is Michel Doucette," Michel replied. "Please give me a call when you have a chance."

He hung up and surveyed the windows of Rhodes's and Ellis's second-floor apartment. A flash of movement caught his eye, and he focused on the open window on the far left. As a warm breeze ruffled the leaves of the adjacent magnolia, the curtain fluttered slightly.

"Let's get out of here," he said.

*****

Michel watched Sassy make her way slowly to the front porch, fighting the urge to get out and help her. Finally, she climbed the stairs and took out her keys. She turned and gave a half-hearted wave before letting herself into the house. Michel stared at the closed door for a moment, wondering if her coming back to work had been such a good idea, then pulled out his cell phone and hit speed dial.

Chance picked up after the first ring.

"Hey," he said in a noticeably tentative tone.

"Hey," Michel replied. "What are you up to tonight?"

There was a long pause, and Michel smiled, picturing the anxious look on Chance's face.

"It's okay," he said reassuringly. "No fancy restaurants, no talking about last night...or this morning. I just wanted to hang out. We can do whatever you want."

"Honestly," Chance replied after another brief pause, "I'm pretty beat from last night...and this morning. Would it be okay if we just ordered pizza or something and watched a movie?"

"Perfect," Michel replied. "How about seven?"

Chapter 13

Michel was being chased by a horde of pale, humanoid mutants, but he was no longer afraid. So far, they hadn't been able to catch him, and he knew that in a minute the music would finish and the whole scene would begin again. He kept running, his breathing oddly easy.

Finally the music ended. Michel stopped running and turned around. He was alone again. After a few seconds, the melancholy throb of the horns and the angelic, wordless choir started again. Soon the kettle drums would join them and the rhythm would grow faster, then the creatures would reappear. He relaxed and waited.

Suddenly the music was joined by a more insistent trilling. Michel's eyes snapped open. Colors and shadows danced across the ceiling directly above him. He lifted his head, groaning at the stiffness in his neck, and looked at the TV. The selection menu for the *I Am Legend* DVD flickered back at him. The display on the cable box read 1:22 AM.

Michel looked down at the shiny black hair against his left shoulder, then tilted his head down until he could see Chance's face. Chance was sound asleep. Michel looked to his right. Blue was curled up on the sofa beside him, her nose nestled behind his right hip.

Isn't this cozy? he thought.

His cell phone rang one more time, then went silent. Michel gently lifted Chance's head, then scooted forward a few inches, twisting his torso to his left. Slowly he lowered Chance into the gap behind him. Blue's eyes remained closed, but her tongue shot out and licked the top of Chance's head once.

Michel stood and stretched. His phone began ringing again. Quickly he padded down the hall to the kitchen and grabbed it off the counter. Skylar Ellis's number lit the display.

"Hello," Michel answered quietly.

"Did I wake you?" Ellis replied.

His voice was too loud, his words slow and thick.

"No," Michel lied.

"Good," Ellis replied. "Do you want to come over?"

Michel crossed into the bedroom and closed the door.

"Well, no," he replied.

There was a long pause, then Ellis sighed loudly.

"I thought that was why you called," he said with a mixture of wounded pride and bitterness. "I thought you'd changed your mind about letting me fuck you."

Michel registered mild surprise. He'd assumed that if he and Ellis had had sex, the roles would have been reversed. He sat on the bed.

"Sorry," he said without apology.

There was another long pause as he waited for a response, but all he heard was deep breathing.

"So why didn't you tell me you and Cam are boyfriends?" he asked finally.

"Because it's none of your fucking business!" Ellis shot back angrily. "Just leave us alone."

"You know I can't do that," Michel replied calmly. "His mother hired me to find him."

"Well, that's your fucking problem," Ellis replied.

Michel rolled his neck slowly from side to side.

"Unfortunately, it's also Cam's problem," he replied.

"Not for much longer," Ellis replied. "In six months he'll be 21 and get control of his trust. He won't need that bitch's money anymore, and then we're going to leave and she'll never see him again."

"Where are you going to go?" Michel asked casually.

"Nice try," Ellis replied with a small giggle.

He began humming a fast tune, punctuating it with verbal drums beats and cymbal crashes. Michel guessed he'd just gotten home from a club. Then suddenly Ellis stopped.

"Why does she want to find him, anyway?" he whined. "So she can bribe him with another car or a trip? Just tell her not to worry. Cam doesn't give a shit about her or Scotty-boy. He won't cause any trouble."

Michel sat up straighter. He was surprised at Ellis's insight into Trish's fears.

"I wish I could take your word for that, Skylar," he replied, "but I really need to talk to Cam."

"Well, he doesn't want to talk to you," Ellis replied with dramatic finality.

"How about if you and I get together to talk then?" Michel asked.

"Sure, come on over," Ellis replied, with a coarse attempt at sounding seductive, "though I don't think we'll be doing too much talking."

"I meant tomorrow," Michel replied flatly. "When you've sobered up."

"I'm not drunk," Ellis replied indignantly. "Besides, I'm busy tomorrow. I've got things to do, and I'm working."

"Look, Skylar..."

"Sky!" Ellis interrupted irritably. "I like to be called Sky."

"Okay, *Sky*," Michel replied. "I'm not going away until I have a chance to talk with Cam. Let him know that."

Michel could hear the click of a lighter and Ellis inhaling. After a few seconds, Ellis exhaled loudly.

"Fine," he said with clipped impatience. "We're done."

The line went dead.

*****

Michel walked back into the living room. The couch was empty. He looked toward the patio. An ember glowed orange in the dark beyond the open door. He grabbed his now-watery drink from the coffee table and went out. Chance was sitting on the edge of the fountain, smoking. Blue was sprawled on the flagstones a few feet away.

"A booty call?" Chance asked.

Michel didn't sense any accusation in it.

"If he'd had his way, yes," he replied, smiling. "It was Skylar Ellis, the roommate-slash-boyfriend of Cam Rhodes, the kid we were hired to find."

"What did he want?" Chance asked.

"Sassy and I stopped by to see him today but he wasn't there, so I left a message. He apparently thought I wanted to take him up on the offer he made me the other day."

"I guess he must have heard about your reputation for sleeping with witnesses and suspects," Chance said.

"Must have," Michel replied.

He poached the cigarette from between Chance's fingers and took a drag, then handed it back.

"Is he cute?" Chance asked.

Michel nodded.

"So why didn't you sleep with him?"

Michel pretended to ponder it for a moment.

"Too young," he replied finally, with an offhand shrug. "I like my men older and more grizzled."

"Older and more grizzled, huh?" Chance asked.

"Relatively speaking," Michel replied.

"Well, don't let me stop you," Chance replied breezily. "It's not like you're the only action I'm getting. In fact, I hooked up with three guys after I left here this morning. That's the real reason I was so tired tonight."

"Oh really?" Michel replied, laughing.

"You didn't think it was because of you, did you?" Chance asked. "I barely broke a sweat last night." He gave Michel a teasing sideways glance, then added, "Or at least that's the way I remember it."

Michel leaned forward suddenly and kissed him.

"Then maybe I'll have to refresh your memory," he said.

"Maybe you will," Chance replied.

Chapter 14

Michel arrived at the office just after 9:30 AM. The door was already unlocked, and he braced himself for another reprimand from Sassy. Instead, he found Russ Turner sitting on the edge of Sassy's desk. He looked exhausted, and his face was lined with worry.

"Is Sassy all right?" Michel asked immediately, his pulse quickening.

Turner gave him a weary smile, then leaned forward to scratch Blue's ears.

"Yeah," he said, "but she had a little episode last night."

"What kind of 'little episode'?" Michel asked uneasily.

"Chest pains, heart palpitations, trouble breathing," Turner replied. "She was convinced it was a heart attack, so I took her to the emergency room. The doctor said it was just a panic attack, and sent us home after a few hours. He gave her some pills to help her sleep."

"A panic attack?" Michel replied. "Was this the first one?"

He settled into the chair closest to Turner. He felt both wired and suddenly very tired.

"Not this bad," Turner replied. "She's been having anxiety issues since she found out about the cancer. Insomnia, no appetite, mood swings, that sort of thing. But nothing like last night. It's actually been getting better lately. I figured she'd turned the corner."

"I'm sorry," Michel replied. "I didn't know."

Turner nodded kindly.

"I know."

The simple words felt weighted with meaning, and Michel wondered if Turner knew the reasons why Sassy had been pushing him away. He fought the impulse to ask, knowing it wasn't the right time. Blue seemed to sense his disquiet and walked over. He felt immediately calmer as he began rubbing her neck.

"How bad has it really been, Russ?" he asked.

"Pretty bad," Turner replied. "I know it's been tough on you being shut out, but believe me, you got the better part of the bargain. Sassy hasn't been the same person since she got sick."

"How so?" Michel asked.

Turner was quiet for a moment. His usually steady eyes were anxious.

"I was prepared for anger or bitterness or fear," he said finally, "but I wasn't prepared for her to just give up."

"Give up?" Michel repeated.

Turner nodded gravely.

"But that doesn't make sense," Michel replied. "Not with everything she's been through in the past. She crawled down three flights of stairs with a bullet in her leg when Joshua Clement tried to burn a house down around her. She didn't just give up."

"I know," Turner replied, "and she's told me about Carl and losing the baby. If anything, those things seemed to have made her stronger, but for some reason, this was different. I've seen enough people who've given up on life, and for a while there, I could see that same look in her eyes."

Michel felt his throat tighten.

"Did you talk to Pearl about it?" he asked.

"She doesn't understand it either," Turner replied, "and since Sassy hardly talks to her...."

"I'm really sorry, Russ," Michel replied, feeling helpless.

Turner accepted the sympathy with a stoic nod. Blue walked back over to him and laid her head on his knee.

"Why didn't you tell me before?" Michel asked.

"I didn't feel like it was my place," Turner replied. "You and I are friends, but Sassy's my wife, and I figured that if she wanted to talk to you about it, she would. Besides, you've had your own stuff to deal with. But now, I feel like I don't really have a choice. You need to know."

For a split second, Michel wondered if Turner had considered him too emotionally frail to deal with the reality of the situation. He let the thought go.

"Is there *anyone* she's been talking to?" he asked.

"She talks to Chance every few weeks," Turner replied, "and Stan Lecher. A few others."

"Chance?" Michel replied, more emphatically than he'd intended.

Turner nodded. "She seems fine talking with friends. The people she's pushed away are the ones closest to her. I think she would have shut me out entirely, too, if she could have. She certainly tried."

Michel blinked at him distractedly for a moment, then realized what he'd said. He studied Turner's face to see if he was exaggerating.

"I won't lie," Turner continued. "It's definitely tested our marriage. There were more than a few times when she invited me to leave, and a few times more than that when I wanted to pack up and take Corey to a motel. But I knew I couldn't."

Michel gave him a sympathetic half-smile.

"I think it's been hardest on Corey," Turner said, "because he doesn't understand what's happening." He shook his head. "Hell, I don't understand, so how could he? But at least I can rationalize it. He can't. He just sees Sassy shutting him out."

Michel grimaced. That his own perception had been the same as that of a seventeen-year-old boy wasn't lost on him.

"Sassy told me they've been having problems," he said quickly. "I thought maybe he was acting out because he was afraid of losing another mother."

"I'm sure that's part of it, too," Turner replied, "but if Sassy hadn't pushed him away, I don't think it would have been so hard for him. He thinks she's stopped loving him, and on some level I think he's blaming himself. Who knows? Maybe he blamed himself for Thesalee's dying, too, and I didn't know it."

They were both quiet for a long moment. Blue turned to Michel, then looked back up at Turner, as if waiting for a cue on whom to comfort next. Finally she lowered her head and walked to her corner to lie down.

"What do you think we should do?" Michel asked.

"I don't know," Turner replied. "When she decided to come back to work, I thought she'd finally turned the corner, but now I'm not so sure it was the right thing to do."

Michel nodded thoughtfully.

"It seems like the perfect case to get her feet wet again," he said. "A few interviews, follow-up on a couple of leads, wait for the kid to resurface, and call mommy and daddy."

Turner pursed his lips.

"Did anything else happen yesterday?" he asked. "Maybe something outside of the case?"

Michel thought he detected a hint of accusation, but let it pass. He thought about the events of the previous day. Other than his revelation about sleeping with Chance, nothing had been out of the ordinary. In fact, it had felt almost like old times. He shook his head.

"I wish I could think of something, but it was pretty average. We interviewed a girl, had lunch, then dropped by to see if the missing kid's roommate was home."

"And Sassy seemed fine?" Turner asked.

"Other than some cramping."

"I thought we were done with that," Turner sighed, closing his eyes.

Michel noticed that the lids appeared almost bruised from lack of sleep. Turners eyes fluttered back open, and he fixed Michel with a probing look.

"And you're sure there was nothing else?" he asked, sounding more like a diligent cop than a worried husband now.

Michel nodded.

"Okay, then I guess we'll just wait to see what happens," Turner replied. "Maybe she was just overly tired."

"And if she wants to come back to work?" Michel asked.

"I'm not going to stop her," Turner replied, "but I'll be counting on you to keep an eye on her." He pushed tiredly to his feet. "I guess I better get going. My shift starts at eleven."

He started for the door, then turned back.

"By the way, this conversation never happened. I was just supposed to call and tell you she wasn't feeling well."

"Understood," Michel replied.

*****

Miss May Nettles had been a teacher in Baton Rouge until she'd retired some ten years earlier and moved back to Butte La Rose. On summer days, after Sassy finished her chores, Miss May would let her read through old textbooks, then quiz her on what she'd learned. Sassy thought that Miss May was about the nicest and smartest person she'd ever met.

But now, as she approached Miss May's house, Sassy had butterflies in her stomach. It had been a few months since she'd seen Miss May, because Miss May had gotten sick. Sassy didn't know what was wrong with her, but knew it must be bad because she'd never known anyone to be sick for so long.

Sassy's mother and a few of the other ladies had taken to bringing food for Miss May, but today they were all busy preparing for the church supper, so Sassy's mother had told her to bring Miss May's lunch. Sassy didn't know why, given how much she liked Miss May, but she felt nervous.

Despite the fact that it was just after noon, it looked to be close to dusk. A storm had blown in that morning and, though the rain had passed, thick gray clouds still hovered overhead. Sassy turned the bend in the road and saw no lights on in Miss May's house. She cursed under her breath, then quickly apologized to God.

She walked up the three wooden steps onto the porch, then looked for a place to set the tray with Miss May's soup and biscuits. The railing was too narrow and frail, and the low bench and wood planks of the porch were covered by a thin film of slimy moss. Sassy frowned. The tray was much too valuable to risk ruining it by resting it on the wet, dirty wood.

It was a family heirloom. Her mother's parents had brought it back from the 1933 World's Fair in Chicago. It was made of a light yellow wood, and had an image of the city lacquered onto the center. The buildings had been painted in bright red, blue, orange, and yellow, and formed together into an almost-perfect triangle. Below them was a black bridge, and under that, a gold banner emblazoned with the words: *A CENTURY OF PROGRESS*. The tray held a place of honor in the house, on the cupboard just outside the kitchen. Sometimes when she was alone, Sassy would take it down and study it, trying to imagine the people living in the buildings and driving across the bridge.

She looked around one more time for a place to set the tray, then carefully shifted it onto just her right hand. She stared at it for a moment to make sure it was balanced, then knocked on the door with her left hand. She waited a moment, but didn't hear anything. She hesitated a few seconds more, then undid the latch and pushed the door open a few inches. The soup bowl began to slide forward, but she quickly righted the tray by grabbing the side with her left hand.

"Miss May?" she said in a small voice, leaning forward into the darkness. "It's me, Sassy. I brought you some soup."

She paused, but still didn't hear anything. She opened her mouth to speak again, then gagged as the smell of feces and stale sweat washed over her. She jerked back involuntarily, and the soup bowl chattered loudly on the tray. Sassy tried to steady herself.

"Miss May?" she called again more loudly, desperation creeping into her voice.

She wanted to leave the soup on the doorstep and run home, but she'd promised her mother she'd stay and make sure Miss May ate it all. She looked back at the road hopefully, willing someone to come along to go inside with her, but no one materialized.

She took a few quick breaths through her mouth, then slowly pushed the door open a few more inches with her left elbow. Suddenly it jammed, and a corner of the tray bumped against it. Sassy heard soup slop onto the floor and looked down.

In the dim light, she could see a stick lying just inside the door. At first she thought it was a broom handle, but the wood was darker, and the end was gnarled and knotted, like the top of a walking stick. Sassy squatted down, balancing the tray on her knees, then reached out to move the stick. It was soft and warm. Suddenly it twitched, and spidery fingers spasmed open from the gnarled end. They began clawing at the dusty floor.

Sassy fell back, and the tray flipped over on top of her. Hot soup ran down her inner thighs, pooling on the dirty planks and mixing with her own urine. She tried to scream, but her vocal chords were frozen. She scrambled backward toward the stairs as black clouds began swirling in front of her eyes. Then her arms buckled, and she felt damp cold against the right side of her face.

*****

Sassy woke with a gasp, her heart racing, her body coated in cold sweat. Still locked in the memories of her eight-year-old self, she looked around the darkened room in panic, trying to make sense of the strange yet familiar shapes. Finally things began to fall into place, and she took deep, calming breaths.

"Goddamn you, Miss May Nettles," she whispered.

Chapter 15

Michel opened the outer door and unhooked Blue's leash. She trotted down the hall, sniffed the air curiously, then went into the office. He heard her voraciously lapping water.

"Don't forget to come up for air," he called, leafing through the mail.

"I won't," a voice replied.

Michel looked up startled, as Blue bolted back into the hallway and up the stairs. Michel walked to the end of the hall and looked up. Chance was squatting on the second-floor landing, accepting Blue's enthusiastic licks with mock distaste.

"Hey," Michel said, his mood brightening after the visit from Russ Turner. "What are you doing here?"

"I own the place, remember?" Chance replied.

"Yeah, I remember," Michel replied dryly, "but it's been at least a year since you've been here."

Blue finished her greeting and shot past Chance into the apartment. Chance stood and wiped saliva from his left cheek.

"That you know of," he said, starting down the stairs. "Maybe I bring all my tricks here late at night."

"I'm pretty sure all my tricks would have noticed," Michel replied, smiling sweetly.

Chance smiled back even more sweetly. "Even with those bags over their heads?" he asked, as he reached the bottom stair.

For a moment they hovered, then Michel leaned forward and kissed Chance. It felt forced and unnatural. He hoped that Chance hadn't felt it, too.

"That was weird," Chance said immediately.

"Um, yeah," Michel replied self-consciously.

"Like you were kissing your grandmother, or something."

"Oh, come on, it wasn't that bad," Michel said, annoyed that Chance was trying to pin the awkwardness entirely on him.

"Yeah, it really was," Chance replied. "Maybe we should have taken our pants off first."

Though his tone was outwardly teasing, Michel thought he caught a slight edge, and wondered if it had been more than just a casual joke.

"Do you want to try again?" he asked.

"With or without pants?"

"With."

Chance pretended to weigh it for a few seconds, then shook his head.

"No, I'm good."

He skirted past Michel into the office, and sat on the edge of Sassy's desk. Michel stood in the hallway feeling foolish a moment longer, then followed.

"So what are you really doing here?" he asked, leaning against the door frame.

Chance's expression turned suddenly uncertain.

"My lease is up at the end of the month," he said, "and I was thinking it's kind of stupid to pay rent when I have this place."

He seemed to be testing the waters as he said it, and Michel could see him watching carefully for a reaction. He suspected that if he responded too enthusiastically, Chance would get spooked and reconsider.

"Makes sense to me," he replied, trying to strike the right note of practical nonchalance.

Chance studied him a moment before nodding.

"That's what I thought, too. I just didn't want you to think I was moving back because of you."

"The thought never crossed my mind," Michel lied. "So when would you move?"

"I was thinking about this weekend," Chance replied. "I already started packing yesterday."

"Oh," Michel replied, surprised that Chance hadn't mentioned it the previous night or that morning. He suspected Chance hadn't fully made up his mind until that moment. "Do you want some help?"

"That would be cool," Chance replied casually. "You may as well use your butch truck to haul something besides pansies."

Michel flirted with a remark about Chance being the only pansy he'd ever had in his truck, but decided against it. The set up had been too easy. He suspected Chance already had a comeback prepared.

"Yeah, may as well," he replied, stifling a smile when he saw the flicker of disappointment in Chance's eyes.

They heard feet thundering down the stairs, then Blue cantered into the room. She ignored them and went directly to her usual spot.

"Damn it," Chance exclaimed. "Did you eat my sub?"

Blue stared at him with round-eyed innocence as the roast beef hanging from her mouth suddenly disappeared.

"I'm sure she left anything green, and most of the bread," Michel said.

"You and I need to have a talk about respecting other people's food," Chance said, shaking a finger at Blue.

She turned her head as though he were talking to someone behind her, then lowered her head and burped.

"She clearly gets her manners from you," Chance said, scowling at Michel, then nodded at Sassy's chair. "So, where is she, anyway? She's the one I was *really* hoping to see."

"At home," Michel replied. "She had a panic attack last night, and went to the emergency room. Russ stopped by this morning to tell me."

"And you didn't think that was something you should tell me before you started slobbering all over me?" Chance asked.

"Sorry," Michel replied.

"So, is she okay?"

"I guess so."

"You guess so?" Chance made a face. "You haven't called?"

"Not yet," Michel replied. "The doctor gave her something to sleep. I didn't want to wake her."

"Did Russ say what caused it?" Chance asked.

"He doesn't know," Michel replied, then paused a beat before adding, "but he said you've been talking to her."

Chance heard a note of something new he couldn't identify in Michel's voice. "So?" he asked warily.

"So, I was just wondering if she mentioned anything that might explain the panic attack," Michel replied.

It sounded stilted. Chance was sure there was more to it.

"I haven't talked to her for a few weeks," he said.

"And she didn't mention anything that was bothering her then?" Michel pressed.

This time Chance recognized the tone. "Oh, you mean like cancer?" he asked sarcastically, then shook his head in dismay. "Wow, you're fucking unbelievable."

"What?" Michel asked, his expression an unintentional parody of Blue's feigned innocence.

"Your best friend had cancer, and now she's having panic attacks, and all you care about is why she hasn't been calling you?" Chance replied.

"That's not what I meant," Michel protested, though he realized immediately it was a lie. It hadn't been conscious, but he'd let his own neediness overshadow his concern for Sassy.

"I realize this may be a blow to your huge ego," Chance said, "but you're not a big topic of conversation." He searched Michel's face for a moment, then his expression softened slightly. "The truth is that we don't talk about much of anything. Just my classes and that kind of shit." He raised his eyebrows. "Does that answer your question?"

"I'm sorry," Michel said with a sheepish nod, "and thanks for calling me on my bullshit."

"Anytime," Chance replied. He looked at Blue, and seemed to debate saying something more, then the moment passed. He stood, stretched, and yawned elaborately. "I should probably finish cleaning so I can get home and pack some more," he said.

Michel nodded, but didn't move. Chance took a few steps toward the door, then stopped and gave him an expectant look. Michel looked back blankly.

"You're kind of in the way," Chance said.

"Oh yeah, sorry," Michel said. He pushed off the door frame and stepped to the side.

Chance took another few steps.

"I guess I'll see you before I leave," he said.

Michel nodded again, then smiled and put his right arm across the doorway.

"What the fuck?" Chance said, laughing nervously.

Michel moved closer and pressed his body into Chance, pinning him against the door. Chance's eyes became suddenly anxious and he tried to pull his head back, but Michel leaned in until their lips touched. For a few seconds, Chance's body remained rigid, his lips pressed tightly shut, then he gave in and returned the kiss.

After nearly a minute, Michel stepped back.

"How was that?" he asked.

"Pretty good," Chance replied with a teasing smile, "but I still think it would have been better without pants."

He reached down and made a show of adjusting himself, then slipped under Michel's arm. Michel smiled as he walked to his desk.

Chapter 16

Michel shut down his computer. Blue immediately lifted her head and gave him a quizzical look.

"In a few more minutes, sweetie," he replied. "I have to make some calls first."

Blue groaned softly as she lowered her head back between her front paws. Upstairs, Chance dropped something heavy and unleashed a loud, "Fuck!"

Michel smiled, flipped open his cell phone, and hit REDIAL. After the increasingly annoying greeting, he left his third message of the day for Skylar Ellis. He hung up and looked at the time: 4:12 PM. If Ellis had been telling the truth about working that night, he was probably already at Jacques-Imo's. Michel debated whether to pay him a visit there.

His deliberation was broken by the phone's ringing. He looked at the display and saw Sassy's number.

"Hey, I was just getting ready to call you," he answered. "How are you feeling?"

"Not good," Sassy replied quickly. "I fucked up."

"What do you mean?"

"Rachel Davis left me three messages last night, but I didn't check them until just now. Rhodes showed up at Gaudreau's place last night."

"Shit," Michel replied. "Have you talked to her yet?"

"I just got off the phone with her," Sassy replied. "She's on her way to pick me up, then we'll come there."

Michel looked at Blue and felt a twinge of guilt.

"Why don't you meet me at my place instead?" he said. "Blue's had her legs crossed for the last half hour. I need to take her for a walk. We should be there in about twenty minutes."

"Okay," Sassy replied. "And I'm really sorry."

Michel knew he couldn't fault her given what had happened the previous night, but also knew that if he let her entirely off the hook, she'd realize Russ had told him about it.

"Yeah, well, I guess you're out of practice," he said with what felt like an appropriate mix of annoyance and poorly disguised disappointment, "but don't make it a habit, okay?"

"I promise," Sassy replied, then hung up.

Blue immediately jumped up.

"How come you can hear that, but can't hear me telling you not to eat a rock from five feet away?" Michel asked.

Blue looked at him blankly.

"Come on," Michel said, shaking his head. "We just have to let Chance know we're leaving."

Blue ran out of the office and up the stairs.

"What do you want, you little thief?" Chance's voice wafted into the stairwell. "You ate it all, and now I'm starving."

Michel reached the top of the stairs. Chance was squatting in the middle of the kitchen, rubbing both sides of Blue's face. He was shirtless, and his hair stuck out at odd angles. Michel found the tableau amazingly sexy.

"I didn't realize this was one of those stripper cleaning services," he said.

"I didn't want to get my shirt all sweaty," Chance replied.

"Because it's your only one?" Michel asked.

"Because I was thinking about going for a drink and didn't want to have to go home to change first," Chance replied.

"What happened to packing?" Michel said.

"I'm kind of over that for today," Chance replied. "Cleaning was a lot more work than I expected. Any chance you could help me move on Sunday instead? That way I'll have tomorrow to finish packing."

"Sure," Michel replied. "I get home from church at ten."

"Funny," Chance replied, standing up.

As he put his hands on his hips, his cargo shorts rode down a few inches to reveal the low waistband of black briefs. Michel wondered if it had been deliberate.

"So?" Chance asked.

Michel blinked at him uncertainly, his face growing warmer.

"So, what?" he managed.

"So did you want to go with me?" Chance asked with exaggerated exasperation. "You know, for a drink?"

"Oh. Um, yeah, sure," Michel stammered, "But I have to meet with Sassy first."

Chance's face brightened.

"Would it be okay if I came along?" he asked.

"Actually, it's business," Michel replied.

"Oh." Chance's disappointment was clear. "Okay."

Michel felt a pang of sympathy.

"But it shouldn't take too long," he added, "and I'm sure she'd love to see you. Why don't you come by the house in an hour. That should give us enough time. Then you can visit with Sassy for a while, and we'll go for a drink after."

"You're sure?" Chance asked.

Michel nodded enthusiastically as he said a silent prayer that Sassy wouldn't mind.

"Cool," Chance replied. "That'll give me a chance to take a shower first."

He lifted his right arm and grimaced as he pretended to take a long sniff. Michel had a sudden vision of pinning him against the wall and licking his armpits.

"Okay," he said quickly. "Blue and I better get going. See you in an hour."

Chapter 17

"He showed up a little after nine," Rachel Davis said.

"Alone?" Michel asked.

Davis shook her head.

"He was with Charlie Manson's twin."

"The meth cooker?" Sassy asked. She cut a look at Michel. "I thought you called Al about them?"

"I did," Michel replied. "He said he'd pass the information along." He turned back to Davis. "Had you ever seen them together before?"

"I'm not even sure how they'd even know each other," she replied, shaking her head. "That crew didn't show up until a few days after Fierce and Rhodes had their fight."

"Maybe," Sassy replied.

Michel and Davis both looked at her expectantly.

"They may not have shown up at Gaudreau's until a few days ago, but that doesn't mean they weren't already in town," Sassy explained. "Maybe Rhodes already knew them. In fact, maybe he's the one who sent them to Gaudreau's."

Michel raised his eyebrows, waiting for her to continue, but she just stared back at him.

"Do you have a theory you want to share?" he prompted.

"No, I'm just saying it's a possibility," Sassy replied.

Michel tried to read her expression and tone, but couldn't.

"Yeah, that's true," he agreed with a slow nod, "but we don't have any evidence to support that yet. Maybe we should just focus on getting the facts first."

A slight tightening of Sassy's lips told him he'd said the wrong thing. Sassy quickly looked at Davis.

"So what happened next?" she asked.

What *just* happened, Michel wondered.

"Like I said, they arrived a little after nine," Davis replied. "Rhodes left mini-Manson on the street and went in. He came back out about ten minutes later, and they both went in."

"Did you follow them?" Sassy asked.

"Just inside," Davis replied. "Then they went up to Fierce's apartment."

"Do you know if anyone else was up there?" Sassy asked.

"I don't think so," Davis replied. "The rest of the inner circle were all downstairs."

"How long were they up there?" Michel asked.

"About a half hour," Davis replied, "then mini-Manson came down by himself and left."

"How did he seem?" Sassy asked.

"Not as tightly coiled as usual."

"What about Rhodes?" Michel asked. "When did he leave?"

Davis shrugged.

"I stayed until after midnight, but I never saw him again."

Michel looked at Sassy.

"So maybe he's still there," he said.

"At the very least, he and Fierce seem to have made nice again," she replied, "so chances are he'll be back."

"But it's going to be tough to stake it out," Michel said. "There are too many approaches to cover, and I can't just stand on the corner because Rhodes knows I'm looking for him."

"I can check it out and call if he's there," Davis offered.

Michel and Sassy exchanged a look of concern. Davis caught it and smiled reassuringly.

"It's no big deal," she said. "I'll be there anyway."

"But what if someone notices?" Michel asked.

"Notices what?" Davis replied. "Me talking on my cell phone? Like that's really suspicious behavior?"

She laughed, and Michel blushed slightly.

"You're sure you don't mind?" Sassy asked.

Davis shook her head.

"Like I said, I'm going to be there anyway."

Sassy considered it, then nodded.

"Okay, but be careful, and don't try to engage him in conversation. If you see him, just call."

"I promise," Davis replied.

She raised her right hand and pantomimed swearing a vow. Sassy nodded again, then studied her for a few moments.

"You certainly are diligent about your research," she said. "I'm surprised you don't have plans with friends on a Friday night. Or a date."

Michel noticed a new, maternal tone in her voice.

"Actually, I'm meeting friends for dinner," Davis replied. "I'll go to the party afterward."

"By yourself?" Sassy asked.

Davis nodded casually, but Sassy suddenly leaned forward, as though she'd caught the faint hint of an intriguing scent. She stared at Davis curiously for a long moment, then narrowed her eyes slightly. Davis responded with a girlish laugh.

"Yes, there's a guy," she said. "His name is Jesse."

Sassy smiled with self-satisfaction, while Michel wondered what he'd missed.

"Good for you," Sassy said, "I've never met a boy named Jesse who wasn't cute. But are you sure keeping an eye out for Rhodes isn't going to cramp your style?"

Davis shook her head.

"I probably won't talk to Jesse, anyway," she replied. "I'm just observing right now. Figuring out if he's worth my time."

Michel let out a snorting laugh, imagining it was the exact sort of thing a younger Sassy would have said. As the women simultaneously turned to him, he covered his mouth and pretended to cough.

"Sorry," he said, gesturing to his throat. "A tickle."

"Smart girl," Sassy said, fixing Michel with a hard look, "because clearly, most of them *aren't* worth it."

She looked back at Davis, and they shared a quick conspiratorial smile.

"Well, I should probably get going," Davis said. "Do you want a ride home?"

"Thanks, but you go on," Sassy replied. "I need to talk to Michel for a little while."

Davis nodded.

"So who should I call if Rhodes shows up?" she asked.

Sassy immediately pointed at Michel.

"If it's after nine, I'll be sound asleep," she said.

Michel pulled a card from his wallet and wrote on the back.

"That's the home number," he said, handing it Davis. "My cell is on the front. Either one should be okay. I'm not planning on going anywhere."

Davis nodded and tucked the card into the front pocket of her shoulder bag.

"Hopefully, you'll be hearing from me later," she said.

*****

"Thanks for throwing me under the bus," Sassy said as soon as Michel had closed the door.

He turned to face her. She was standing at the end of the hallway, her arms folded across her chest.

"What are you talking about?" he asked.

"'*Do you have a theory you want to share?*'" Sassy replied in a high, mocking voice. "'*Maybe we should focus on getting the facts instead of you just pulling stuff out of your ass.*'"

"I didn't say that last part," Michel replied.

"You might as well have," Sassy snapped back.

"Was I wrong?" Michel asked defensively.

Anger flashed in Sassy's eyes, then her whole body seemed to deflate. Michel thought she suddenly looked exhausted.

95

"No, but you didn't have to make me look like an idiot," she replied in a small, plaintive voice. "I already felt stupid enough that I missed her messages. I was just trying to help."

"And you did help," Michel replied. "Once you stopped with all the crazy talk."

"It wasn't crazy," Sassy replied, seeming slightly mollified. "It just didn't make sense."

They were both quiet for a moment, then Michel cocked his right eyebrow.

"So what was that all about, anyway?" he asked.

Sassy let out a deep sigh, and slowly shook her head.

"Insecurity, I guess."

"Because of Rachel?" Michel asked.

"Because of her. Because I haven't done this in so long. I guess I wanted to prove I still had it. Not very successfully."

Michel smiled warmly.

"You know you don't need to impress me."

Sassy gave him a playfully imperious scowl.

"I should hope not."

"And I think Rachel is plenty impressed with you already."

A small, pleased smile curled Sassy's lips.

"Of course she is," she replied, all theatrical bluster. "Why shouldn't she be?"

"Exactly," Michel replied.

"After all, I'm Sassy Jones," Sassy said, regally lifting her chin. "Beautiful Nubian queen, and mistress of all I survey."

Michel held up his hands.

"Uh, no," he said. "This is all my shit. I'm the queen here. You're just visiting royalty."

Sassy stared him down for a moment, then shrugged.

"Okay, I can accept that," she said.

"Good," Michel replied. His expression grew more serious. "Just relax and work your way back into things. This isn't a murder case. No one's life hangs in the balance. It's just some stupid kid hiding from his parents."

Sassy took a cleansing breath, then smiled and nodded. "You're right," she said. "And thank you."

"You're welcome," Michel replied. "Now can we sit down?"

Chapter 18

"So what have you been up to all day?" Sassy asked, taking the wine glass from Michel.

"Checking into Rhodes and Ellis," Michel replied.

He settled onto the couch to Sassy's right.

"Why Ellis?" she asked.

"In case they make a run for it," Michel replied. "Obviously they wouldn't go to Trish, but I thought they might pay a visit to Ellis's family."

"And?"

"Doubtful. His parents are Holy Rollers."

"What flavor?"

"Assemblies of God. His father has his own congregation in West Monroe."

"I think it's a pretty safe bet they won't be welcoming their son and his boyfriend for a visit," Sassy agreed. "Anything else?"

Michel shook his head.

"Nope. Just your average small town girl with big city dreams," he intoned dramatically. "Just like you."

Sassy rolled her eyes.

"Don't make me slap you. So what about Rhodes?"

"Well, he shares his mother's penchant for substance abuse, but not her resolve to quit. According to the Boston gossip rags, he's been in rehab at least three times. He was also arrested on a DUI at 18, though no charges were ever filed."

"Trish must have called in a lot of favors to pull that one off," Sassy replied. "Anything else of interest?"

"His best friend committed suicide during their senior year of high school," Michel replied.

"Jesus," Sassy replied, grimacing. "How?"

"Ate a bullet."

"That doesn't leave much room for interpretation," Sassy replied sympathetically. "Definitely not just a cry for help."

"No," Michel agreed.

Sassy took a long sip of her wine. Michel noticed that she suddenly seemed anxious.

"What?" he asked.

Sassy hesitated a moment, then leaned forward and set her glass down on the coffee table.

"Would you ever do it?" she asked quietly.

Michel blinked at her.

"You mean kill myself?"

Sassy's head nodded almost imperceptibly, as though she were afraid to affirm the question too strongly.

"No, of course not," Michel replied, his attempt at certainty undercut by the awkward pitch change of his voice.

"But when you went after Joshua Clement, you were ready to die then," Sassy said.

Michel sipped his drink as he considered his response.

"I knew it was a possibility," he said carefully, "and maybe I was even prepared, but that's not the same thing as wanting to die, or trying to kill myself."

Sassy nodded more comfortably.

"And you never considered it after Joel died?" Sassy asked.

"No," Michel replied, shaking his head slowly but emphatically. He paused, staring down at his drink for a moment, then gave Sassy a probing look. "So is this just about me, or are you trying to tell me something?"

Sassy smiled softly.

"Being sick has definitely made me think about my own mortality," she said, "but no, I haven't been thinking about killing myself. I was just curious about you."

There was more she wanted to say, but decided against it.

"*Would* you ever consider it?" Michel asked.

Sassy shrugged.

"Under the right circumstances, I suppose."

Michel studied her.

"But not now, right?" he asked, the need for assurance clear in his voice.

"No, not now," Sassy replied. "But at some point down the road, if I were alone and in pain, it might be an option."

They sat in contemplative silence for almost a minute, then Sassy picked up her wine and drained it.

"Well, that was cheery," she said, holding out the empty glass.

Michel laughed and took it.

"Hey, you brought it up," he said, walking into the kitchen.

"I know, and now I'm going to change the subject," Sassy replied, suddenly all business again. "Did you have a chance to check out our buddy Fierce at all?"

Michel refilled the glass and carried it back into the room.

"No, but I asked Al to see if they have anything on him or the house."

He handed the wine to Sassy.

"Hopefully it won't matter," she said. "Hopefully Rhodes will show tonight and it'll be over. If not, we'll pick it up again on Monday."

She raised her glass in a toast to the resolution of the case.

"So you'll be back?" Michel asked, then silently cursed himself as he realized what he'd said.

"Why wouldn't I be?" Sassy replied suspiciously, lowering her glass.

Michel struggled to come up with a plausible response.

"Gee, maybe because you've been back to work for two whole days and you're already faking sick?" he said, adopting a teasing tone. "I'm really feeling the commitment to the job."

"I was *not* faking," Sassy replied.

"Oh, sorry," Michel replied elaborately. "I certainly didn't mean to impugn your work ethic...after you've taken the last two years off."

Sassy narrowed her eyes, then broke into an amused chuckle.

"Fuck you," she said. "And it's only been a little over a year and a half."

"Whatever," Michel replied quickly, hoping to move on before Sassy realized he'd glossed over her question. "So, any exciting plans for the weekend?"

"Just the usual," Sassy replied. "Cleaning, laundry, waxing my head."

"Can't you just say no?" Michel asked.

"No," Sassy replied, then paused and gave him an overly sweet smile. "And what about *you*?" she asked in a saccharine singsong. "Do *you* have any plans? With *Chance*?"

Michel raised his eyes to the ceiling and sighed tolerantly.

"As a matter of fact, we do," he replied, bracing himself for the inevitable. "I'm helping him move."

"Move?" Sassy cried. "When did you become lesbians?"

"Not into my house," Michel replied. "He's moving back above the office."

"Oh," Sassy replied, sounding only slightly deflated. "Well, won't that be convenient?"

"Are you done?" Michel asked.

Sassy pursed her lips in deliberation for several seconds, then nodded.

"Yeah, I suppose so."

"Good," Michel replied.

"So did you two talk about Joel yet?" Sassy asked.

Michel shook his head.

"Not yet."

Sassy frowned her disapproval.

"And what about what's going on between you? Did you talk about that?"

"No," Michel replied. "Right now we're still working on the hello kiss. Once we get past that, we'll figure out the rest."

"I'm going to assume that was a joke," Sassy replied.

"Assume whatever you want," Michel replied.

Sassy gave him a puzzled look that turned to concern.

"And that doesn't worry you?" she asked.

"The kissing part?" Michel replied.

"No, the not-talking part, smart ass," Sassy replied.

"No," Michel replied, matter-of-factly. "I already told you, I know we need to talk about Joel, and we will. As for '*us*,'" he said, making air quotes, "I think it's a little premature for that."

"Hey, it's your life," Sassy replied, putting her hands up in surrender. "Like I said, I just don't want to see either of you get hurt because you're not on the same page."

"I think we're fine for now," Michel replied. "We're just taking things one day at a time."

"Like alcoholics working a program," Sassy muttered.

Suddenly Blue jumped up, followed a split second later by the doorbell.

"Speaking of," Michel said.

"Chance?" Sassy replied.

Michel nodded.

"That's a nice surprise," Sassy said.

"I was hoping you'd think so," Michel replied. "Can you stay for a while?"

Sassy shrugged.

"I don't know why not," she said. "Russ is working until eight, and Corey's supposed to be having dinner at a friend's house. It was just going to be me, Pat, and Vanna tonight."

Michel gave her a look of mock pity.

"Wow, you really do need to get out more often," he said.

Chapter 19

Michel dropped the empty takeout carton in the trash. He felt more contented than he had in a long time. The evening had been just like old times. He almost hoped that Rachel Davis wouldn't call. He refilled his glass with ice water and walked to the patio door. Sassy had taken the nearest chaise, and Chance was perched on the wall of the fountain. Blue was lying halfway between them.

"You really like it?" Sassy was asking, pretending to fluff a mass of invisible curls.

"Yeah," Chance replied. "It definitely suits you."

Michel debated where to sit, finally opting for a spot next to Chance, where Sassy wouldn't be bothered by his smoking. He noticed that Chance looked mildly irritated, and that he immediately shifted a few inches away.

"It's too bad Russ couldn't join us," Michel said, mostly meaning it, "though this was nice with just the three of us."

Sassy nodded contentedly.

"So why aren't you drinking, anyway?" Chance asked, making a face at Michel's glass. "Did the Jack Daniels factory burn down?"

"It's called a distillery, and no," Michel replied. "We're hoping Cam Rhodes is going to show up tonight, so I want to keep my wits about me."

Chance snorted laughter. "Wouldn't that assume you had some about you in the first place?"

Sassy's deep chuckle rose above the burbling of the fountain.

"Well, it's nice to see things haven't changed just because you two are 'doing the do' now," she said.

Chance's head jerked toward Michel and his eyes widened.

"What? Did you put up a billboard so everyone would know?" he asked.

Michel was relieved that Chance seemed surprised but not angry.

"You didn't see it?" he replied, "I also hired a plane to fly a banner around the city."

"You probably did," Chance said. "I'm sure it's the most exciting thing that's happened to you all year."

Michel started to protest, but realized it was probably true.

"I've got a reputation to protect, you know," Chance said, shaking his head.

Although his tone was still joking, Michel thought he heard a note of discomfort. He looked at Sassy and caught a slight smirk on her lips. He knew immediately what she was thinking, and realized she was right. He and Chance would have to talk sooner than later.

His cell phone rang and he was happy for the distraction. He eagerly pulled it from his shirt pocket and looked at the display.

"It's Rachel," he said.

*****

"I've got to hurry," Michel said when he hung up.

"Why, what's happening?" Sassy asked.

"Rachel just got to Gaudreau's place. Rhodes and Ellis are there, but they're not planning on sticking around for long."

"Why not?"

"They're going camping."

"Camping?" Sassy replied. "Rhodes didn't exactly look like the camping type in those photos."

"It gets weirder," Michel said. "Gaudreau is going, too."

"That *definitely* doesn't sound right," Sassy said.

"I know," Michel agreed. "Goths in the wilderness. But Rhodes said they're going camping down in Florida."

"Wait a second," Sassy said, concern creasing her forehead. "Rachel talked to him? She wasn't supposed to do that."

"She didn't," Michel replied. "She said Rhodes had an RV parked out front, and he and Gaudreau were out there telling people about the trip."

Sassy frowned.

"That sounds suspicious."

"That's what Rachel thought," Michel replied. "She said it seemed staged, like they wanted to make sure everyone knew the official story."

"So what do you think is really going on?" Sassy asked.

"They're definitely going somewhere," Michel replied. "Maybe Rhodes has a surprise planned for Trish."

"Do you think you should call her?" Sassy asked.

Michel shook his head.

"I'd rather just try to head him off. I can always call her later if I miss him."

He stood up and looked at Chance.

"Are you going to stay here? I don't think it'll take long."

"I guess so," Chance replied without much enthusiasm.

"I can call you when I'm finished, and we can meet up somewhere for a drink," Michel offered.

"Okay," Chance replied, brightening slightly.

Michel turned to Sassy.

"I'll call and let you know what happens."

"You want some company?" she asked.

"Sure." Michel replied, surprised. "You really want to go?"

"May as well," Sassy replied. "Russ can just as easily pick me up there. Besides, I'm curious to see this Fierce in person."

Chapter 20

The street was empty, and the doors of the building were shut, though a slash of dim light was visible along the bottom of the middle one. Even with the truck's windows closed, they could hear the muffled throb of pulsing music.

"Rachel said she'd be waiting out front," Michel said, searching the shadows around them.

"I don't like this," Sassy said. "There's no RV, and there should be people out here. Something's wrong."

"Let me try calling her," Michel said.

He pulled out his phone, but the truck was suddenly filled with a loud, thumping bassline. He looked at the now-empty passenger seat.

"Wait!" he called as Sassy slammed the door shut.

Michel dropped the phone back into his jacket pocket and jumped out of the truck.

"Wait!" he called again.

Sassy was already at the door. She turned to face him. Michel could see the worry in her eyes.

"Shouldn't we at least have some kind of plan?" he asked.

"We have a plan," Sassy replied tersely. "We go inside and ask nicely if anyone knows where Rachel is, and if we don't get an answer, I start slapping people."

She turned, yanked the door open, and slipped inside. Michel could feel the music pounding against his chest, as if it were trying to keep him out. He took one last look around the street for Rachel, then sighed and followed.

He stood just inside the door, waiting to acclimate to the sudden sensory overload. In addition to the pain in his ears and dizziness from the flash of strobe lights, the thick smells of burning wax, incense, cigarettes, and stale perfume were making him slightly sick. He was suddenly glad he hadn't had anything to drink. He took a few deep breaths through his mouth, and closed his eyes for a moment. When he opened them again, he saw Sassy on his right, watching him. She nodded straight ahead, and they began moving slowly down the center of the room.

At one point, the open two-story space had probably housed heavy machinery, but now it looked like a cross between a dance club and a Victorian bordello. The centerpiece was a massive, gaudy crystal chandelier that spun slowly fifteen feet above the floor. Its faux-candle fixtures were unlit, but the beams of four strobing laser lights refracted through the crystals, swirling bands of color on the brick walls like a giant rainbow disco ball.

The left half of the room was divided into several small seating areas of ornate furniture, arranged around expensive-looking oriental rugs. Dozens of half-full glasses and lit pillar candles covered the tops of coffee and side tables, but the sofas and chairs were all unoccupied. Michel noted that most of the glasses were coated with fine sweat.

They reached the base of an intricately carved "wine glass" pulpit near the back wall. From the expression on Sassy's face, Michel could see she'd reached the same conclusion he had: a lot of people had left very recently. The question was why.

"What do you think we should do?" he shouted, barely able to hear his own voice.

Sassy pointed to her ears and shook her head in frustration. Michel took a quick look around, and saw cables snaking upward from the back of the pulpit to speakers mounted high on the wall. He walked to the gracefully curving staircase, and climbed up into the pulpit.

A bank of sound and lighting equipment had been mounted into a metal rack in the front. He knelt and studied the various components and controls for a moment, then hit the OFF button on the top left unit. As the echo of the music faded, an eerie silence took its place.

Michel stood and surveyed the room from his raised vantage point. In the back right corner, nearly hidden behind tall book shelves, was another grouping of sofas and chairs. Like the rest, they were unoccupied. He sighed and started to turn away, but a sudden movement caught his eye. He jerked his head back and stared at the spot where he'd seen it.

"Hello?" he called tentatively.

He heard what sounded like the sob of a child in response. He leaned forward to see Sassy, but she was already moving toward the corner. He hurried down the stairs after her.

As they got closer, they could hear low murmuring, punctuated by occasional gasping breaths, but still couldn't see anyone through the gaps on the shelves. Michel unholstered his gun and quietly racked the slide. Sassy stopped and gave him a questioning look. He replied with a "you-never-know" shrug, then nodded down at her belt. Sassy shook her head. Michel took the lead and they began moving forward again.

When they reached the end shelf, they paused. Michel flipped off the safety and brought his gun up to the high ready position, then stepped around the corner. A dozen pairs of eyes stared up at him with terror.

"Please don't hurt us," a girl with spiked blue hair and a nose ring pleaded in a small voice.

Even with her severe make-up and black satin bustier, she looked like a frightened child.

"We're not going to hurt you," Sassy said soothingly as she came up beside Michel.

She knelt and quickly searched the faces of the small group huddled together on the floor. Rachel wasn't among them.

"What happened?" she asked.

Although there were no obvious physical injuries, the haunted eyes and slack expressions indicated shock.

"What happened?" Sassy repeated more urgently. "Where's Rachel Davis?"

Wide eyes stared back at her, but didn't seem to register the question.

"Mistress Nightshade," Michel said. "Do you know where she is?

A boy toward the back of the group began crying. Michel's pulse quickened.

"Jesse went to look for her, but he didn't come back," another boy in a leather harness said. "I thought they were just hooking up, but..."

He trailed off and his eyes became unfocused, then his narrow shoulders and chest began to spasm. Michel wondered if he was having a seizure and took a step closer. Suddenly the boy jackknifed forward and began retching, though nothing came up. Only a few delicate threads of spit dangled from his open mouth, slowly stretching toward the carpet. He gasped for air, and dry heaved again, his whole ribcage convulsing. Michel leaned forward and put a steadying hand on his back.

Finally, after nearly a minute, the boy sat up and looked at Michel with red, glassy eyes. Snot and spittle covered his mouth and chin, and he tried unsuccessfully to wipe them away with the back of his left hand.

"It didn't seem real," he said in a dazed whisper. "I thought someone was playing a joke."

"What?" Michel asked. "What didn't seem real?"

Sassy took a deep breath, fighting to hold back her rising panic. She realized she no longer had the ability to emotionally detach that she'd had when she was working homicide.

"Where?" she asked, her voice shaking.

The boy pointed to door in the opposite corner.

"In the playroom."

*****

The black rubber floor beneath the St. Andrew's Cross was slick with blood. Rachel's naked, battered body was still strapped in place by the wrists and ankles. Her head hung back and slightly to the left, the slit in her throat gaping open as though in a silent scream.

On the floor to her right lay the body of a male. He was dressed in immaculate black trousers, a red silk waistcoat, and a gray frock coat, but his bow-tied neckcloth and Grafton shirt collar were soaked through with blood. The features of his face were no longer distinguishable.

Chapter 21

Sassy took another sip of tepid coffee and pulled Michel's jacket tighter around her shoulders. Despite the warm night air, she couldn't shake the chill that seemed to have settled deep in her bones. The guilt, sadness, and anger she'd been feeling a half hour earlier had faded to numbness for now, but she knew they'd be back.

"I just don't understand it," she said, shaking her head. "Why would Rhodes kill her? It doesn't make sense."

Michel didn't reply, knowing the question was rhetorical. He took a cigarette from his pack and clamped it between his lips. As he lit it, he saw Al Ribodeau come out of the building. Ribodeau seemed to have aged dramatically in the two-plus years since he'd been promoted to homicide detective. He'd also put on at least thirty pounds, and his walk had slowed considerably. Michel wondered unconsciously how long it would be before he had his first heart attack.

Ribodeau spotted them leaning against Michel's truck and walked over.

"I thought you said you weren't going to fuck up my nice peaceful summer," he said without humor.

"Sorry about that," Michel replied. "I thought we just had a kid hiding out from his parents. I wasn't expecting this."

"So what happened?" Sassy asked.

Ribodeau sighed with frustration.

"I don't know if it's because they're all in shock or high or what, but we're having a tough time getting a cohesive story."

"Well, what do you know so far?" Sassy asked more sharply than she'd intended.

Ribodeau nodded, acknowledging her anxiousness.

"We know the Rhodes kid and his buddy Ellis showed up around 8:30 PM," he said. "They were in a tan or off-white motorhome. One of those big jobs you usually see being driven down the middle of two lanes by someone's grandfather. Sounds like it was a newer model, possibly with Georgia tags."

Sassy nodded impatiently.

"Davis showed up just before nine," Ribodeau continued, "A girl by the name of..." he paused to consult his notepad, "...Kimberly Buchanan...remembers her coming up the block from the direction of Esplanade. That's when things get a little fuzzy. According to Buchanan and another kid by the name of Kenny Dixon, Davis disappeared a few minutes later."

"Probably to call me," Michel said. "Why is that fuzzy?"

"Because the rest of them either don't remember her being there at all, or think she was out on the street the whole time," Ribodeau replied. "Of course, there's also some confusion about whether Gaudreau had a duffel bag with him when he came out of the building, whether he'd told anyone he was going away, and the day of the week. Buchanan and Dixon seem to be the most reliable, but that's not saying much."

He mimed taking a hit off a bong, and rolled his eyes.

"Did either one of them see Rachel again?" Michel asked.

Ribodeau shook his head.

"And where was Rhodes after she disappeared?" Sassy asked.

"Out front," Ribodeau replied. "He was out there when she arrived, and stayed there until he, Ellis, and Gaudreau took off about 10 minutes later."

"So he didn't have anything to do with her killing?" Michel asked, surprised.

"I don't see how he could," Ribodeau replied.

"Are you sure he was out there the whole time?" Michel asked. "You said the other witnesses are fuzzy on the details."

"That's the one point everyone agrees on," Ribodeau said. "Rhodes and Gaudreau were both out there the whole time."

"Maybe the others are trying to cover for them," Sassy said.

"Maybe," Ribodeau replied, "but I think at least one of them would have slipped up. They're all pretty shaken."

"What about Ellis?" Michel asked. "Where was he?"

"In the front of the RV," Ribodeau replied. "The Buchanan girl said he seemed to be sulking."

"I wonder what that was about?" Michel said. "Ellis didn't strike me as the sulking type."

Ribodeau shrugged.

"Have you got an ID on the other victim yet?" Michel asked.

"According to the license in the wallet we found on him, his name was Jesse Woods."

"One of the kids said Jesse went to look for Rachel." Michel said, nodding.

"That was probably Dixon," Ribodeau replied. "He said that Woods and Davis had been circling one another for a while. Woods noticed she was gone and told Dixon he was going inside to look for her. He never came back. We're guessing he interrupted the assault and got killed."

"Was she raped?" Sassy asked quietly.

Ribodeau studied her a moment, then nodded. Sassy let out a small moan, but her gaze remained steady.

"Who found the bodies?" Michel asked.

"Dixon and some friends," Ribodeau replied. "Everyone came back inside after Rhodes and the others left, and a few of them headed for the 'playroom.' At first they thought it was some kind of joke or a performance art thing, then one of the friends noticed that Davis was still bleeding."

"And then everyone just ran away," Sassy said bitterly.

"Pretty much," Ribodeau replied.

"Did Dixon see anyone back there?" Michel asked.

"No," Ribodeau replied, "but he gave us the names of his friends. We'll question them. Right now it looks like it all happened while everyone was outside, and the killer—or killers—took off before they came back in."

"No one even tried to take her down," Sassy said, her voice breaking slightly.

Michel and Ribodeau both looked at her.

"They did the right thing," Michel said gently. "They would have contaminated the crime scene."

"I know that," Sassy said, her tone suddenly much harder, "but it's not natural. To see something like that...someone you *know* like that, and not do anything about it." She paused as she blinked back tears. "They didn't even call a fucking ambulance. They just hid."

Michel knew better than to try to justify it, and shot Ribodeau a warning glance.

"It just wasn't right," Sassy said.

*****

Michel pulled up in front of Sassy's house and cut the engine. Neither had spoken during the five-minute drive.

"It wasn't your fault," Michel said.

"I know that," Sassy said softly, her eyes still fixed on the dashboard. Michel tried to read her expression, but couldn't.

"So then what is it?" he asked.

Sassy's mouth twitched slightly, then she sighed deeply.

"It's just that...I keep thinking about how scared and helpless she must have felt," she said, "and I just wish that somehow I could...comfort her. Take away the pain, make it so that she didn't feel so alone." She stopped and gave Michel a sad smile. "I know I can't, and I know it's stupid to even think about, but I can't disconnect emotionally anymore."

"That's not necessarily a bad thing," Michel said.

"I know, but in this case it would help," Sassy replied.

They were both quiet for a long moment. Michel fought the urge to light a cigarette.

"So do you still think Rhodes has something to do with it?" he asked finally.

"Who else could it be?" Sassy asked.

Michel shrugged.

"We didn't know anything about Rachel. Maybe she had a crazy ex-boyfriend stalking her, or owed millions to a Mexican drug cartel. Or maybe it was just some random psycho."

"Who just happened to show up tonight?" Sassy asked, arching her brow skeptically.

"But Rhodes was outside the whole time," Michel argued.

"Exactly. Conveniently surrounded by dozens of witnesses who can give him an alibi," Sassy replied. "Just because he didn't do it himself doesn't mean he wasn't responsible."

Michel shook his head wearily.

"It's a big jump from runaway to murderer," he said. "I don't see it. All she did was give us a little information."

"Then who?" Sassy asked.

"What about Gaudreau?" Michel offered. "Maybe he found out she was studying the group, and didn't like it."

"Now who's reaching?" Sassy replied.

They were both quiet again for a moment, then Sassy cracked open the passenger door. The dome light cast harsh shadows across her face.

"I'm tired, Michel," she said. "I'm tired of being sick. I'm tired of people being killed."

Michel nodded.

"Does that mean you won't be back on Monday?"

"Oh no, I'll be back," Sassy said. "I'm not going anywhere until this is done."

Chapter 22

Michel snatched his buzzing cell phone from the night stand and slipped out of bed.

"Hey, what's up, Al?" he answered softly as he stepped into the hallway, closing the door behind him.

He winced, and shielded his eyes from the pale morning sun streaming through the patio doors.

"The Rhodes kid," Ribodeau started in immediately. "He wouldn't be about six-three, a hundred-and-ninety pounds, sandy hair, would he?"

"No, smaller and darker. Why?" Michel asked.

"They just pulled a body matching that description out of the river in Gretna," Ribodeau replied.

Michel's senses came fully alert.

"Skylar Ellis," he said.

"I figured it might be one of them," Ribodeau replied.

"Why? What happened?" Michel asked.

"An insomniac neighbor reported a vehicle with no lights heading toward the river behind the Domino Sugar warehouse at around three this morning. When the patrol car arrived, they found a partially submerged Airstream Land Yacht with Georgia tags. They hauled it out and found the body inside."

"Accident, suicide, or murder?" Michel asked.

"Murder," Ribodeau replied. "His throat was cut."

"Just like Rachel Davis," Michel said.

"Exactly," Ribodeau replied. "And it looks like he was severely beaten first, too."

"Jesus," Michel whispered. "What about sexual assualt?"

"Not sure yet," Ribodeau replied, "but the body was nude."

Michel grabbed his cigarettes and lighter from the dining room table on his way to the patio. Blue suddenly materialized by his side, her tail surprisingly lively given the early hour. Michel opened the door and she sniffed the air before sauntering out.

"That doesn't make any sense," Michel said, following her. "The matching MO can't just be coincidence, but we know that Ellis left with Rhodes and Gaudreau, and they couldn't have killed Rachel."

He dropped into his usual chair and lit a cigarette.

"I know," Ribodeau replied, yawning.

Michel took a meditative drag.

"So does this mean Rhodes and Gaudreau are suspects?"

"Or victims," Ribodeau replied.

Michel felt the hair on the back of his neck prick up, and straightened in the chair.

"We're going to be cooperating with the boys in Gretna since the murders appear to be linked," Ribodeau continued. "We'll need you to bring in whatever you've got on Rhodes."

Michel didn't respond for a moment. He knew someone would have to call Trish Taylor, and wondered if he should do it himself or let the police handle it. He decided he owed it to her, though he wasn't looking forward to the conversation.

"Yeah, no problem," he replied finally. "Okay if I come in in a few hours?"

"Sure," Ribodeau replied. "I'm still at home working on my first gallon of coffee. How 11?"

"Fine. I'll see you then," Michel replied.

*****

He finished his third cigarette and walked into the kitchen to refill his coffee. He was feeling restless, his mind racing and his body wired with nervous energy. He checked the clock on the microwave, willing it to jump forward another hour.

"Fuck it," he whispered to himself.

He crossed to the bedroom door and silently pushed it open, then stuck his head into the room. Chance was sprawled face down across a mound of pillows, his naked body managing to take up a disproportionate amount of space for his size. Michel could hear deep regular breathing, and see the steady rise and fall of his back.

He focused on Chance's face and shouted, "Wake up! Wake up! Wake up!" in his mind. Chance didn't stir. Michel frowned, knowing there was no reason they should both lose sleep just because he was keyed up. He withdrew his head and started to pull the door shut.

"Is everthing okay?" Chance asked.

Michel jumped a little, then stuck his head back into the room and smiled guiltily. Chance was sitting up now, trying to untangle the sheet, blanket, and comforter at the foot of the bed. He managed to wrestle the sheet up to his waist.

"Sorry, I didn't mean to wake you," Michel said. "Go back to sleep. It's not even six yet."

"Why? So you can watch me again?" Chance asked. "That's kind of creepy, you know."

He propped a few pillows against the headboard and pushed back into them.

"Seriously, what's up?" he asked.

Michel hesitated a moment, then stepped into the room.

"Al Ribodeau called a little while ago," he said. "Skylar Ellis's body was found early this morning."

"Holy shit," Chance said, any trace of sleep leaving his face. "Was he killed?"

Michel nodded.

"His throat was cut, just like Rachel Davis."

"I'm sorry," Chance said, though he seemed uncertain it was the correct response. "Did you want to talk about it?"

Michel walked over and sat on the edge of the bed. Chance immediately grabbed his coffee and drank half of it.

"A little more sugar next time," he said with a sour face as he handed it back.

"I'll remember that the next time you're planning to drink my coffee," Michel deadpanned.

"So?" Chance asked.

Michel considered what to say, then shrugged.

"Ellis is dead, and I have to be at the station at 11," he said, feeling stupid. "That's pretty much it. I guess I was just feeling kind of restless, and didn't want to be alone anymore."

He immediately realized the potential for a more profound interpretation of the words, and hoped Chance wouldn't read more into them than he'd intended. At some point they'd have to talk about what was going on between them, but for now, it just felt good being together.

"Do you think the Rhodes kid killed him?" Chance asked, apparently oblivious to any other interpretation.

"The police are considering him a potential suspect and a potential victim," Michel replied. "And I'm the lucky one who gets to tell his mother."

He gave a long put-upon sigh.

"Oh, poor you," Chance replied with exaggerated sympathy.

"What's that supposed to mean?" Michel asked.

"Let's just keep a little perspective here," Chance replied. "I mean, yeah, it sucks a little for you, but it's going to suck a lot more for her. It's her son. Even if she *is* a shitty mother."

Michel realized how ridiculous he'd sounded, and nodded.

"Are you always so clear-headed when you first wake up?" he asked.

"Obviously *way* more than when I go to bed," Chance teased, making a show of looking Michel up and down. Then his expression grew more serious. "So do you want me to go home so you can get ready for it?"

Michel studied him a moment, then shook his head.

"No. There's nothing I can do right now except obsess."

"Then let's take your mind off it," Chance said.

"That is *so* inappropriate," Michel replied, feigning shock. "I can't believe you'd even suggest something like that at a time like this." Then his eyes dropped to the sheet, and he leered with comic lasciviousness. "But if you insist..."

"I meant breakfast," Chance replied flatly.

Michel's shoulders dropped, and a small pout rounded his lower lip.

"Oh," he said. "I suppose we could do that, too."

Chapter 23

Al Ribodeau was hunched crookedly in his chair, the phone receiver wedged between his right ear and shoulder as he rummaged through the top right drawer of his desk.

"Yeah, that's right. R-I-B-O-D-E-A-U," he was saying. "Same as it's always been."

He waved Michel into the chair on the far side of the desk, then plucked a half roll of Rolaids® from the drawer, triumph lighting his face.

"Tuesday the 24th at 10 AM," he said. "Got it. Thanks."

He hung up and quickly jotted a note on his desk calendar.

"Sorry about that," he said, looking up. "My gut's been killing me lately. I decided it was time to see my doctor."

He ripped an uneven spiral of paper and foil from the roll, and popped two tablets into his mouth.

"Maybe you should try laying off the fast food and cut down on the coffee," Michel offered.

Ribodeau silently chewed for a moment, then took a swig of cold coffee, swished it around a few times, and swallowed.

"That's heresy," he said. "You know cops can't live without fast food and crappy coffee. It's in the book. By the way, how are those smokes treating you?"

Michel smiled.

"At least I'll leave a fashionably thin corpse."

He took a look around the squad room. Not much had changed in the three years since he'd been kicked off the force. He noticed a few familiar faces pointedly ignoring him.

"So any news?" he asked.

"We may have caught a break," Ribodeau replied. "A guy who lives a few blocks from the Domino warehouse reported an RV stolen sometime during the night."

"Another Airstream?" Michel asked.

Ribodeau shook his head.

"Smaller. A Lance camper on a Ford F-250 frame. The Gretna PD put out an APB, and a scanner junkie working the counter at a truck stop on I-55 reported that a vehicle matching the description stopped for gas around 7 this morning."

"Whereabouts?"

"A few miles outside of Jackson, Mississippi."

"At least that narrows the search direction," Michel replied.

"Maybe, maybe not," Ribodeau said. "The guy said it was being driven by a woman, and he didn't get a plate number, so we're not sure it's a match. Gretna alerted the cops in the major towns north of there, just in case."

Michel nodded. "What about the Airstream? Any idea where it came from?"

"Stolen," Ribodeau replied. "Thirteen days ago in Cordele, Georgia, wherever the hell that is."

"So Rhodes or Ellis either borrowed a stolen motorhome, or went to Georgia to steal one themselves?" Michel replied skeptically. "That doesn't make any sense."

"No," Ribodeau agreed.

Michel frowned.

"Has the forensics team come up with anything yet?"

"The Davis crime scene is like a damn cesspool," Ribodeau replied, grimacing. "There's hair, bodily fluids, and God knows what else on everything. Even if we had a suspect in custody, it would take weeks to isolate samples to see if we have a match."

"And what about the Airstream?" Michel asked.

"You mean the one that was filled with a thousand gallons of pure, clean Mississippi River?" Ribodeau asked.

"Forget I asked," Michel replied.

"Actually, the Gretna forensics guys are pretty sure Ellis wasn't killed in it," Ribodeau said.

"How's that?"

"No blood on anything above the water line, and only a small stain on the carpet below."

"Couldn't it have washed away?"

"They said it was unlikely in such a short period of time, especially given that the water in the shallows is pretty still."

"So that means there's another crime scene somewhere," Michel said.

"Most likely," Ribodeau replied, nodding.

Michel's attention drifted to a handsome younger detective emptying the dregs from the communal coffee pot into a white mug. The coffee looked thick and inky, and the stained and scratched pot clearly hadn't seen a scrubber in years. Michel marveled that the New Orleans Police Department still hadn't managed to provide its officers with a decent cup of coffee.

"Let me ask you something," Ribodeau said, snapping Michel's attention back. "Does it maybe seem staged to you?"

Michel's brow furrowed with confusion.

"The dump scene," Ribodeau clarified. "Presumably, they were trying to sink the RV to hide the body, right? But they drove it into six feet of water. That's either really stupid, or maybe they actually wanted the body to be found. I mean, why try to sink the RV in the first place, especially if Ellis wasn't killed in it? It would have been much easier to just dump the body in the river and abandon the RV somewhere else."

Michel remembered what Trish Taylor had said about Rhodes's need to draw attention to the things he'd done, but dismissed it. It was a huge leap from taunting his parents with his sexuality to staging scenes with his dead boyfriend's body.

"It could have just been a fuck up," he said. "Maybe the killer got nervous and hit the accelerator instead of the brake, or maybe the moon was playing tricks and he didn't see the edge of the water."

Ribodeau mulled it for a moment, then nodded.

"Okay, so then let's assume we're talking either an accident or a legitimate attempted sinking," he said. "If it's the latter, that suggests that the killer isn't a local."

Michel gave him a perplexed look.

"You lost me."

"A local would know the waters in that part of the West Bank are too shallow," Ribodeau replied as though the answer were obvious.

"Then how come I didn't know?" Michel replied.

Riboeau chuckled softly.

"Probably because you grew up on the wrong side of the bridge and never fished for alligator gar as a kid."

Michel looked at him like he was speaking in tongues.

"Yeah, I'm pretty sure I never did that," he said.

Ribodeau gave a small smile, then a larger frown.

"Think we're getting ahead of ourselves?" he asked.

"Maybe," Michel replied, "but until there are some solid leads, it doesn't hurt to speculate."

"I suppose," Ribodeau replied, "but I hope we'll get something concrete when we interview more of the kids from Gaudreau's last night."

"Can I watch?" Michel asked immediately.

The smile that played across Ribodeau's thin lips suggested he'd just won a bet.

"I already cleared it with the Captain," he said. "The first is at 2, then every 15 minutes until we're done. We've got 15 coming in so far."

"Not like I have anything better to do," Michel replied. "Especially since I can't get in touch with my clients."

"The Taylors?" Ribodeau replied. "They're on their way down. I spoke to them just after I called you this morning."

"Oh," Michel replied. "Because I tried calling them, but their assistant said they were traveling and..."

He stopped, feeling both embarrassed and slightly hurt.

"Sorry. I guess I should have told you I was going to call them," Ribodeau said. "I just assumed..."

"No, that's okay," Michel replied quickly. "After all, it is a police investigation now, right?"

"Yeah, but still," Ribodeau apologized.

Michel shook his head emphatically.

"Really, it's no big deal," he said almost convincingly. "Do you know where they're going to be staying?"

"The Ritz," Ribodeau replied.

"Like I couldn't have guessed that?" Michel said, attempting an easy smile.

They sat in awkward silence for a few seconds, each studying his own hands, then Ribodeau sat up straighter and flipped open his notebook.

"So," he said, pretending to lick the nib of his pen, "tell me everything you know about Campbell Rhodes."

Chapter 24

The digital display read "71 MPH." It was only a few miles over the speed limit, but twenty-two-year-old patrolman Eddie Pike of the Russellville Police Department was feeling restless. He dropped the radar gun on the seat, threw his car into gear, and flipped on the siren. A cloud of pale dust kicked up from under the rear tires as the car lurched down the embankment and onto I-40. Almost two hundred yards ahead, the top of the beige camper disappeared over a low rise.

Pike pushed the accelerator nearly to the floor, and the old Crown Victoria responded smoothly. As he crested the hill, he could see that he'd already closed the distance by thirty yards, and was gaining quickly. The camper's brake lights came on, and Pike eased off the gas. Both vehicles slowed, coasting to a stop along the right side of the narrow two-lane highway.

Pike put the car in park and jotted down the Louisiana plate number, then reached for the radio. As the back door of the camper swung open, he felt a quiver of apprehension, and his right hand drifted to his holster. The only warning before the shot was a quick glint of sunlight on steel.

Pike's head snapped back as dozens of tiny lead balls crazed the safety glass in front of his face. He rolled to his right and managed to unbuckle his seat belt as the second blast rained chunks of glass down on him.

"Dispatch, this is Pike," he yelled into the microphone, vaguely aware of how high-pitched and fast his voice sounded. "I'm under fire. Do you copy?"

"Copy," a woman's voice came back. "What's your 10-20?"

"I-40 westbound," Pike managed, though he was having trouble breathing now. "Just past the Mission Road overpass."

"Copy," the woman replied, followed by a louder, more authoritative, "All units, we've got an 11-99. Interstate 40 West, just west of Mission Road. Officer under fire. Repeat, officer under fire. All units respond."

Pike dropped the microphone to the floor. His eyes stung, and he tried blinking the sweat away.

"Fuck, fuck, fuck," he whispered as he inched toward the passenger door.

Suddenly a shadow moved over him and he froze. He closed his eyes tightly, unable to breath, waiting for the inevitable shot. A muffled pop rang out, followed quickly by two more. Pike let out a small, strangled cry.

"What the fuck?" a voice growled behind him.

The shadow moved to the left. Pike sprang up and managed to fumble his pistol from its holster. He could see a bearded man standing along the left side of the hood, cradling a shotgun. The man was looking toward the camper, his face working angrily.

"What the fuck do you think you're doing, you stupid cunt?" he yelled, then took a step forward.

A loud, clear shot cracked the air, and the man staggered back a few steps. He tried to raise the shotgun, but another shot dropped him. Pike heard the shotgun clatter on the asphalt.

Pike's head spun toward the camper. A young woman with long blond hair was slowly walking toward the car, her eyes focused on the ground by the driver's door, a small pistol braced with both hands trained on the same spot.

"Stop," Pike cried weakly as the girl reached the front of the patrol car, but she didn't show any sign that she'd heard him.

She took another few steps until she was even with the side mirror, then fired down toward the pavement.

"You piece of shit," she said coldly.

She laid the gun on the hood of the car, then looked up at Pike. Her pale green eyes were calm, almost peaceful.

"It's okay," she said. "They're all dead."

Chapter 25

Michel looked down at the list of names and yawned. After three hours of interviews without a break, he was finding it hard to muster any enthusiasm.

He looked up at the preppy blond in khakis and a pale pink button-down shirt, then back at the list to make sure he hadn't made a mistake. It was hard to reconcile the Kenny Dixon sitting on the other side of the observation window with the scrawny leather-harnessed kid cowering behind the bookcases at Gaudreau's. Michel remembered what Rachel had said about bored rich kids, though he'd thought that applied only to the outsiders who came just for the parties.

He shifted in his chair, trying to get comfortable, then took out his cigarettes.

"Don't even think about it," a low voice just behind his left shoulder.

Michel flinched.

"Jesus, I didn't even hear you come in," he said, turning to his former commander, Captain Carl DeRoche.

"Obviously," DeRoche replied with a ghost of a smirk. "I thought you'd quit those things."

"They didn't want to stay quit," Michel replied.

DeRoche gave a small grunt of disapproval.

"I was sorry to hear about the Davis girl," he said. "Did you know her well?"

"We just met her the other day," Michel replied, "but I liked her. She reminded me of a younger Sassy."

He assumed the next question would be about Sassy, and considered how much to say.

"Have they been at it long?" DeRoche asked instead, nodding toward the interview room.

"No, they're just starting," Michel replied, surprised.

"So do you think this one is just a witness, or a potential suspect?" DeRoche asked.

"He could be either, I suppose," Michel replied.

"But what does your gut say?" DeRoche asked with a hint of impatience.

"Witness," Michel replied immediately. "Why?"

"Because we'll have to reschedule him," DeRoche replied.

"What's going on?" Michel asked.

"I think I should discuss that with my detective first, don't you?" DeRoche replied.

Michel noted the mild rebuke, but decided to ignore it.

"Do you want me to finish it up?" he offered, unable to disguise his enthusiasm.

DeRoche let out a short, percussive laugh.

"I'm sure that would do wonders for my career if the Commissioner found out I was letting dismissed officers conduct official interviews in murder investigations," he said. He stared through the observation window for a moment, then dropped his eyes to Michel's cigarettes and smiled slyly. "But you might want to go outside and have a smoke now."

*****

Dixon ambled out of the station and stood blinking in the late afternoon sun for a moment. When he spotted Michel standing in the shade on the opposite side of the street, his eyes flashed recognition, then wariness. He seemed to debate what to do before crossing the street.

"You were the guy at Fierce's last night, right?" he said, more statement than question.

Michel nodded as he pressed a cigarette between his lips. He held the pack out toward Dixon.

"Thanks, I've got my own," Dixon replied, fishing a pack of Camel Lights from the right front packet of his khakis. They both lit up. "So are you a cop?" Dixon asked, squinting through the smoke.

"Not anymore," Michel replied.

"So then what were you doing there?" Dixon asked. "And how come you're here now?"

"How about I buy you a cup of coffee and we talk about it?" Michel asked.

Dixon took an elaborate drag on his cigarette. Michel noticed that his mannerisms had a louche, languid quality that contrasted sharply with his current appearance. He imagined Dixon was far more comfortable in his harness, lounging on a velvet settee at Gaudreau's.

"How about a cocktail instead?" Dixon asked.

Chapter 26

Michel set the martini glass in front of Dixon, and slid onto the opposite banquette. He lit a cigarette.

"So who are you, Michel Doucette?" Dixon asked across the top of his cosmopolitan before taking a delicate sip.

It seemed practiced, down to the intense, probing gaze. Michel imagined it was usually successful with younger men convinced of their own inherent interest to others.

"I'm just a private investigator," he said, keeping his tone neutral. "I was hired to find Campbell Rhodes."

Dixon's eyes narrowed slightly, his curiosity plainly piqued.

"So then why were you looking for Mistress Nightshade?"

"She was helping out," Michel replied, seeing no reason to hide the truth. "Just keeping an eye out for Rhodes."

"Was she like an undercover cop?" Dixon asked.

"What makes you ask that?" Michel asked.

"It just always felt like she was watching everybody really closely," Dixon replied. "Like she was there, but never really part of things because she was too busy watching. You know?"

"You're observant," Michel replied, nodding admiration, "but she wasn't a cop. She was a psychology student."

"She was studying us?" Dixon asked.

"Pretty much," Michel replied. "She was interested in cult behavior and saw some similarities in your group."

He expected defensiveness or anger, but Dixon just shrugged.

"Yeah, I can see that," he said, "though it's mostly an illusion. At least within the inner circle."

"How so?" Michel asked, his own curiosity piqued now.

"Everyone assumes that we're like Fierce's disciples or something, but it's not like that at all. Yeah, we keep things under control, but that's just because we don't want the place to get busted."

"Because you'd end up on the streets?" Michel asked.

Dixon shook his head and lit a cigarette.

"That's another part of the illusion," he said. "None of us actually live there. Except Fierce. The main building, the place next door, and the corner market are all connected. There's another entrance off Piety, through the market. We just show up before the parties."

"So you just pretend to live there?" Michel asked. "Why?"

"It was Fierce's idea," Dixon replied. "He thought it would create caché."

"I don't follow," Michel replied.

Dixon let out an impatient sigh.

"It's like with nightclubs," he said. "If you let just anyone in, then no one wants to go. But if you keep some people out, then it seems exclusive, and everyone wants in. Fierce figured that if we created the illusion of this fabulous inner circle who all live and party together, everyone would want to be part of it. It was actually pretty genius because people kiss our asses hoping they're going to be invited to live there."

"That sounds a tad manipulative," Michel said.

Dixon's expression clearly said, "Your point being?" Michel decided to let it drop.

"So how did you make it into the inner circle?" he asked.

"I've known Fierce the longest," Dixon replied.

"How long is that?"

"About two years," Dixon replied. "I met him when he first came down here."

"He's not from New Orleans?" Michel asked.

"New York," Dixon replied, shaking his head. "I met him at Oz when he was on vacation, and invited him to a few parties.

133

Introduced him around the scene. He started talking about buying a place down here where everybody could party every night. I figured it was bullshit, but six months later he called and told me he'd done it."

"It sounds like you're close," Michel said.

Dixon took a long, ruminative drag on his cigarette. Michel sipped his Jack Daniels.

"We were," Dixon said finally, "but then he started to change. Instead of it being about the group, it became all about him. That's when the whole Fierce God thing started."

"I hadn't heard the God part before," Michel replied.

Dixon gave a humorless laugh.

"When I met him he was just plain old Frankie Pierce."

"So where did Gaudreau come from?" Michel asked, noting he'd been substantively right about the derivation of "Fierce."

Dixon shrugged.

"Maybe it's a family name, or maybe he thought it made him sound more like a native. He was already using it when he moved down, then about a month later he claimed some kid at a party came up with Fierce God. I think he made it up himself, but it was obvious he wanted us all to start calling him that. It just grew from there. He cultivated a whole new persona."

"So why did you stick around?" Michel asked. "Sounds like he became kind of a dick."

"At first, I guess I felt kind of sorry for him because it was obvious how desperate he was to be liked," Dixon replied, "and because sometimes he still acted like the old Frankie."

Michel nodded. It had sounded sincere.

"And now?" he asked.

"The drugs and liquor are free, and it's easy to get laid," Dixon replied, enthusiasm overwhelming sincerity. "And since he and Cam became buddies, he's hardly ever around anyway."

"Where's he been?" Michel asked.

"In his apartment," Dixon replied. "He and Cam are always holed up in there."

"Do you think they're lovers?" Michel asked.

"In Cam's fantasies, maybe," Dixon replied, "but not in the real world."

"How can you be so sure?" Michel asked.

"Fierce used to be fat when he was a kid," Dixon replied. "He's got like that whole body dyslexic thing..."

"Body dysmorphic disorder?" Michel interrupted.

"Yeah, where he thinks he's still fat even though he's like skinnier than I am. I tried to hook up with him when we first met, but he wouldn't even let me take his shirt off. I kept trying, and finally he started crying and told me about being fat and everything. I tried to tell him he was hot, but he wouldn't believe me."

"I don't think he could," Michel replied, deciding not to antagonize Dixon by adding, *That's why it's called a disorder.* "So do you think Rhodes is in love with Fierce?" he asked.

"Love," Dixon repeated, seeming to taste the word. "That sounds a little too healthy. I think Cam wants to possess Fierce. Or maybe be him. It's more like obsession."

"That's what Rhodes's boyfriend said," Michel replied.

"Poor pathetic Skylar," Dixon said, shaking his head.

"Why do you say that?" Michel asked.

"When Cam first started hanging out, he was always fucking with other guys," Dixon replied. "Then he'd bring Skylar and introduce him to the guys, and you could see in Skylar's face that he knew what was going on. I think Cam got off on humiliating him, and he was willing to put up with it."

Michel wondered if the drunk, angry Ellis who'd called him was closer to the truth than the relentlessly sunny version he'd met at the apartment.

"Because he loved Cam, or because he was afraid to leave?" he asked.

"More likely afraid of leaving Cam's money," Dixon scoffed. "And Cam's never going to dump him because he likes having someone to abuse. The whole relationship is pretty twisted."

135

"Was," Michel corrected.

Dixon gave him an uncomprehending look.

"Skylar's dead," Michel said. "His body was found early this morning over in Gretna."

Dixon's features went slack for a moments, then his eyes widened as he registered what Michel had said.

"Fuck, I had no idea," he whispered. "Now I feel like shit for saying that about him."

"I'm sorry," Michel said. "I assumed Detective Ribodeau had already told you."

Dixon blinked a few times, and quickly downed the rest of his drink.

"What happened?" he asked, his tone awed.

"He was murdered," Michel replied.

He waited for Dixon to come to the next logical question.

"Holy shit," Dixon exclaimed suddenly, rocking forward. "What about Fierce? Is he all right?"

His reaction made it clear he still cared about Gaudreau. Michel decided to exploit it.

"We're not sure," he replied evenly. "He and Rhodes are still missing." He paused and affected a worried expression. "Is there anyone outside the group he might contact if he needed help? Maybe family in New York?"

"He has a sister," Dixon volunteered quickly, "but I'm not sure where she lives. I don't know if his parents are still alive."

"Do you remember his sister's name?"

Dixon's face set in concentration, then he shook his head.

"He never told me her real name," he said, frustrated. "He always just called her Daisy."

"How do you know that's not her real name?" Michel asked.

"Because they're from New York, not West Virginia," Dixon replied, with surprising vitriol. "Besides, I asked him about it once. He said it was a private nickname, but didn't tell me what it meant, or her real name."

"It's a start," Michel said. "What about Rhodes? Was he

close with anyone besides Fierce? Anyone he might call? Rachel mentioned someone named Sparkle."

"Yeah, they were close," Dixon replied, "but Sparkle hasn't been around since December. He said he was going home to visit his family for Christmas, but never came back."

It was the same story Rachel had given.

"Any idea where home is, or his real name?" Michel asked.

"Yeah, we hooked up a few times," Dixon replied. "Angel Peterson. His family lives in Indiana. Someplace just over the border from Cincinnati. I don't remember the name."

"That's fine," Michel said. "That's actually really helpful."

Dixon brightened slightly.

"Anyone else I should talk to?" Michel asked.

Dixon started to shake his head, then stopped.

"There was a girl," he said. "She came to a few parties with Skylar. She worked with him. I don't remember her name, but she was a typical fag hag. Chunky, trying too hard to be fabulous. Always got drunk and hit on all the gay guys, then cried about how lonely she was when they rejected her."

"That will be really helpful to know if she happens to be drunk when I find her," Michel replied.

Dixon nodded, the sarcasm apparently lost on him.

"Cam might have called her," he said. "Especially after what happened to Skylar."

Michel doubted that was the case. If Rhodes knew Ellis was dead and had access to a phone, he was probably the killer.

"Thanks. I'll check her out," he said.

Dixon gave his empty glass a meaninglful look which Michel ignored.

"You wouldn't happen to have a picture of Fierce would you?" he asked.

"Yeah, right," Dixon replied with a derisive laugh. "He never lets anyone take his picture. If he even sees someone taking pictures, they're banned. I think it's because of the body dysphobic thing."

This time Michel suspected Dixon was playing dumb, mistakenly thinking it was cute. He also suspected Gaudreau had more practical reasons for not wanting his picture taken.

"This has been really helpful," he said abruptly.

He swallowed the rest of his Jack Daniels and stood up. Dixon looked mildly annoyed, then stood, too. Michel was struck again by how different he looked from the previous night.

"So I'm curious," Michel said. "Which is the real you?"

Dixon responded with a blank look.

"The harness or this?" Michel said, nodding down at Dixon's clothes.

Dixon's expression softened and he laughed.

"It's all just drag, isn't it?" he said. "This is my work drag, the harness is my play drag, and then I've got some for special occasions." He smiled flirtatiously, and cocked a curious eye at Michel. "So what's your drag?"

"Human," Michel replied.

*****

As Michel turned onto Royal Street, he checked his phone. He'd had one call each from Sassy and Chance, and three from Al Ribodeau. He decided to call Ribodeau first.

"It's about time," Ribodeau answered on the first ring.

"Sorry," Michel replied. "I was talking with Kenny Dix..."

"The camper turned up," Ribodeau cut him off. "A local cop in Arkansas pulled it over for speeding, and almost got his head blown off."

"By Rhodes and Gaudreau?" Michel replied.

"No. A guy named Bobby Lee Collins. Sound familiar?"

"Should it?"

"He had a warrant from Gainesville."

"One of the meth labbers?" Michel replied.

"You got it," Ribodeau replied.

"But how the fuck...?" Michel began, then stopped. He

took a slow breath, trying to clear his mind. "Were Rhodes or Gaudreau there?" he asked.

"No sign of them," Ribodeau replied.

"Did Collins say anything about them?"

"He couldn't," Ribodeau replied. "He's dead, along with a second man and two women. A third woman shot them all when Collins went after the cop."

"Holy fuck," Michel replied. "Did she say why?"

"They haven't had a chance to question her yet," Ribodeau replied. "She was in rough shape, so they airlifted her to a hospital in Little Rock. The sheriff said she's under sedation, but they're hoping to transport her in the morning."

"Where?" Michel asked.

"Here."

"How did that happen?" Michel asked. "The Feds don't have the case?"

"They do, but apparently two unsolved murders and two missing persons trumps four dead meth heads," Ribodeau replied. "Especially when one of the missing is Trish Campbell Rhodes Taylor's kid. So we're getting a crack at the girl."

Michel felt a giddy rush, but held his tongue, determined not to sacrifice his pride by asking to be involved again. "Please, please, please," he mouthed, as the silence stretched out.

"So do you want to be there, or not?" Ribodeau asked finally.

"Well, if you think you could use my help," Michel replied with exaggerated breeziness.

"Don't push it," Ribodeau growled.

Michel smiled to himself.

"Yes, I do, Al. Thanks."

"You're welcome," Ribodeau replied. "I'll call you in the morning when I'm sure she's on her way."

Michel hung up and considered calling Sassy and Chance. He decided to wait until he got home.

Chapter 27

Michel unlocked the door and pushed it open. He expected Blue to come charging toward him, but the house was still.

"Hello?" he called apprehensively.

"Out here," Chance's faint voice came back.

Michel moved through the house to the open back door. Chance was lying on a chaise in a narrow wedge of sunlight along the back patio wall, wearing just boxer shorts that he'd bunched up to expose more of his thighs. Blue lay a few feet away, panting in the shade.

"Hey," Chance said, shielding his eyes from the sun. "I hope you don't mind."

Michel nodded blankly, not sure exactly how he felt.

"What's up with her?" he asked, nodding at Blue.

Though she hadn't acknowledged him yet, she suddenly rolled onto her back, her legs splayed out to the sides. Michel walked over and began rubbing her belly. The sparse fur was damp and warm.

"She's exhausted," Chance replied. "I ran into my friend Ramon while we were walking and he invited us to his place to go swimming. She was in the pool for almost two hours."

"She can swim?" Michel asked, suddenly noticing the light odor of chlorine.

"She can now," Chance shrugged.

Michel felt like a parent who'd missed his child's first steps.

"So what happened to packing?" he asked, aware that it had sounded almost accusatory.

A momentary frown creased Chance's brow.

"Well, I was going to go home, but then I figured I'd wait and take her for her noon walk in case you got tied up," he said. "Then it turned into a whole adventure, so I figured I'd hang out and see if you wanted to have dinner or something."

Michel felt a pang of guilt, followed by a flood of anxiety. His chest suddenly felt tight, his breathing became shallow.

"Yeah, sure," he managed. "I just have to check in with Sassy, then we can figure out what to do."

He stood and walked stiffly back into the house. He felt oddly like a stranger, as though everything had changed while he was gone. He went into his rarely used office, closed the door, and dialed Sassy.

*****

"Hmmm," Sassy murmured when Michel finished filling her in on the day's events. "This is all getting very interesting. I wonder if Al would let me tag along, too."

"Probably," Michel replied. "I'll ask."

He let out an unconscious sigh.

"What the hell's wrong with you?" Sassy asked.

"Nothing," Michel replied too quickly.

"Then why does it sound like you're hooked to a damn respirator?" Sassy replied, heaving a dramatic sigh of her own. "I'd think you'd be creaming yourself with excitement about tomorrow."

"Gross. And I am," Michel replied unenthusiastically.

"So then what *aren't* you excited about?" Sassy pressed.

There was a long pause. Michel knew Sassy was going to chide him if he told the truth, but he needed to vent.

"The babysitter seems to have moved in," he said finally, bracing himself for the reaction.

"'The 'babysitter' being Chance?" Sassy asked.

"Yes."

"I assume you don't mean literally?"

"No," Michel replied, "but when I got home, he was lying out on the patio in his underwear. And Blue totally ignored me."

He realized how whiny he sounded, but didn't care.

"So basically you feel like he's intruding into your life, and usurping your place with Blue?" Sassy asked.

"Yeah, basically."

"But let me guess," Sassy said. "You also kind of like it?"

Michel considered it for a second, then nodded to himself.

"Yeah, how did you know?"

Sassy chuckled.

"What's so funny?" Michel asked.

"You've got 'new boyfriend syndrome,'" Sassy replied.

"He's not my boyfriend," Michel argued like a sullen child.

"Maybe not, but he's starting to act like one," Sassy said, then laughed again, this time sympathetically. "I went through the same thing when Russ started coming down to visit. I wanted him to feel comfortable in my house, but if it seemed like he was getting too comfortable, I'd get all worked up, convinced he was trying to take over my life. I'd start obsessing over his towel and toothbrush cluttering up the bathroom, and his clothes on the bedroom floor, and how I couldn't just sit on the couch and eat a whole package of Oreos for dinner."

"Again, gross," Michel said.

"When he wasn't there," Sassy continued, "I couldn't wait to see him, but a day or two after he'd arrive, I'd start feeling trapped. Like I was suffocating."

Michel thought about the sudden tightness in his chest.

"So what did you do about it?" he asked.

"I told him the truth," Sassy replied. "That I loved him, but that I'd been on my own for a long time and I was used to having my own space and doing things my way, and that he was going to have to be patient until I got used to him being around. After that, whenever I started to lose it, I'd just let him know and he'd disappear for a few hours."

Michel nodded to himself again. Though he and Chance still weren't technically dating, their relationship had clearly moved beyond just friendship.

"'New boyfriend syndrome?'" he said.

"Yup. It's kind of like new car smell," Sassy said. "Nice, but annoying at the same time."

Michel laughed. "That doesn't even make sense."

"No, I suppose it doesn't," Sassy agreed, then turned more serious. "You know what you need to do."

"Yeah, I do," Michel replied. "I'll talk to him tonight. Thanks. And I'll let you know what Al says about tomorrow."

"Okay," Sassy said. "Good luck."

Michel hung up and stared at the phone for a moment. He wanted a cigarette. He opened the door and stepped into the hall. Chance was sitting crossed-legged at the end, still in just his boxers, Blue curled up on the floor beside him.

"So were you hiding from me?" he asked.

It hadn't sounded hurt or angry, but Michel still fought the urge to give reflexive reassurance.

"Maybe a little," he admitted.

"I'm sorry," Chance replied. "I should have called to make sure it was okay for me to hang out. I was just trying to help out with Blue, then by the time we got back it was already 2:30, so... I really am sorry. I didn't mean to like take over your house."

Michel felt the tension in his shoulders ease a bit, and decided that the big talk could wait a while longer. He walked over and extended his right hand.

"It's okay," he said, pulling Chance to his feet. "I just wasn't expecting you to be here, and freaked out for a minute." He smiled an apology. "So what have you been doing all afternoon?"

They headed toward the patio, Blue trotting ahead of them.

"Reading your magazines, eating your food, snooping through your stuff," Chance replied casually. "You've got some nasty porn. Freak."

Michel laughed, knowing the closest he had to porn was an International Male catalog.

"So I guess you're not moving tomorrow," he said.

"No," Chance replied. "I'm too lazy to pack."

Or unsure about the move, Michel thought.

"Actually that kind of works out," he said. "The camper stolen in Gretna this morning showed up in Arkansas, and one of the occupants killed the other four. She's being brought here tomorrow for questioning. Al invited me to observe."

Chance stopped short and turned to face Michel.

"So you were planning to blow me off to watch an interview anyway?" he asked.

Michel smiled sheepishly.

"And I suppose you're hoping I'll look after Blue while you're gone, too?" Chance asked.

"If you wouldn't mind," Michel replied, trying for endearing, but managing only mildly cute.

Chance shook his head, and started back toward the patio.

"You are *so* taking advantage of me," he said. "One of these days you're going to have to start paying for all this babysitting."

Michel felt his face flush, wondering if Chance had been listening outside the office door.

"With or without pants?" he asked quickly.

Chance stopped just inside the patio door, turned again, and smiled. He hooked his thumbs inside the waist band of his boxer shorts.

"Definitely without."

Chapter 28

The cracked and dirty concrete sidewalk in front of Tulane Medical Center's Aron Pavilion gave way to only slightly less worn and dirty brick in front of the main hospital. The building was set back thirty feet, with two patchy plots of grass bracketing a cluster of concrete benches, trash receptacles, and cigarette urns just to the left of the entrance. Al Ribodeau was on the bench closest to the building, sheltered from the early afternoon sun by two palm trees. He was sitting straight up, but his eyes were closed and his chin rested on his chest. His head rose and fell with each slow breath.

"Al," Michel said, gently touching Ribodeau's right shoulder. "Are you all right?"

Ribodeau's eyes blinked open, and he looked around as though surprised to find himself there.

"Oh, hey," he blustered. "I was just resting my eyes."

He tried to stifle a yawn, then cover it by rubbing his hand over his face. As his thick fingers pulled his fleshy cheeks down, he looked like an exhausted bloodhound.

"You sure you're okay?" Sassy asked, watching him carefully. "You look like hell."

"Did you pull another all-nighter?" Michel added.

Ribodeau shook his head.

"No, I was in bed by nine. I just couldn't seem to get comfortable. Damn indigestion."

Michel and Sassy exchanged concerned looks. Ribodeau gave an unconcerned shrug.

"So what are you doing out here?" Michel asked. "I thought we were going to meet inside?"

Ribodeau looked momentarily confused, then seemed to find his bearings.

"Oh yeah," he said, "I just wanted to fill you in on what the girl told the Feds before we go up."

Sassy made a face.

"Out here? In the middle of the day?"

"It's not so bad," Ribodeau replied.

Michel nodded at Ribodeau's blue shirt.

"Yeah, those two half moons of sweat accentuate your breasts really nicely."

Ribodeau looked down and frowned.

"Okay, maybe we should go someplace cooler," he said.

*****

"Her name's Jami-Lynn Dale," Ribodeau said, as they settled in at a corner table in the nearly-empty cafeteria. "Eighteen-years-old, from Ocala, Florida. Her folks reported her missing last July. The local cops checked it out, found that she'd taken most of her stuff and emptied her bank acount, and classified her as a runaway. End of story."

"How did she end up with Collins's crew?" Michel asked.

"Essentially, she was kidnapped," Ribodeau replied. "Collins's girlfriend..." he checked his notes, "...Cissy Yates, picked her up hitchhiking a few days after she left home, and offered her a place to stay for the night. They never let her leave. Collins and the other guy, Clay Bettis, raped her, then locked her up in a shed. They'd bring her out at night and take turns with her, then lock her back up."

"Did Yates and the other woman know?" Sassy asked.

Ribodeau nodded.

"They watched. Apparently it was all just part of the party."

Sassy's jaw tightened, but she didn't say anything.

"But when we saw them outside Gaudreau's, she didn't seem to be a prisoner," Michel said.

"Dale said they kept her locked up for about a month, then started letting her out for short periods of time," Ribodeau replied. "After another month or so, she was allowed to roam free, except at night. For the past few months, they didn't even lock her up at night."

"So why didn't she make a run for it?" Michel asked. "They couldn't have been watching her constantly."

"She tried once," Ribodeau replied. "They found her, and Collins told her that if she tried it again, he'd kill her, go to her parents' house and kill them, and bring her 14-year-old sister back to take her place."

"No wonder she killed them," Sassy growled in a low voice.

"After that, she started using meth and stopped thinking about getting away," Ribodeau continued. "Eventually she settled into the role of a younger sister to the other two women. Of course, it was a pretty incestuous family."

"So what happened in the camper?" Michel asked.

"Apparently Dale finally snapped," Ribodeau replied. "When they got pulled over, Collins started ranting that it was because of 'that nigger bitch and her boyfriend.' He went after the cop, and Bettis made the mistake of putting his gun down. Dale grabbed it, shot him, and the two women. She got the drop on Collins because he was too arrogant to believe she'd shoot him until it was too late."

"Wow. I wonder what finally pushed her over the edge?" Michel said.

Ribodeau shrugged.

"Hopefully we'll find out." He pushed to his feet, then stopped. "Oh, and one other thing. We got the Coroner's report on Skylar Ellis. There were no signs of sexual assault, but they did notice something unusual."

Michel and Sassy both looked at him expectantly.

"A half dozen shallow stab wounds to his chest," he said.

"Pre- or post-mortem?" Sassy asked.

"Pre-," Ribodeau replied, "and none more than a quarter-inch deep. Painful, but not deadly."

"Were they made with the same knife used to cut his throat?" Michel asked.

"They couldn't be sure because only the tip was used."

"So what did they make of it?" Sassy asked.

"Not much," Ribodeau replied, "but they said the pattern was random, and the edges of the wounds were rough, indicating quick jabs rather than steady pressure."

Michel looked at Sassy, hoping she might offer a theory. She just shrugged.

"One more mystery to add to the pile," she said.

Chapter 29

The elevator glided to a stop, the doors opened. They stepped out and followed the signs for 4 West. As they entered the in-patient wing, they could see a uniformed officer standing outside a closed door at the end of the hall. Michel's stride faltered as he flashed back to the night Joel was shot.

"Are you okay?" Sassy asked, turning back to him.

The emotional memory had been so unexpected and so intense that Michel couldn't reply for a moment. He just gave a quick, unconvincing nod, and started walking again. Sassy and Ribodeau exchanged curious looks, then followed.

"Hey, Butch. I thought there'd be someone from the Bureau out here," Ribodeau said, as they approached the door.

He and the officer clasped hands like old friends. Michel noted that the other man was older than he'd appeared from a distance, his thick mustache gone mostly gray, and that he had sergeant's insignia on both sleeves. His nameplate read RYAN.

"The last two left about a half hour ago," Ryan replied.

"So she's alone in there?" Ribodeau asked, surprised.

Ryan pulled a business card from his right shirt pocket and handed it to Ribodeau.

"They said to give them a call when you're done."

Ribodeau nodded, then gestured toward Sassy and Michel.

"Butch, this is Sassy Jones and Michel Doucette. They used to work homicide. They're doing the private investigation thing now. I've invited them to observe because the girl may be involved in a case they're working."

Ryan gave a perfunctory nod, showing no apparent interest in the reason for their presence.

"So how does she seem?" Ribodeau asked.

"A little spacey, but responsive," Ryan replied.

Ribodeau turned back to Sassy and Michel.

"You ready?"

They both nodded.

"If it's all right with you," Ryan said, "I'm going for coffee."

"Take your time, Butch," Ribodeau replied. "I'm sure we'll be a while."

Ryan gave Sassy and Michel a two-finger salute, then squeezed Ribodeau's left shoulder and headed down the hall.

"So does this mean we can come in?" Michel asked eagerly, as soon as Ryan was out of earshot.

"It's not like they have an observation room, so yeah," Ribodeau sighed, quickly adding, "Assuming the girl doesn't object and you promise to sit quietly and just watch,"

He kept his attention focused on Michel. Michel quickly crossed his heart.

"Anything else you think we should know?" Sassy asked.

Ribodeau thought for a moment, then pulled out his note pad and ran his index finger down the page.

"Oh yeah," he said, stopping near the bottom. "The Feds found 10 grand hidden behind the crapper in the camper."

*****

She looked younger than she had on the street, though still several years older than her actual age, and the toll of crystal meth use was apparent in the sores on her arms and neck and her brittle, stained teeth. Still, it was easier to get a sense now of the girl she'd once been.

"Miss Dale, my name is Al Ribodeau," Ribodeau began. "I'm a homicide detective with the New Orleans Police Department. I'd like to ask you some questions."

"About the girl they killed?" Dale asked, her hard flat accent evoking the parts of Florida still more closely aligned with the Confederacy than New York or Cuba.

Ribodeau nodded.

"These are colleagues of mine, Miss Jones and Mr. Doucette," he said. "They're private investigators. Would it be all right with you if they observed?"

Dale cast a wary look at Sassy and Michel. She had the anxious face of someone who constantly tries to please, but knows she's most likely going to be rewarded with the back of a hand.

"I guess so," she said.

Ribodeau took the chair to the left of the bed. Michel and Sassy sat by the foot, under the muted TV.

"What can you tell us about Rachel Davis' killing?" Ribodeau asked.

"Nothing," Dale replied with an apologetic shrug. "I didn't know anything about it until we got pulled over and Bobby Lee said it was probably because of..."

She stopped and cut a nervous look at Sassy.

"It's okay," Ribodeau reassured her. "The FBI told us what he said. You don't have to repeat it."

Dale gave him a cross between a grateful smile and a wince.

"So neither Collins nor Bettis said anything about the murder until that moment?" Ribodeau asked.

"No, sir," Dale replied.

"So then what reason did they give you for going on the run?" Ribodeau asked.

"They didn't," Dale replied. "When they came back that morning, they just said they'd gotten some seed money and we were going to Tulsa because Bobby Lee's sister has a farm there where we could stay."

Michel was struck by the way she referred to Collins as though he were a friend or family member. It seemed both grotesque and completely natural.

151

Ribodeau frowned.

"Okay, so let's back up a little bit. An Airstream motorhome was recovered from the river in Gretna early that morning, a few blocks from where the camper you were in was stolen. Do you know anything about the Airstream?"

Dale nodded.

"The car broke down on the way to Atlanta, so Bobby Lee borrowed it," Dale replied.

"From?"

"I didn't ask," Dale replied quickly.

From her expression, it was clear she never asked.

"You said you were heading to Atlanta," Ribodeau continued. "How did you end up in New Orleans?"

"Bobby Lee talked to a friend here who said he could help us out," Dale replied.

"Another friend you didn't ask about?" Ribodeau asked.

Dale gave another pained smile.

"And you never met this friend?" Ribodeau asked.

"I don't think so," Dale replied.

"What about anyone else?" Ribodeau asked. "Did anyone ever stop by? Or did you visit anyone?"

"There was a boy named Cam," Dale replied. "I don't know his last name, but he came by a few times."

"But you don't think he was the friend Collins mentioned?" Ribodeau asked.

"I don't know," Dale replied. "Maybe, but I never heard Bobby Lee say that name before, and he talked about people he knew in other places all the time. He had a lot of friends."

"I'm sure," Ribodeau replied dryly. "So did he or Bettis ever mention loaning the Airstream to this Cam?"

"Not that I remember," Dale replied, "but they didn't usually talk things over with me. Or even with Cissy or Christy that much. They just kind of told us what to do and we did it. You know what I mean?"

Ribodeau nodded sympathetically.

152

"So tell me about that night," he said. "The night before you left New Orleans."

Dale blinked her large green eyes a few times.

"Bobby Lee and Clay left about five in the afternoon," she said. "They said they had a job to do, and wouldn't be back until late. They told us not to leave the house while they were gone."

"Any idea where they were going?"

"No, sir," Dale replied again, this time almost moaning it.

It was clear she wanted to be helpful.

"When did they get back?" Ribodeau asked.

"About four in the morning."

"And they were in the camper by then?"

Dale nodded. Ribodeau knew better than to ask if Collins or Bettis had explained what happened to the Airstream.

"And then what?" he asked.

"Like I said before, they told us we were going to Tulsa," Dale replied, "so we packed up the camper and left right away."

"You didn't think that was strange?" Ribodeau asked. "That they wanted to leave so quickly?"

Dale's expression turned hurt.

"With Bobby Lee, things like that happened all the time," she said defensively. "It was best *not* to think about it."

"I'm sorry," Ribodeau replied. "I didn't mean it as an accusation. I'm just trying to piece things together."

Dale studied him for a few seconds, then nodded eagerly.

"When Collins and Bettis came back, did you notice any blood on them, or anything unusual?" Ribodeau continued.

Dale tilted her head up toward the TV, but her eyes were fixed on a spot just above Michel's head.

"They were both wet," she said after a moment, looking back at Ribodeau, "and they stunk like swamp water, but they didn't even wash up. They just put on some dry clothes."

Ribodeau exchanged quick looks with Sassy and Michel.

"That's very helpful," he said with gentle encouragement. "Just a few more questions and we'll be out of your hair."

Dale flashed a broken smile, seeming more relaxed now.

"Did Collins or Bettis mention Cam while you were on the road?" Ribodeau asked. "Or someone named Fierce Gaudreau?"

"Not while we were on the road, but Bobby Lee mentioned Gaudreau a few times," Dale said. "I remember because at first he didn't like him."

"Any idea why?"

"Because he said that Gaudreau acted like his shit didn't stink," Dale replied. "Bobby Lee didn't like people looking down on him."

"You said, 'at first,'" Ribodeau replied. "But later on he started to like him?"

Dale nodded.

"I heard him tell Clay they had an arrangement, but I don't know what about."

Ribodeau looked at Sassy and Michel again, and raised his eyebrows. Michel shook his head, but Sassy leaned forward in her chair.

"What made you decide to kill Bobby Lee and the others?" she asked.

Dale's eyes dropped to her lap. The fingers on her left hand twitched slightly, as though she were fighting the impulse to scratch the sores on the back of the right.

"I knew what that poor girl went through," she said finally, looking up. Her voice was surprisingly passionate. "I knew how scared she was, and it pissed me off. They needed to be stopped so they couldn't do it again."

Sassy nodded sympathetically. She understood exactly how the younger woman had felt, and was glad that Rachel had finally had someone to stand up for her.

"But why the women?" she asked. "They didn't kill Rachel. "They weren't even there."

For the first time, Dale's eyes betrayed anger.

"Because Bobby Lee and Clay were just being men," she said, then smiled in a way that suggested she might not be

154

entirely sane. "But Cissy and Christy let it happen. They were supposed to be like sisters. That's much worse."

Sassy felt a chill as she realized they were no longer talking about Rachel Davis.

Chapter 30

"Okay, so what do we know for certain?" Ribodeau asked, a green marker poised in his right hand.

"Number one, Collins 'borrowed' an Airstream Land Yacht in Georgia," Sassy said, making air quotes.

Ribodeau began chicken scratching on the dry erase board.

"Number two," Sassy continued, "Rhodes, Ellis, and Gaudreau were last seen together in that Airstream."

"Number three," Michel said, "that same vehicle ended up in the Mississippi with Ellis's body inside."

"Number four," Ribodeau muttered, writing quickly, "Collins said he'd made an arrangment with Gaudreau."

"Five, Collins and Bettis were wet when they got back to their place that morning," Michel said. "And six, the camper they were driving in Arkansas was stolen a few blocks from where Ellis's body was dumped, at about the same time."

"Good," Ribodeau said. "Seven?"

"The Feds found ten grand in the camper," Sassy said.

There was a long pause while they all studied the board.

"Anything else?" Ribodeau asked finally.

"Collins and Bettis admitted to killing Rachel Davis and Jesse Woods," Michel said.

"That's not entirely accurate," Sassy said, "though I think we can assume that's who they meant by 'that nigger bitch and her boyfriend'."

Michel gave her a consoling look, while Ribodeau added it to the board.

"And number nine," Ribodeau said, still writing, "Rachel Davis and Skylar Ellis were both beaten and killed using the same method."

He capped the green marker and put it down, then picked up a red one.

"Okay, now what can we speculate based on the facts?"

"Either Collins and Bettis killed everybody but we haven't found all the bodies yet, or Gaudreau and/or Rhodes paid them to kill Davis and Ellis."

"What about Woods?" Ribodeau asked.

"I think we can assume he was just collateral damage," Sassy said. "Wrong place at the wrong time."

Michel nodded.

"Agreed," Ribodeau said.

He wrote down both hypotheses, then turned back.

"What about kidnapping, or an unknown party with a grudge?" he asked without much conviction.

"If Rhodes or Gaudreau had been kidnapped, there would have been a ranson demand by now," Michel replied. "And so far there's nothing to suggest another party."

"So is that it?" Ribodeau asked, jerking a thumb over his shoulder toward the board.

"I think so," Sassy replied, as Michel nodded.

"Okay, evidence against the first theory?" Ribodeau asked, switching to a black marker.

"Rhodes and Gaudreau were with Ellis," Sassy replied. "If Collins and Bettis killed them, why weren't all three bodies in the Airstream?"

Ribodeau wrote it down.

"What else?" he asked over his shoulder.

"It wouldn't explain the money," Michel offered.

"That's not exactly going to hold up in court," Ribodeau replied, chuckling, "but I'll note it."

He finished writing and turned back.

"What about the second theory?"

"That one definitely fits the evidence," Sassy replied. "The vehicle trail, the money in the camper, Collins and Bettis being wet, and Rachel and Ellis being killed the same way."

Ribodeau nodded.

"Evidence against?"

Sassy shrugged. Michel felt a niggling sense of disquiet in the back of his mind, but couldn't pinpoint the reason.

"Nothing for the moment," he said.

"What about a motive to support it?" Ribodeau pressed on.

"I don't know about Rachel," Michel said, "but Rhodes may have wanted Ellis out of the way so he could be with Gaudreau."

"A simple break-up email wouldn't do?" Sassy deadpanned.

"Maybe not," Michel replied. "Kenny Dixon told me that Rhodes used to hook up with a lot of guys and rub it in Ellis's face, but so far as we know, they were still together. Maybe Ellis wouldn't go away that easily."

"But murder?" Sassy asked, looking at him skeptically.

Michel shrugged.

"I'm just saying it's a possibility."

"But Rachel said she didn't think there was anything sexual going on between Rhodes and Gaudreau," Sassy said.

"Dixon said the same thing," Michel agreed, "but he also said he thought Rhodes wanted to possess Gaudreau, and Ellis said Rhodes was obsessed."

They both suddenly turned to Ribodeau, like children imploring a parent to settle an argument.

"I say we include it," he said after a moment's deliberation.

He added it to the board, then turned back.

"So what are we missing?"

"I think that's it for now," Sassy replied.

"Me, too," Michel replied.

"Good enough," Ribodeau said.

He checked his watch, then ran his thick fingers through his thinning hair and yawned.

"I guess I better get started on my report on the Dale interview," he said with a blatant lack of enthusiasm.

Michel looked at him curiously.

"Al, I just realized something," he said. "Why don't you have a partner?"

Ribodeau grunted.

"She's out on maternity leave," he replied.

"Again?" Michel replied. "Didn't she just have a kid like two years ago."

"Different partner," Ribodeau replied.

"This is the third one, right?" Sassy asked.

Ribodeau nodded wearily.

"Apparently Al has some serious fertility mojo," Sassy said.

"With everyone except my ex-wife," Ribodeau replied, "though I'm not sure anything could have turned that barren wasteland fertile."

"Wow. Bitter much?" Michel asked.

"Only that she left me," Ribodeau replied. "So you two calling it a day, or heading back to your office?"

"I was thinking about swinging by Jacques-Imo's," Michel replied. "Dixon told me Ellis was close with one of his coworkers. I figured she might have some insight into the relationship."

"Would you mind dropping me at home before you go?" Sassy asked.

"No, that's fine," Michel said. "I can stop by the house and see if Chance wants to go with me and have dinner. Ellis said the food is great."

"Like two alcoholics," Sassy said under her breath.

"I almost forgot," Michel said, ignoring her and looking at Ribodeau. "Dixon gave me two other leads that are probably more up your alley."

"Shoot," Ribodeau said, taking out his note pad.

"Apparently Gaudreau's actual name is Frank Pierce. Dixon said he grew up in New York, and has a sister he calls Daisy, though that's not her real name. Dixon didn't know where she lives, but thought Gaudreau kept in touch with her."

"I can handle that," Ribodeau replied. "What else?"

"He also gave me a name for Sparkle," Michel said.

"What the fuck is Sparkle?" Ribodeau asked, making a face.

"A friend of Rhodes," Sassy replied.

"Rachel said they were pretty close," Michel added. "Maybe Rhodes called him."

Ribodeau nodded.

"Real name?"

"Angel Peterson," Michel replied. "He went to visit his family for Christmas, and apparently didn't come back. The family lives in Indiana, somewhere in the southeast corner."

Ribodeau finished writing and flipped the pad shut.

"I'll see what I can find out," he said.

Chapter 31

"So what's wrong?" Sassy asked as they stopped in front of her house. "You haven't said a word since we left the station."

Michel cut the engine and turned sideways on the truck's faded blue bench seat.

"Does it make sense to you that Collins and Bettis would go to the trouble of trying to sink Ellis in the river, but leave Rachel and Woods out in the open like that?" he asked.

"They couldn't very well carry them out of the building in front of everyone," Sassy replied.

"Dixon told me there's a back way out," Michel said, "but even if they didn't know that, why not at least hide the bodies? I mean, you'd think they'd have wanted to get as far away as possible before the cops showed up."

"Maybe they were interrupted," Sassy replied.

Michel shook his head.

"I don't think so. It feels to me like they were trying to make a statement. The savagery of the beating, the rape...they don't fit if it was just a killing for pay. It felt personal. Like they were punishing her."

Sassy didn't reply for a moment. Her eyes were fixed on the dashboard. Finally she let out a ragged breath.

"Why didn't I see that before?" she said, her voice barely more than a whisper. "But why would they want to punish her? From what she told us, she didn't even know them."

"Maybe just for who she was," Michel said.

Sassy stared at him for a moment, then slowly nodded.

"Smart, black, and female."

"We know what they called her," Michel said, "and how they treated Jami-Lynn Dale."

Sassy nodded again, though her gaze was suddenly distant. When she looked back at Michel, he could tell she'd reached the same conclusion he had.

"Ellis's killing was personal, too," she said.

Michel nodded.

"Seems that way."

Sassy slumped back against the seat.

"I think we better go inside and have a drink," she said.

*****

Michel walked back into the living room from the garden. Sassy had a tumbler of Jack Daniels waiting on the coffee table.

"Thanks," he said, settling onto the other end of the sofa.

"Did you reach Chance?" Sassy asked.

"Yeah, he's actually making dinner," Michel replied, "so we won't be going to Jacques-Imo's tonight. I'll call tomorrow. See if they'll give me a name and number for Ellis's friend."

"I didn't know Chance cooked," Sassy said.

"Me, neither," Michel replied, "though he wouldn't tell me what he's making, so it could just be something from a box."

He gave a worried frown, then sipped his drink.

"So why didn't you mention your theory to Al?" Sassy asked.

"I didn't come up with it until we were in the car," Michel replied. "I just knew something didn't feel right."

Sassy nodded.

"So if Collins and Bettis didn't kill Ellis, how did they end up with the stolen camper, and where did they get the money?"

"I don't think they *killed* Ellis, but I think they were paid to get rid of his body."

"And you're basing that on what?" Sassy asked.

"Intuition?" Michel tried half-heartedly.

"You're going to have to do better than that," Sassy said.

"It would explain the money, the camper, and how they got wet," Michel offered.

"True," Sassy replied, "but that's a lot of money just for dumping a body on the other side of the river. Especially since they fucked it up."

"I know," Michel said. "I've been thinking about that. I mean, if I were going to pay someone to dispose of a body, I'd want to make sure it ended up somewhere it either wouldn't be found, or wouldn't be easily connected back to me."

"Like Tulsa?" Sassy said.

"Or along the way there," Michel said.

"That would certainly be worth a lot more," Sassy agreed, "but then what changed the plan?"

"I don't know," Michel said. "It's like they got spooked."

"Because they left so quickly?" Sassy asked.

"Exactly," Michel replied. "If you'd been in that part of the river, wouldn't you want to at least rinse off first?"

"Or bathe in bleach and disinfectant," Sassy replied.

Michel nodded.

"So why the sudden urgency to get on the road?"

"Trying to beat rush hour?" Sassy replied.

Michel fixed her with a deadpan look.

"Assuming Collins was telling the truth about Tulsa," he continued, "he must have been in touch with his sister."

"Sounds like we need to get in touch and find out if—and when—she was expecting him," Sassy said.

"I'll call Al and let him know," Michel replied.

He and Sassy sipped their drinks in silence for a moment. Michel took out his cigarette pack, but only toyed with it.

Finally Sassy spoke. "So I guess Rhodes and Gaudreau are our primary suspects for Ellis's murder now."

"I guess so," Michel replied.

"I wonder how Trish is going to take that?" Sassy asked.

Michel made a sour face.

"I've left a few messages for her at the hotel, but haven't heard back yet. I'm sure it won't be pretty when I do." He sighed, downed the rest of his drink, then shrugged the thought away. "So where are your menfolk tonight, anyway?" he asked, looking around.

"Russ is still at work, and Corey better be in his room studying for finals," Sassy replied.

"Things haven't gotten any easier?"

"No," Sassy replied, staring down at her glass. "I've tried to engage him more, but he's moved from sullen indifference to sullen hostility. It's going to be hell when school ends next week and he's around all the time."

"Make him get a job," Michel suggested.

Sassy's head whipped toward him so quickly that he let out a small reflexive gasp.

"Why is it that people who don't have children are always so anxious to give advice on raising them?" she snapped.

Michel was shocked by the ferocity of her reaction.

"Sorry, I was just trying to be helpful," he said defensively. "Can you please spit my head back out now?"

Sassy blinked a few times, then closed her eyes and took a few calming breaths.

"I didn't mean to take it out on you," she said after a moment. She opened her eyes and offered a contrite smile. "It's just such a sore subject. I've never felt like such a failure at anything in my life."

"You're still pretty new at all this," Michel said, "and let's face it, things haven't exactly been normal lately. You've been sick, and Corey's in that stage between being a kid and being a man, where he wants the freedom and respect but not the responsibility. Don't worry, it'll work itself out."

He cringed mentally. It had sounded like the sort of trite aphorism that people always trotted out at funerals, like "God never gives us more than we can handle," or "Everything happens for a reason."

"I better get going," he said, leaning forward and squeezing Sassy's right hand. "I don't want to get blamed if the Hamburger Helper is burned."

Chapter 32

Virtually every pot and pan he owned was out. A few were on the stove, but most were either stacked on counters or lying on the floor in front of open cabinet doors. All but a few appeared to be unused, though most were at least spattered with grease or dusted with flour.

"Sorry, I'm a little messy when I cook," Chance said, "but don't worry, I'll clean up."

"I'm not worried," Michel managed, despite the sudden tightness in his chest and pounding in his temples. "So what is it?"

"Grillades and grits," Chance said. "At least I hope so. You didn't have a lot of the spices, so I had to improvise. Hopefully it'll still be all right."

"It smells good," Michel said automatically.

"Thanks," Chance replied.

He gave the roux a quick stir, then lay the whisk directly on the tile counter, next to the spoon rest. Michel's jaw tightened, but he tried to smile.

"So do you cook much?" he asked.

"Not so much anymore, but I used to," Chance replied. "Before I left home. The only thing my father could make from scratch was scrambled eggs, so I had to learn."

Michel nodded dully, fighting the urge to put things away and wipe the counters.

"Joel's grandmother taught me the basics," Chance said.

He picked up the cutting board and pushed most of the

diced onions, celery, and green peppers into the cast iron skillet. The rest bounced across the stove top or onto the floor. Michel decided it was time for a drink.

"Have you spoken to her recently?" he asked, as he filled a glass with ice.

"Last week," Chance replied. "She told me to say hello."

Michel was sure it was a well-intentioned lie. He poured three fingers of Jack Daniels into the glass and took a long sip.

"So, anything I can help with?" he asked, hopefully.

"No, I think I've got it covered," Chance replied.

He stirred vigorously, sending more green and white chunks over the side of the skillet.

"How about if I set the table?" Michel offered.

He began stacking plates, cloth napkins, and silverware without waiting for an answer, then put his drink on top. He carefully picked up the pile, and turned around. Chance was poking the handle of a wooden spoon at a piece of green pepper that threatened to catch fire under the burner grate.

"I'll be outside." Michel said.

"I'll be here," Chance replied distractedly.

Michel walked out to the patio and set the dishes on the wrought iron table. Blue suddenly appeared at his side. He knelt and kissed the top of her head.

"Where have you been?" he asked. "Hiding from Hurricane Chance?"

Blue pushed her head into his chest, and Michel scratched her back haunches. Suddenly his cell phone rang. Blue immediately backed away.

"Sorry about that," Michel said. He pulled his phone from his jacket pocket and checked the display. The number was local, but unfamiliar. "Hello?" he answered tentatively.

"Mr. Doucette?" a man's voice asked.

"Yes."

"This is Scott Taylor."

"Oh, hello, Mr. Taylor," Michel replied. "I've been trying to reach you and your wife."

"Yes, I know," Taylor replied, his voice low and anxious, as though he were afraid of being overheard. "I'm sorry to bother you so late, but I was hoping you could come by the hotel."

Michel looked through the patio window. Chance suddenly appeared in the hallway and picked something up from the floor. He seemed to contemplate eating it for a moment before walking back into the kitchen. Michel felt the tension in his chest and shoulders ease a bit, and smiled to himself.

"I'm afraid I've already got plans tonight," he said. "Could we make it tomorrow morning?"

There was a long pause, and Michel began to wonder if Taylor had hung up.

"I'm afraid that if you don't come here, she's going to go there," Taylor replied finally. It sounded more like a considerate warning than a threat. "I wouldn't bother you if it weren't important," he continued, his voice taking on an edge of near-desperation. "I don't think it will take long."

Michel sighed acquiescence.

"Would 8:30 work? I'm just about to have dinner."

"Sooner would be better, if possible," Taylor replied. "Trish...isn't feeling well. She should get to bed soon."

Michel was certain there was more to it, but decided it didn't matter.

"Okay, I'll get there as soon as possible," he said.

"Thank you," Taylor replied, his relief palpable through the phone. "We're in the Ritz-Carlton Suite."

Michel hung up and slipped the phone back into his pocket, then finished setting the table. He picked up his drink and walked back into the kitchen.

"It'll just be another minute," Chance said.

His face was flushed, though Michel couldn't tell if it was with pride, or from the heat. He decided it was probably more the former, and felt a pang of guilt.

"Great," he said stiffly, "but I'm going to have to go out for a little while afterward."

"Oh," Chance replied, disappointment clouding his eyes.

"Scott Taylor just called," Michel said. "I have to meet with them in their hotel suite."

"You *have* to?" Chance replied. "I thought the point of your own business is so you can stop being a dancing monkey."

To Michel's surprise, the tone was more teasing than angry.

"I'm not a 'dancing monkey,'" he protested weakly. "I chose to go." He sipped his drink, then quickly added, "Besides, they're probably going to fire me."

Chance snorted and shook his head.

"Oh, don't even *try* that with me."

"Try what?" Michel replied, a lame parody of innocence.

"Poor me, I'm going to get fired," Chance replied in a high, whining voice. "Feel sorry for me even though I'm blowing you off after you spent all afternoon slaving over a hot stove for me."

Michel couldn't help but laugh.

"You're not getting any sympathy here," Chance continued, dropping his voice to its normal register, but bobbing his head from side to side. "Not from me *or* Blue. Uh uh. We're tired of being neglected."

Michel suspected there was at least a kernel of truth behind the theatrics.

"I really am sorry," he said. "I swear I'll make it up to you when I get back."

"Oh, and don't be thinking you can buy me off with sex, either," Chance replied, waving his hands dismissively. Then his expression turned serious. "But what if they actually *do* fire you?" he asked.

"I'd get over it," Michel replied.

"That's not what I mean," Chance replied. "Would you still try to find Rhodes and Gaudreau?"

Michel hadn't considered that possibility yet.

"I don't know," he replied honestly. "Probably."

"Why not?"

Michel's ears burned suddenly. He felt oddly vulnerable.

"That's a way more profound question than I'm prepared to answer right now," he said, laughing to cover his discomfort.

Chance studied Michel, then nodded.

"That's okay," he said. "Dinner's ready anyway." He grabbed two serving bowls from the cabinet to his left, then turned back to Michel. "But you should probably figure that out at some point."

Chapter 33

Trish Campbell Rhodes Taylor was curled up against the left arm of a cream and gold brocade sofa, a half-empty glass of amber liquid resting in her right hand. For a moment, she didn't notice Michel standing in the doorway with her husband. Her bright green eyes remained fixed blankly on a spot just above the coffee table. Then suddenly they focused and locked on him.

"*Bravo*," she said too elaborately. She banged her glass down on the ornate side table and pushed forward. As she rose unsteadily to her feet, she began a slow clapping. "Not only were you unable to find my son, but now he may be dead. Well done, Mr. Doucette."

Michel wasn't sure how to respond. He looked at Scott Tayor, who seemed equally at a loss. The clapping stopped abruptly and Trish reached for her drink.

"Do you know why we hired you in the first place?" she asked, the words fuzzy around the edges, but the taunting tone clear. "Because you're a faggot. A faggot who likes 20-something-year-old boys. We thought if anyone could find Cam, it would be you."

"Trish, I think that's..." Scott Taylor started, then faltered as his wife turned her cold glare on him.

She took a slow sip, then looked back at Michel and smiled. The exaggerated sweetness turned it into a mocking leer.

"Yes, I know all about your dead boyfriend," she said. "I always do my research before I put anybody on my payroll. I'd offer you my condolences, but I'm too busy worrying about my son at the moment, thank you."

Michel felt suddenly dizzy with anger.

"Pity you didn't start worrying years ago," he said in a tight voice. "Maybe we wouldn't be here right now."

Trish took a shaky step toward him, her knuckles turning pale as she gripped the glass more tightly.

"You have no idea what kind of relationship I have with my son," she said.

"Yes, it's obvious you were very close," Michel replied, nodding at the glass.

Trish stared at it for a moment, then her anger seemed to drain away. Her shoulders dropped and she wobbled slightly from side to side.

"Alcoholism is a disease," she murmured. "We both suffer from it."

Michel let out a contemptuous bark of laughter.

"How convenient. A disease. So I guess that means neither of you has to be responsible for anything you do?"

Trish's jaw tightened, but she didn't respond.

"Let's face it," Michel said, "the problems with your son started a long time ago. You just hired me to clean up the mess before it got out of control. Unfortunately, it was too late. But I don't think you have to worry about him being dead. You need to worry about what happens when the cops find him and charge him with Skylar Ellis's murder."

Trish's body immediately stilled.

"What are you talking about?" Scott Taylor said. "I thought Ellis was killed by those drug dealers?"

Michel knew he'd already said more than he should, but he wanted to hurt Trish Taylor now.

"Maybe," he replied, "but Collins and his friends were carrying $10,000 in cash when they were killed." He paused a beat, then added, "By the way, do you know how much money Cam took in cash advances on his credit card?"

For the first time, he saw doubt cloud Trish's eyes.

"You're trying to twist things," she said. "Trying to turn Cam from a victim into a criminal."

"I never said he wasn't a victim," Michel replied. "I just said I don't think anyone killed him. I'm pretty sure he's been a victim most of his life, *Trish*."

A few drops spattered Michel's chest and left shoulder as the glass sailed past his head. It shattered against the wall. Trish closed the distance before Michel could react.

"That's enough," Scott Taylor shouted, stepping between them and grabbing Trish's left arm.

She tried to take a step back, then looked at her arm with confusion. She seemed genuinely surprised to see her husband's hand there. Then the surprise turned to anger, and she ripped her arm away.

"Be careful which side you're on, Scott," she warned.

"I'm on your side," Taylor replied, his tone even but firm, "and I want to make sure you don't do anything you're going to regret in the morning."

He took a step forward and gently squeezed Trish's shoulders. For a moment, she looked ready to pull away again, then her whole body slumped forward as though overcome with exhaustion.

"I think you should go to bed," Taylor said.

Trish stared up at him, tears welling in her eyes.

"I'm sorry," she said.

"I know," Taylor replied, pulling her closer and resting her head against his chest. "It's okay. You're under a lot of stress."

Trish nodded and let out a wet gasp.

"I am," she managed in a ragged voice.

"I know," Taylor soothed, stroking her hair. "You just need some rest."

Trish stayed pressed against him for a few moments longer, then stepped back. She wiped her eyes and attempted an embarrassed smile.

"Good night," she said quietly.

"Good night," Taylor replied.

He leaned forward and kissed her forehead. Trish turned and walked to the bedroom door. She put her left hand on the handle, then turned to Michel as though she were going to say something. After a few seconds, she seemed to change her mind, and gave a small fluttery wave instead. Michel thought it was an oddly vulnerable and girlish gesture. For a second, he felt almost sorry for her.

Chapter 34

"I'm sorry," Scott Taylor said. "If I'd known that was going to happen, I wouldn't have asked you to come over. Hopefully she got it all out of her system."

"That's all right," Michel replied. "I've been called far worse than 'faggot'."

Taylor gave a thin smile. "Can I get you a drink?"

"Sure, if there's any left," Michel replied.

Taylor picked up a bottle of Johnnie Walker Blue Label and displayed it toward Michel. The liquor was barely an inch below the base of the neck. Michel gave him a bemused look.

"Is that the second bottle?"

"I guess she doesn't have much tolerance, anymore," Taylor replied, shaking his head. "She only had three light drinks, but it hit her about five minutes after she took the first sip." He poured scotch into two glasses. "Neat or on the rocks?"

"Rocks, please," Michel replied.

Taylor picked up the tongs, then set them down and dropped a handful of ice into each glass. It struck Michel as surprisingly informal, and he wondered if it had been calculated to put him at ease.

"Here you go," Taylor said, handing him a glass. "Why don't we go outside. I need a cigarette."

"I wouldn't have pegged you as a smoker," Michel replied.

Taylor gave a soft chuckle.

"When you're running for office, you have to be discreet about a lot of things," he said.

175

It could easily have sounded suggestive, but Michel didn't pick up any sexual vibrations. They walked out onto a terrace surrounded by a white marble rail. To their left, the bend in the Mississippi was visible beyond the French Quarter, its usually brown water turned pale blue by the late-evening sky. Michel noticed that the ashtray on the round glass-topped table was already full with white and cork-colored cigarette butts.

"So has this been going on for a while?" he asked, nodding back toward the suite and lighting a cigarette.

"The drinking?" Taylor replied. "No. At least not so far as I know. I've never seen her have even a glass of wine before."

He sipped his drink, then lit his own cigarette and took a long drag. Michel decided to let him lead the conversation.

"You were a little hard on Trish," Taylor said after a moment, his tone matter-of-fact.

"I think it was pretty mutual," Michel replied. "Just because I'm 'on the payroll,'" he air-quoted, "doesn't mean my personal life is fair game. Especially since I don't need the job."

"Fair enough," Taylor replied, without apparent irony.

He took another sip and watched the ribbons of smoke curl up and dissolve in the light breeze, then looked back at Michel, his expression more serious.

"You don't really think Cam was involved with Ellis's murder, do you?" he asked.

Michel shrugged noncommittally.

"They all left together, and Ellis turned up dead. Plus Collins's crew had the money."

"They were drug dealers," Taylor replied. "It could have been their own."

"Doubtful," Michel replied. "Their operation in Florida was busted. What are the chances they were carrying that much cash when it happened? Of course, they may have stolen it, but no one's reported it missing yet."

Taylor's brow furrowed slightly.

"Okay, assuming they were paid to kill Ellis, what makes

you so sure it was Cam?" he asked. "What about Gaudreau? Maybe he wanted Ellis out of the way."

Michel nodded.

"The thought occurred to me, and the truth is that I'm not sure it was Cam. It's too soon to be sure of anything."

Taylor studied him for a moment, then nodded. His whole body seemed to relax slightly.

"So basically you were just fucking with Trish because she pissed you off," he said.

"Yeah, basically," Michel agreed, though he knew it was only partially true.

Taylor gave him a wry smile.

"You have an interesting way of dealing with clients."

"And sometimes they have an interesting way of dealing with me," Michel replied.

"Touché," Taylor replied, raising his glass.

He drained it in one long gulp, then looked at Michel's still nearly-full glass.

"Can I freshen that up for you?" he asked.

Though he'd been hoping to get home early, Michel sensed that Taylor had something more on his mind. He downed half his drink, then handed it to Taylor.

"Sure, why not?"

*****

"I think you may have been given the wrong impression about Trish's and Cam's relationship," Taylor said, handing Michel his glass and taking the chair to Michel's left.

"How so?" Michel asked.

"They used to be very close. Maybe too close."

"You mean she smothered him?" Michel asked.

Taylor shook his head. "It was on Cam's part."

"I guess that doesn't seem unusual given what happened with his father," Michel replied.

"It was more than that," Taylor said. "Most kids try to assert their independence by lying and keeping secrets from their parents. Cam was the opposite. It was like he had a compulsion to share everything with Trish. He treated her more like his best friend than his mother. She tried to maintain appropriate boundaries, but he never recognized them."

"Even after she married you?" Michel asked.

Taylor snorted humorlessly.

"A few months after we married, we had to put a lock on our bedroom door because Cam kept crawling into bed with us in the middle of the night."

Michel quickly did the math.

"He must have been at least 12 by then."

Taylor nodded, and sighed.

"I understood why he'd become dependent on Trish," he said, "but he seemed determined not to outgrow it."

"That must have created some tension between the two of you," Michel said.

"Some," Taylor agreed, "but for the most part, we got along. I don't think Trish and I would have lasted if we hadn't."

Michel was sure the last part was true, though he suspected Taylor was glossing over some of the thornier aspects of his early relationship with his stepson.

"Maybe on some level Cam understood that Trish needed me," Taylor continued, "but for whatever reason, he never treated me like a threat. I think he even considered me a father of sorts after a while. At least for a few years."

Michel decided that Taylor was far more accessible in person that he appeared on TV, and far more likable than he'd been during their first meeting.

"So when did things between Cam and your wife start to change?" he asked.

"Initially during his junior year in high school," Taylor replied, "though at that point, the changes were positive."

"Was there any particular catalyst?" Michel asked.

"A new boy moved to town," Taylor replied. "Damian Pope."

"The boy who committed suicide," Michel replied.

Taylor nodded, and Michel saw what seemed to be genuine sadness in his eyes.

"Until Damian moved in, Cam had never had any friends," Taylor said.

"None?" Michel asked skeptically.

"Trish said it was because he had trouble relating to kids his own age," Taylor replied, "but honestly, I think it was because he made other kids feel uncomfortable."

"Why?" Michel asked.

"It was just one of those things, I guess," Taylor shrugged, "but it was pretty obvious. Whenever he was with a group of kids, you could see them keeping their distance him."

Michel suddenly wondered if Rhodes had been drawn to Gaudreau because outcasts and misfits were actually celebrated in his world.

"That must have been hard on him," was all he said.

Taylor nodded.

"And Trish. I think she had a hard time understanding it."

Michel didn't doubt that. He was certain Trish Taylor had never had any trouble making friends.

"So what was so different about Damian?" Michel asked. "Why did he and Cam click?"

"I'm not sure," Taylor replied, "but for that year before Damian died, they were almost inseparable."

"What was Damian like?" Michel asked.

Taylor studied his glass for a moment.

"Smart. Personable," he said with an almost-wistful smile. "Sure of himself without being arrogant. I liked him."

"And your wife?" Michel asked, sensing a "but."

"She was...less enthusiastic," Taylor replied diplomatically.

"Why's that?"

"She was worried that he was going to take advantage of Cam," Taylor replied.

179

"Sexually?"

"No. At that point the incident with the gardeners had already taken place." Taylor shook his head. "She was more concerned about him being exploited emotionally. It was clear that Cam worshipped Damian, and Trish thought Damian might use that to manipulate him."

Michel was reminded of the way Ellis, Rachel Davis, and Kenny Dixon had all described Rhodes's relationship with Gaudreau. There seemed to be a pattern.

"And what did you think?" he asked.

"I thought she was being paranoid," Taylor replied. "I think she'd spent so much time around politicians that she had a hard time believing anyone could be just what they appeared to be."

Michel nodded. "So how did their relationship change once Damian came along?"

"It became more...*mature* is a good word, I think," Taylor replied. "They were still close, but there was a healthier distance between them. And Cam stopped antagonizing Trish."

"Antagonizing?" Michel repeated.

The sudden anxiousness in Taylor's eyes suggested he'd spoken more freely than he'd intended. He looked quickly toward the door, then down at his drink.

"What Trish so euphemistically referred to as *trying to get her attention*," he said. "I always thought there was more to it. I think he was testing her, trying to find out how far he could push before she'd stop loving him."

Michel remembered what Dixon said about Rhodes flaunting his sexual conquests in front of Ellis. Had those been tests, too?

"But it stopped once Damian came along?" he asked. "At least until recently?"

Taylor hesitated, and shot another look at the door.

"That's what Trish believes, anyway," he said quietly.

"And you?"

"I think he's decided to cut Trish out of his life," Taylor said.

Michel sat back in his chair, and exhaled loudly.

"Kind of dramatic, don't you think?" he asked. "He couldn't just stop calling on Mother's Day?" He looked for at least a half-smile, but didn't get one. "So why do you think that?" he asked.

"He told me as much," Tayor replied. "A few months after Damian killed himself. He said that as soon as he had enough money, he was going to disappear and Trish would never hear from him again."

Michel noted they were almost the exact words Skylar Ellis had used during his drunken call.

"I didn't take him seriously at the time," Taylor continued, "but now I think I was wrong."

"Because he's about to get his trust fund," Michel said, fitting the pieces together.

Taylor nodded. "In another six months, he'll have more than enough money."

"But why not wait until he actually has it?" Michel asked. "That doesn't make sense. Did anything happen that might have set him off?"

"Not that I know of," Taylor replied.

Michel frowned and took a sip of his drink.

"I'll understand if you don't want to answer this," he said, "but why does Cam hate his mother so much? Especially given how close they were."

Taylor hesitated again before answering.

"You have to understand..." he began, then stopped.

Michel raised his eyebrows expectantly. Taylor swallowed half his drink, then fumbled another cigarette from his pack. Michel leaned back in his chair and waited. After nearly a minute, Taylor looked at him and offered a diffident smile.

"When Trish said her alcoholism is a disease, she was just trying to play the sympathy card with you," he started again. "It *is* a disease, but she's never viewed it that way. She's always seen it as a weakness that she overcame."

Until today, Michel thought, but just nodded.

"And despite her own history...or maybe because of it...she can be extremely unsympathetic toward people who are still struggling, or who can't move beyond difficult periods in their lives," Taylor continued. "She doesn't believe in dwelling on problems, or, as she puts it, 'talking things to death.' She believes in moving on. That's what she did when she got sober, that's what she did when her first husband died, and that's what she expects everyone else to do."

Taylor didn't seem to be defending his wife, so Michel didn't bother arguing her viewpoint.

"But when it came to Cam, it was different," Taylor said. "With Cam, she could be forgiving. She never got angry about his alcohol and drug problems, and each time he relapsed, she saw it as just a misstep on his path to recovery."

"When it comes to people we love, I guess we're all more willing to forgive," Michel replied, though he wondered if the opposite was also sometimes true.

"But not after Damian died," Taylor replied.

"How do you mean?" Michel asked.

"When Cam met Damian, he cleaned up his act," Taylor replied. "Damian didn't drink or do drugs, so Cam stopped, too. But when Damian died, Cam went on a binge. At first Trish was sympathetic. She even took him down to the Cape for a week in hopes she could talk him through it, make him realize that it wasn't what Damian would have wanted. But they ended up having a fight instead. When they got back, Trish committed Cam to a treatment facility in the Berkshires."

"I can see how that might have soured things," Michel replied dryly.

"It was a few weeks later that he told me his plan to leave," Taylor replied. "Eventually things thawed out, but it was never the same between them again. I think Cam felt that Trish betrayed him. Obviously he never let go of his resentment."

"I take it you haven't told Trish any of this?" Michel asked.

"How could I?" Taylor replied. "It would break her heart.

She thought she was doing the right thing with Cam. It would kill her to know that he hates her because of it."

"But don't you think you're just postponing the inevitable?" Michel asked. "At some point, she'll either figure it out on her or he'll tell her."

Taylor let out a weary sigh. "Maybe I'm being stupid, but I guess I'm hoping that eventually he'll change his mind, and she'll never have to know the truth."

Michel felt certain things weren't headed in that direction, but gave a supportive smile.

"You never know," he said, "but then why hire me to find him? Seems like it would have been better to just let him disappear for a while."

"I didn't have much choice in the matter," Taylor replied.

Michel nodded. He finished his cigarette and stubbed it out, careful not to knock any other butts or ashes onto the table. "One last question," he said. "Just out of curiosity, why did Damian Pope kill himself?"

Taylor grimaced. "The police thought he was despondent about being gay."

"They *thought*," Michel replied. "They didn't know?"

"He didn't leave a note," Taylor replied, "but they found some internet searches and unfinished emails on his computer that pointed in that direction." He slowly swirled the ice cubes around his glass, then shook his head as though trying to lose a bad memory. "I don't know. It just didn't feel right to me."

"It never feels right when a kid kills himself," Michel replied.

"That's not what I meant," Taylor said. "I meant that I didn't think he was gay."

Michel looked at him curiously. "Did he ever say he was?"

"He told Cam," Taylor replied.

"So then what makes you think he was actually straight?" Michel asked.

"Well, I'm not an expert on these things," Taylor replied, "but he spent a month on the Cape with us that last summer, and I noticed that he never looked at other boys unless Cam pointed them out first. And even then, they didn't hold his interest for very long."

"They may have had very different tastes," Michel replied.

"Maybe," Taylor replied, "but he definitely seemed to notice girls. So much so that I think it made Cam angry."

"It's possible he was overcompensating," Michel offered. "If he really was troubled about his sexuality, he would have tried to hide it. Especially in public."

"But that's the point," Taylor replied, frustration creeping into his voice. "He didn't try to hide anything. He was naturally a delicate kid, almost pretty, and he played it up. Make-up, crazy hair, girl's clothes. I think he liked toying with people's perceptions about his sexuality, but when it came down to it, my sense was that he liked girls."

Michel was intrigued both by Taylor's use of the word "pretty," and by how attuned he'd apparently been to Damian Pope's sexual persona. He wondered if Taylor had dreamed of trading in his cleats and shoulder pads for eyeliner and platform boots at some point in his youth. He pushed the thought aside.

"Did you ever mention your feelings to anyone?" he asked.

"Just to Trish," Taylor replied. "I mean, what could I say? 'I'm so sorry Damian killed himself, but I think he lied about the reason?' His family didn't need to hear that."

"I suppose not," Michel replied, though he wasn't so sure.

Chapter 35

Michel climbed into his truck and checked his phone. It was almost 10 PM. Sassy had called a few minutes earlier, but hadn't left a message. He hit CALL BACK.

"It's about time," Sassy answered, after the second ring. "What were you doing there for so long? Having a threesome?"

"What?" Michel replied. "A threesome?"

"With the Taylors," Sassy replied.

"How did you know I was with the Taylors?" Michel asked.

"I called your house about an hour ago, and Chance told me," Sassy replied.

"He answered the phone?" Michel asked, then cursed himself as he imagined the smirk on Sassy's face. He felt the now-familiar tightening in his chest and shoulders.

"No, he picked up when he heard my voice," Sassy replied, her voice surprisingly neutral.

"Oh," Michel replied, feeling stupid.

"So what happened with the Taylors?" Sassy asked.

"Well, it was mostly the husband," Michel replied. "Trish ripped into me for a few minutes, then went to sleep it off."

"She was drunk?"

"Mmm," Michel replied around the cigarette he was lighting.

"So has she been off the wagon for long?" Sassy asked.

Michel exhaled, squinting against the smoke. He rolled the window down a few inches.

"Not according to Scott Taylor," he said. "He said this was the first time he's ever seen her drink."

He put the key into the ignition, then thought better of it. Driving while smoking and talking on the phone seemed like more than he could safely manage at the moment.

"So what did she say?" Sassy asked.

"Basically that I'm an incompetent faggot who managed to put her son's life in danger."

"That's just wrong," Sassy deadpanned. "I think you're an extremely competent faggot. Maybe the best."

"Thank you," Michel replied.

"So are we out of a job?" Sassy asked.

"Surprisingly, no, but maybe that part slipped her mind."

"So then what did you and Taylor talk about for so long?"

Michel took a long drag. He suddenly wished he were out on the patio with Blue and a fresh cocktail.

"Well, which do you want to hear about first?" he asked. "The part about him sleeping with his 12-year-old stepson, the part about the straight kid who killed himself because he was gay, or the part about Rhodes torching his life?"

There was a long pause while Sassy waited for an indication he was kidding.

"Okay, maybe you better start at the beginning," she said, when it became apparent he wasn't.

*****

"So what makes you so sure Rhodes is doing a slash-and-burn?" Sassy asked when Michel finished.

"Primarily the fact that he won't get control of his trust for another six months," Michel replied. "I understand why he'd want to get away from Trish, but right now she's his only financial support, and based on his apartment, he likes to live well. He's already waited almost three years, so why jump the gun now unless he's not planning to be around in six months?"

"Or if he doesn't need her money anymore," Sassy replied. "Maybe Gaudreau's taking care of him now."

Michel sat up straighter. It was a possibility he hadn't considered.

"Okay, but what about dropping out of school?" he said, not ready to give up so easily. "Not to mention killing his boyfriend. Does that sound like someone planning a future?"

"People drop out of school everyday and go on to live long productive lives," Sassy replied reasonably, "and we don't have any concrete proof that he killed Ellis yet. And even if he did it, he probably thinks he's smart enough to get away with it."

Michel lit another cigarette and smoked it hard.

"It just seems like you're jumping to conclusions," Sassy said, reading his silence. "Do I think we need to find him? Yes. Do I think he had something to do with Ellis's murder? Yes. Do I think he's planning on going out in a blaze of glory next week? No. There's no evidence of that yet."

Michel sighed with resignation, realizing she was right.

"Well, so what do you make of the rest of it?" he asked.

"Interesting," Sassy said. "I don't know what it all means, but it's interesting."

"I wonder why Taylor felt it was so important for me to understand the relationship between Trish and Cam?" Michel said. "I don't know if he just didn't want her to be the villain in the story, or if there was more to it."

"Well, if nothing else, I think we have a much better understanding of what makes Rhodes tick now," Sassy replied.

"True, though I don't feel like we're any closer to finding him or figuring out what actually happened," Michel replied.

Sassy yawned conspicuously.

"Maybe a good night's sleep will help put everything in perspective," she offered.

"Yeah, maybe," Michel agreed.

"And since you'll be sleeping alone tonight, that shouldn't be a problem," Sassy added.

Michel frowned.

"Why will I be sleeping alone tonight?" he asked.

"Oh, didn't I mention? Chance said he was heading home to do some packing," Sassy replied.

"No, you didn't mention it," Michel replied distractedly, more curious why Chance hadn't mentioned it himself. He wondered if it had been a spur-of-the-moment decision, and what had prompted it. He felt suddenly uneasy.

"You still there?" Sassy prompted.

"Yeah," Michel replied, coming back to the moment. "Sorry, I just zoned out for a second."

"Gee, I can't imagine why," Sassy replied.

"What's that supposed to mean?" Michel replied testily.

"You know the old saying," Sassy said. "You made your own bed. Now I guess you've got to sleep in it. Alone."

She hung up before Michel could reply. He gave the phone a cross look, then started the engine.

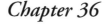

Chapter 36

Michel opened the door to the sound of nails clattering down the hall. Blue stopped a few feet away, stretched and yawned, then cantered excitedly toward him. Michel knelt and they went through their usual greeting ritual, but with Blue stealing expectant looks at the open door.

"Sorry, it's just me tonight," Michel said. "Uncle Chance is sleeping at his own house."

Blue allowed herself another moment of affection, then ran to the back door. Michel pushed himself up with a grunt, shut the front door, and followed. He let her out onto the patio, then walked back to the kitchen and flipped on the light.

"Wow," he said, looking around.

Everything had been put away, and the stovetop, counters, and floor gleamed. He picked up the note in front of the coffee maker and tried to decipher Chance's handwriting.

Michel — I decided it was time to shit or get off the pot, so I went to my place to do some packing. Besides, I figured we could both use some time alone. I'll talk to you soon.
— Chance

"'I'll talk to you soon?'" Michel repeated sourly. "No 'hugs and kisses?' No 'I'll miss you?'"

He put the note down, grunting dissatisfaction, and opened the cabinet to his left. He grabbed a glass and the bottle of Jack Daniels, then went to the fridge and filled the glass with ice.

"'I figured we could both use some time alone,'" he muttered, as he walked through the house. "Like I don't get a say?"

He stepped out onto the patio. Blue was lying in front of the fountain watching him, her ears back, eyes anxious.

"It's okay, I'm not mad at you," he reassured her, the tension in his voice suggesting the opposite.

Blue moved a few feet farther away and lay down again, facing the wall. Michel barely noticed. He dropped into his regular chair and pulled out his cigarettes.

"Why does this feel so complicated?" he asked the moon. "It's not like we're even dating."

The lighter flared, and he inhaled deeply, letting the nicotine go to work. As he exhaled, he felt his muscles relax. He poured an inch of Jack into his glass and took a long sip, then shook his head.

"I'm such a dork," he said with an embarrassed laugh. "I'm the one who was feeling suffocated, and now I've got my panties in a bunch because he went home."

He finished his drink in a single gulp, then checked the time on his phone.

"One more," he said to Blue, "then off to bed."

Blue let out a groan, and seemed to settle more deeply into the flagstone.

*****

Michel opened his eyes and saw night sky, though only a handful of pale stars were still visible. He rolled his head forward and groaned at the pain in his neck. Blue lay sprawled across the red cushion on the chaise to his left, her breathing slow and regular.

He straightened up and felt a jolt of adrenaline as the glass started to slip out of his left hand. It hit his thigh, and he jerked his hand down to catch it. Lukewarm, watery Jack Daniels soaked his lap. Classy, he thought, looking down.

He put the glass on the side table, and slowly pushed himself up. His lower back felt even stiffer than his neck, and his right foot was numb. He shook his leg for a few seconds, then took a tentative step. Pins and needles stabbed at his toes.

Without opening her eyes, Blue suddenly rolled onto her back, hind leg splayed and front legs drawn up like Tyrannosaurus arms. Michel hobbled over and began gently scratching the pale gray fur covering her belly.

"Come on, sweetheart," he said. "We'd better go inside before the rats eat us."

For a moment Blue remained still, her long tongue lolling out of the right side of her mouth. Then her legs came together, and she rolled toward Michel. He straightened up as she stepped delicately down from the chaise and stretched.

"Let's go, sleepyhead," Michel said.

Blue bounded ahead of him into the house. He grabbed his cell phone, and limped after her, turning off lights as he went. By the time he reached the bedroom, Blue was stretched out on the hall carpet outside the door, her eyes closed.

"That was fast," Michel said, carefully stepping over her.

He walked into the bathroom without bothering with the light, and stripped, tossing his wet pants and boxers over the edge of the tub. As the smell of Jack Daniels hit him, he considered a quick shower, but decided it was too much work. He peed, then walked into the bedroom.

The nightstand clock read 3:20 AM. He lifted the rumpled sheet and blanket, and slipped under them. The cool crispness sent a pleasant shiver through his body. He closed his eyes, and his mind immediately began to drift.

Suddenly a thought began to take shape. Something about Trish Taylor's reaction hadn't felt right. He tried to hold onto it, but it moved out of focus. He wished he had a pad to write a note for himself, and suddenly saw one in his hand. He looked around for a pen, but the room was unfamiliar, all four walls lined with drawers that stretched high above his head. He opened one at random. It was empty, and much deeper than he'd expected. He closed it and opened another. It held a massive tangle of rubber bands and paper clips. He began pulling them apart, searching for a pen.

His head rolled to the side as sleep overtook him.

Chapter 37

Michel groaned. The distant ringing stopped. He turned his head to the left and struggled to focus his eyes. The fuzzy red numbers on the clock seemed to mock his effort. He leaned closer and saw he'd been asleep for just over two hours.

"What the fuck," he said, as the ringing began again.

He pushed unsteadily to his feet and lumbered to the door. Blue was still asleep just outside, apparently oblivious to the noise. Michel stepped over her, and headed toward the living room. The ringing grew steadily louder, then stopped as he reached the doorway.

"Motherfucker," he hissed under his breath.

The ringing began again almost immediately, and he spotted the phone's flashing green light on the dining room table. He crossed the room and snatched it up.

"Hello?" he answered, a combination of apprehensiveness and annoyance.

"Michel, it's me," Carl DeRoche replied.

Michel's annoyance died immediately.

"What's wrong?" he asked.

"Al had a stroke," DeRoche replied without hesitation.

It was the directness of someone too accustomed to delivering bad news.

"Is he all right?" Michel replied reflexively.

"He's in critical condition. It's still too soon to tell if he's going to make it, or how much damage was done."

"I'm sorry," Michel replied, unsure what else to say.

"Thank you." DeRoche replied, managing to make it sound more than perfunctory. "I'm sorry to call so early, but I thought you should know."

"No, I appreciate it," Michel replied. "Is there anything I can do to help?"

He suddenly felt as though he were reciting lines in a movie.

"I'm still trying to figure out the reassignments for his cases," DeRoche replied, "but I should have it worked out later this morning. It would be helpful if you and Sassy could come in to review the Rhodes case with whoever takes it over."

"Yeah, of course," Michel replied. "I'll call Sassy and let her know. Eleven?"

"That should be fine," DeRoche replied.

Michel put the phone back down on the table. He decided there was no need to wake Sassy with the news. Another few hours wouldn't make any difference.

He walked into the kitchen and put grounds and water into the coffeemaker. His body still wanted sleep, but his brain was wired now. As the coffee began dripping into the pot, he went into the hall and sat cross-legged next to Blue. He stroked the soft spotted fur along her side.

"You want to go out on the patio with me?" he asked.

Blue snorted in reply, not even bothering to open her eyes. Michel gave a small laugh, but managed only a melancholy smile. He could tell it was going to be a very long day.

Chapter 38

They'd avoided talking about Ribodeau on the drive to the station, instinctively knowing they needed to focus until they'd brought his replacement up to speed. Michel knocked on the open door to DeRoche's office. He motioned them in.

"Close the door, please," he said brusquely.

Michel noticed that the blinds on the windows had been shut. He closed the door and took the chair to Sassy's left. DeRoche opened the center drawer of his desk and took out two black leather billfolds. He tossed them on top.

"What are those?" Sassy asked, eyeing them suspiciously.

"Shields," DeRoche replied, frowning. "I've been ordered to temporarily reinstate you."

"By whom?" Sassy asked.

"Friends of Trish Taylor."

"That doesn't make sense," Michel replied. "Last night she was accusing me of putting her son's life in danger. Now she wants us working with the department?"

"I guess she changed her mind," DeRoche replied, his tone making it clear he wasn't pleased with the situation.

"And what if we don't want to be reinstated?" Sassy asked.

"Then I've been authorized to retain you as consultants," DeRoche replied.

Before Sassy could respond, Michel picked up one of the billfolds. He flipped it open for a moment, then slipped it into his jacket. He raised his eyebrows at Sassy. She hesitated a moment, then sighed and picked up the other.

"So are we just supposed to be finding Rhodes, or trying to figure out who killed Ellis, too?" Michel asked.

"Both," DeRoche replied, "though if you find Rhodes, I suspect your services may no longer be required." He slid a neat stack of folders across the desk. "Here are Al's files. You've been set up with access to our databases. You'll report directly to me. Everything will be standard procedure, except I think it would be better if you work from your own office."

"And why's that?" Sassy asked.

"Al was a popular guy," DeRoche replied. "A lot of people aren't going to be happy about outsiders taking over his case."

"But we're not outsiders," Michel protested. "We've only been off the force for a few years. I'm sure some people still remember us."

DeRoche nodded.

"And some of them probably still think you were on Priest Lee's payroll. For your own sakes, I think it would be better if you kept your distance. If you need anything, just call me."

Chapter 39

"So why do you suppose Trish was so keen to get us reinstated?" Sassy asked, thumbing through a folder on her lap.

"My personal charm must have finally won her over," Michel replied. He turned the truck left onto N. Rampart.

"Seriously," Sassy said, looking up. "Does it that make any sense to you? And what's this bullshit about us working from our own office? Something's not right."

Michel shrugged. "I guess Trish didn't want to wait for someone new to get up to speed."

"That doesn't explain keeping us away from the station," Sassy said. She flipped to a new page, and shook her head. "You know, Al may have looked like a slob, but his notes are meticulous. Anyone could have picked this up and run with it."

"Still..." Michel said, not bothering to finish the thought. He pulled to the curb in front of the office. Sassy closed the folder and looked at him curiously.

"Where's Blue?" she asked. "Did you park her with the babysitter again?"

"I couldn't," Michel replied. "I called twice, but it went straight to voicemail."

Sassy thought she detected a hint of a pout in his voice, but decided to leave it alone. "So where is she?" she asked.

"At home," Michel replied. "I figured I'd go pick her up, and bring us back some lunch."

"Just like old times," Sassy said, sighing. "I do all the work, while you run personal errands and get food."

Michel forced a smile. If only, he thought.

"Close enough," he said, "except that now I'm paying. So what are you in the mood for?"

Sassy folded her arms across chest and pretended to give it serious consideration. "Popeye's," she said after a moment.

"How did I know you were going to say that?" Michel replied, shaking his head.

"What are you talking about?" Sassy replied. "I hardly *ever* eat Popeye's anymore. Especially since that crazy motherfucker Joshua Clement tried to make it my last supper. I'm only doing it because I need to put some meat back on my bones."

"Hey, whatever helps you sleep..." Michel replied breezily.

Sassy's peered at him over the top of her reading glasses. "Hush up and go get my chicken," she said.

*****

"Anything good?" Michel asked, dropping the grease-stained bag on the front edge of Sassy's desk.

Sassy rubbed Blue's neck for another few moments, then kissed the top of her head and straightened up. She closed her eyes and inhaled deeply.

"Did you remember to get my extra biscuit?" she asked suspiciously, her eyes popping open.

"Of course."

"Because I don't smell an extra biscuit."

"Trust me, it's in there," Michel replied.

"It better be," Sassy muttered. She moved the bag to the side, then picked up the file she'd been reading. "So, guess who doesn't really exist?"

"Heterosexual male figure skaters?"

"Nope."

"Surprising," Michel replied.

"Gaudreau," Sassy said.

It took Michel a moment to realize what she'd said.

"How's that possible?" he asked.

"I don't know," Sassy replied, "but Al ran a check, and it came up empty."

"Did he check for Frank Pierce, too?" Michel asked.

"Both Pierce and Gaudreau, Franklin, Frank, and plain old F," Sassy replied. "There are a plenty of Frank Pierces, and a handful of Frank Gaudreaus, but none of either in the right age range, living in New Orleans."

"Maybe he never officially became a resident," Michel replied. "He could still be listed in New York."

Sassy shook her head.

"Or maybe Dixon was wrong about New York," Michel said.

"Maybe," Sassy agreed, unconvinced.

Michel frowned. "We should check the deed for the place on Burgundy. See what name is listed on it."

"The City of New Orleans," Sassy replied.

Michel gave her a questioning look.

"Al already checked it," she replied. "The previous owners didn't carry flood insurance. After Katrina, they couldn't afford to fix up the store and reopen it. They ran up over $50,000 in unpaid taxes. The city finally agreed to forgive the debt in exchange for the property."

"That was big of them," Michel replied. "How long ago?"

"About 20 months."

"So Gaudreau's been squatting there and throwing parties every night for a year and a half, and nobody's noticed?" Michel shook his head incredulously.

Sassy shrugged. "The previous owners left the city, and it's not like there's anyone else on that block to give a shit."

Michel grumbled discontent. "Okay, then who's paying the electric bill?"

"Congratulations, you have your first official task," Sassy replied. "Welcome back to the exciting world of police work."

"Gee, I hope I can handle it," Michel replied.

Sassy gave him a half-smile.

"Of course, the good news is that we won't need a warrant to search the property now," she said. "I already contacted the City Attorney's office, and they've okayed it."

"It wasn't searched after the murders?" Michel asked.

"Only the building where they happened," Sassy replied. "The others weren't considered part of the crime scene."

"That could be interesting," Michel replied, brightening slightly. "Maybe we'll find some pictures of Gaudreau. It would be nice to put a face to the name."

Sassy nodded agreement. Michel took out his cigarettes, then immediately put them back in his pocket when he saw Sassy's scowl.

"So anything else of interest in the files?" he asked.

Sassy slid a piece of paper across the table. The circular emblem of the Alabama Bureau of Investigations was printed in the top left corner.

"Angel Peterson's parents reported him missing on December 23rd," she said. "He called them just after seven that morning to let them know he'd gotten on the bus, but he never made it home."

Michel quickly perused the report. "And they stopped in Alabama for lunch?"

"Just outside of Birmingham," Sassy replied, "When they left, Sparkle wasn't on board. The last anyone remembers seeing him, he was heading toward the restroom in the restaurant."

Michel looked back down at the report again, but didn't see what he wanted. "I wonder if the bus always stops in the same place?" he said.

"Why?"

"If it does, someone could have been waiting for him."

Sassy smiled. "Wow, you're actually starting to think like a cop again."

"And I have my second official task," Michel replied. "I'll contact ABI to see if they know." He looked at the stack of folders with admiration. "Al didn't waste time, did he?"

"No," Sassy agreed. "It was almost like he knew he didn't have much." The words hung there for a long moment before she cocked her head curiously. "So do you feel at all guilty?"

"Why? Because a friend had a stroke and now I get to take advantage of it and play cop again?" Michel replied.

"Yeah, something like that," Sassy replied.

"Never even crossed my mind," Michel replied with a rueful grimace. Then his expression grew more serious. "Yeah, of course I do, even though objectively I know it has nothing to do with me. It's not like I stuck stroke pins in an Al voodoo doll. What about you?"

Sassy shook her head. "It was never *my* dream to be back on the force."

"Thanks a lot," Michel replied.

Sassy chuckled softly. "Look, after what's happened in my life, I know there's no cosmic force balancing things out. Bad shit happens without a reason, and good things happen without someone else having to pay the piper."

Michel gave an appreciative nod. "Do you think he's going to be okay?"

Sassy knew there could be no real answer.

"At the very least, he's probably going to have to go through a long period of rehab," she said. "It's going to be tough. Especially with no one to take care of him."

Michel was struck by the empathy in her voice. He wondered if she was tapping into fears of her own.

"You know, I would have taken care of you if Russ hadn't come along," he said.

Sassy studied him a moment. "Even if Joel were still alive?"

"Of course," Michel replied, sitting on the edge of the desk. "What difference would that have made?"

Sassy smiled softly. "When you're on your own, you can make choices that you can't when other people are depending on you. It's one thing to volunteer to give up part of your own life. It's another to ask someone else to live with that sacrifice."

"Gee, thanks for the warning," Michel joked. "I guess I better not have a stroke."

Sassy looked down at her hands for a moment. Michel couldn't read her expression.

"No, you don't have to worry," she said finally. "You're rich now. You can hire people to pretend that they care about you."

Though her tone was outwardly teasing, there was an unmistakable edge beneath it.

"I'm sorry," Michel said.

"For what?" Sassy asked.

"I'm not quite sure."

"Let me know when you figure it out," Sassy replied.

The office phone rang, and she snatched it up before Michel could reply.

"Jones and Doucette Private Investigations."

There was a brief pause, then she locked eyes with Michel.

"How long ago?" she asked.

A briefer pause.

"We're on our way," she said, then hung up.

Michel raised his eyebrows.

"So much for all of our theories," Sassy said. "That was Scott Taylor. They received a ransom note."

Chapter 40

Trish Taylor was sitting in the same spot where she'd been the previous night, her legs curled beneath her, an unlit cigarette in her left hand. A nearly full coffee cup steamed on the table in front of her. She wore a long white robe embroidered with the Ritz logo, and her damp hair was pulled back into a loose ponytail. Michel thought she was both prettier and more masculine without makeup.

"*Officer* Doucette," she said.

From her tone, it sounded as though she expected a thank you. Michel noticed her voice was raspier than usual, but she appeared to be sober.

"This is my partner, Miss Jones," he said.

"Miss Jones or Mrs. Turner?" Trish replied.

Sassy's expression didn't change.

"I'm Mrs. Turner when I'm out socially with my husband. This isn't social."

Trish's lips pressed together in a hard line.

"Please, have a seat," Scott Taylor said. "Would you like some coffee?"

"No, thank you," Michel said.

Sassy just smiled politely.

They settled into high-backed chairs opposite the couch, Michel directly across from Trish Taylor, Sassy to his right. Scott Taylor sat next to his wife. He reached for her hand, but stopped when he saw the cigarette. He folded his hands together in his lap instead.

"When did you receive the note?" Michel began.

"It was delivered to our townhouse on Beacon Hill this morning," Scott Taylor replied. "The housekeeper found a package inside the storm door when she went to get the mail. She wasn't sure if it was important, so she called. Trish told her to open it."

"What did it say?" Michel asked.

"I wrote it down," Scott Taylor replied, nodding at a sheet of paper in the center of the coffee table.

Michel leaned forward to pick it up. Taylor's handwriting was surprisingly elegant.

$250,000 or you'll never see your son alive again. Small bills. You have 3 days. We'll be in touch with further instructions. Don't contact the police or we'll kill him. You're being watched!

Michel almost laughed. He'd never read a ransom note so cliched, nor so lacking in urgency.

"Obviously the last part is a lie, or it wouldn't have been sent to your house," he said.

Taylor nodded.

"It also seems rather modest," Sassy said.

"Which means what?" Taylor asked.

"Just an observation," Sassy replied. "We'll figure out if it means anything later."

"Was it handwritten?" Michel asked.

Taylor shook his head.

"And was there any indication how the package was delivered?" Sassy asked.

"Fedex," Taylor replied. "It was sent Saturday afternoon for overnight delivery, but apparently Fedex doesn't normally deliver on Sunday."

"If it was Fedex," Sassy said, "there must have been a sender's name on it."

"Bea Bell," Trish Taylor intoned suddenly.

"Excuse me?" Sassy said.

"Bea Bell," Trish repeated. "The return address is her condo in Atlanta."

"And who's Bea Bell?" Michel asked.

"An old friend," Trish replied. "We were in school together at Choate and Vassar."

"And I take it you're still close?" Michel asked.

"Not the way we were," Trish replied, "but yes, we still keep in touch, and get together whenever we happen to be in the same city. The last time I actually saw her was at her daughter's wedding in the Hamptons last June."

"Have you tried contacting her?" Sassy asked.

"Of course," Trish replied with a hint of annoyance, "and she's in Southampton, just as I'd expected. I suggested she call building security in Atlanta and have them check her unit to make sure no one's there."

"I don't imagine whoever took your son would make things quite that easy," Michel replied dryly.

Trish drew herself up as though preparing to attack, but Scott Taylor cut in before she could respond.

"Whoever? You don't think it's Gaudreau?"

"That's our first assumption," Sassy replied evenly, "but it's also possible they were both kidnapped. Gaudreau apparently comes from money, too."

"Why 'apparently'?" Taylor replied. "You're not sure?"

Sassy shook her head. "We're not sure who he really is yet. According to another boy who was part of the same group, his real name is Frank Pierce, but we haven't been able to trace him yet. In any case, at this point we still have to consider other possibilities as well"

Michel turned to Trish. "Who outside your family and friends would know that you and Bea Bell are friends?"

"Anyone who can use a computer to search my name," Trish replied, sighing with exaggerated exasperation. "We've been photographed together literally dozens of times over the years. It's not exactly a national secret." She crossed her arms tightly over her chest.

Sassy leaned forward, and fixed her with a hard stare. "Are you about done?" she asked.

Trish's eyes narrowed. "Excuse me?"

"Because the bitch routine isn't helping," Sassy said. "You're the one who pulled strings to get us on this case. Say the word, and we'll be happy to go home." She straightened up and raised her non-existent eyebrows. "Do we understand one another?"

Michel had to suppress a smile. Trish regarded Sassy coldly for a few moments, then her expression suddenly softened and she nodded penitently. Michel recognized the move immediately. She'd used it during their first meeting, and again the previous night.

"I'm sorry," Trish said. "I'm afraid I'm just feeling a bit overwhelmed by all of this and, as I'm sure your partner told you, I relapsed last night."

Michel wanted to laugh at the blatant play for sympathy.

"I understand," Sassy replied, "but we're on the same team. We need to work together."

Trish looked down at her coffee cup for a moment, then offered an apologetic smile. "Of course."

Michel watched for a sign that Sassy knew Trish was trying to play her, but she offered a smile of encouragement instead.

"I appreciate that," she said. "Now, is there any reason you can think of why the package would have been sent using Mrs. Bell's name? I mean, I'm sure you must have a lot of friends. Were you expecting anything from her?"

"I certainly wasn't expecting anything from her." Trish replied, then paused. Vertical creases appeared between her eyes. "It's actually an odd choice," she said. "Bea is a friend, but I wouldn't expect her to send me anything that demanded immediate attention. At least not without calling first. In fact, if I'd been home, I might not have opened it for days."

She fell silent, absently tapping the unlit cigarette as she stared down at her coffee again. Michel studied her. For the first time, her reaction seemed genuine.

"I'm assuming you haven't contacted the Boston police yet?" Sassy asked.

"No, it didn't occur to us," Scott Taylor replied.

"That's fine," Sassy said. "We'll get in touch with them and have them book the note and package into evidence. I imagine the FBI may also be getting involved since the package was sent from Atlanta. That could mean that Cam was taken across state lines."

Michel noticed Trish Taylor's body stiffen slightly, though her expression remained fixed, brooding. He had a feeling the FBI wouldn't be getting their hands on the case anytime soon.

*****

"So what do you think?" Michel asked as the elevator doors glided shut.

"I think she must be out of practice," Sassy replied.

Michel raised a questioning eyebrow.

"Meaning?"

"She was a much more convincing liar when her late husband was running for president," Sassy replied.

Michel smiled.

"I was afraid you didn't notice."

Sassy cut him a sideways look.

"I had a hysterectomy, not a lobotomy."

Chapter 41

"So what do you think's really going on?" Michel asked as he eased the truck out of the garage, onto Dauphine Street.

"I think Rhodes is faking his kidnapping," Sassy replied, "and I think Trish knows it."

Michel nodded. "Something was bothering me last night as I fell asleep, but I couldn't put my finger on it until just now. Her reactions are wrong. Last night she supposedly thought her kid might be dead, but I didn't see any grief, and now she supposedly thinks he's been kidnapped, but she doesn't seem scared. She skipped straight to pissed off and hostile."

"So I noticed," Sassy replied, "but I think you're wrong about her not being afraid. I think she's plenty scared about what he's planning to do."

"So then why doesn't she just come clean and ask for our help, and why bother getting us reinstated?" Michel asked.

"I have a feeling she knew about the ransom note *before* she got us our badges," Sassy replied.

"In other words, we got the case so the real cops wouldn't?"

Sassy shrugged matter-of-factly.

"I suppose it would make sense if she knows he's just playing games," Michel replied.

"Killing Ellis was more than just a game," Sassy said, a bit more stridently than she'd intended.

"Yeah, I know," Michel replied. "Sorry."

They rode in silence for a minute.

"Taylor doesn't seem to be in on it," Sassy said.

"Mmmm," Michel mumbled.

Sassy studied his profile. He seemed suddenly distracted.

"So what's going on in that big old head of yours?" she asked.

Michel blinked, then gave her a crooked half-smile. "My head is *not* big," he said.

Sassy chuckled. "Okay, so then what's going on in your normal-sized head that's just disproportionately large for your tiny body?"

"Assuming we're right about it being a fake, what's the point?" Michel asked. "If Rhodes needed cash, he'd have put a tighter deadline on it."

"Being kidnapped is a pretty good way to throw off suspicion that you killed your boyfriend," Sassy replied.

"True," Michel replied, "but it makes Gaudreau the primary suspect, which would pretty much kill the theory that they're working together."

"So what are you saying?" Sassy asked. "You think the kidnapping might be real now?"

Michel gave a vigorous head shake. "No, it's definitely fake. I just can't figure out the reason, or why the package was addressed from Bell. There has to be some significance to that."

"I'm pretty sure Trish is wondering the same thing," Sassy replied. "I guess we need to check old Bea out."

They were quiet for another block.

"There's one other thing I'm wondering about," Michel said. "Why would Rhodes send the ransom note to the house?"

"Maybe he wasn't sure where they'd be staying down here."

Michel gave a dubious look. "I think the only question was which suite they'd be in."

Sassy considered it for a moment. "Maybe he just didn't think Trish cared enough to actually come down here."

"Now *that* I'd believe," Michel replied. He reached into his jacket for his cigarettes, then looked at Sassy guiltily.

"Go ahead," she said. "After all, how many times can I die?" Her tone was light, teasing.

"You're not dying," Michel said, anyway. "And thank you."

He rolled down the window and lit a cigarette.

"We need to call the Captain and let him know what's going on," Sassy said.

Michel savored the smoke in his lungs for a moment, then blew it out the window.

"My guess is he already knows," he said. "I'll bet Trish was on the phone the minute we left, making sure the case doesn't get reassigned."

He turned up the radio and began a soft, off-key duet with a Foreigner ballad from the 80s that Sassy vaguely remembered.

"You know who has a *crazy* big head?" he asked suddenly.

Sassy stared blankly at him. "Who?"

"Babar," Michel said.

Sassy frowned. "The elephant?"

Michel nodded and smiled. Sassy looked annoyed, then began laughing.

"Yeah, I guess he does, now that you mention it," she said. "The whole family, actually."

"But especially Babar," Michel said. "It's fucking huge."

Chapter 42

"I guarantee that when we get to the end of the trail, Rhodes will be there. Probably laughing at us," Michel said.

"Just so long as he isn't dead," Carl DeRoche replied. "That's something I can't risk by assuming the whole thing is just a hoax."

He'd arrived at the office on N. Rampart ten minutes earlier.

"So you want us to actually follow up on it?" Sassy asked.

DeRoche shook his head. "You've got enough on your plate. We'll handle it internally."

"I don't think Trish is going to like that," Michel said.

"What she doesn't know won't hurt us," DeRoche replied.

"So you want us to just pretend we're taking it seriously?" Sassy asked.

"More or less," DeRoche replied.

Sassy gave him a skeptical look, though she also felt relieved.

"How are you going to swing it so Trish doesn't find out?" Michel asked. "You don't think her very important friends are going to notice?"

"I'm sure they're too busy wasting taxpayer dollars to watch what we're doing," DeRoche replied. "Just so long as she doesn't complain, we should be fine, and for the moment, she thinks she has exactly what she wants. Let's keep it that way."

Michel nodded, but Sassy cocked her head curiously. "So who's going to handle it?" she asked.

A flicker of discomfort in DeRoche's eyes told her he didn't like the question.

"I'm not sure yet," he said, "but I'll be the liaison between you. If anything pertinent comes up, I'll let you know."

"A real name for Gaudreau would be helpful," Michel said.

He caught a small frown of disapproval from Sassy and gave her a questioning look, but she seemed suddenly entranced by the top of her desk. DeRoche nodded, finished his coffee, and stood to leave.

"One more thing," he said, reaching into his jacket pocket. He took out a small spiral-bound notebook with a battered black cover, and handed it to Michel. "The hospital found this in Al's jacket."

"How is he?" Michel asked.

"No change," DeRoche replied.

*****

"What was that about?" Michel asked.

"I just wanted to see where we really stand," Sassy replied.

"Meaning?"

"Our badges may as well be plastic. I'd be willing to bet that the only people who know we're working this case are you, me, DeRoche, and whoever's on the other end of the strings Trish is pulling. It's all just a show to keep her happy."

Michel blinked at her. "What makes you think that?"

"You heard him," Sassy replied. "He won't even risk ignoring an obviously fake kidnapping. Do you really think he'd let us handle a murder investigation involving Rhodes? We're not exactly at the top of our games anymore."

"Hey, I never retired," Michel protested with a mixture of hurt and offense.

"I know," Sassy replied, "but you haven't investigated a murder in a few years either."

She smiled sympathetically. Michel frowned back.

"Why not just be honest with us then?" he asked.

Sassy shrugged.

"Maybe he was afraid we'd get pissed and tell Trish, or maybe he didn't want to hurt our feelings," she said. "I mean, does a farmer tell a horse when he's putting it out to pasture?"

"Please don't confuse me with farm metaphors," Michel replied.

"Look, I'm not sure why he didn't tell us, but having another team working behind the scenes is the right thing to do," Sassy said. "Trish is forcing him to go along with this farce, but if anything happens to Rhodes, you can bet it would be the Captain's ass on the line. He has to do the responsible thing."

Michel nodded reluctantly. "So what do we do? Quit?"

Sassy gave him a sly smile. "Seems to me we're actually in a pretty good position."

"How do you figure?"

"No one's expecting us to solve shit, so we can only exceed expectations."

Michel let out a wry chuckle. "That's one way to look at it."

"I'm serious," Sassy said. "We've got nothing to lose. Let's find these fuckers, prove they killed Ellis, and go out in style. We'll make the department wish they'd never let us go."

"That sounds pretty ambitious for a couple of has-beens who aren't at the top of our games," Michel replied.

"Oh, please," Sassy said. "On my worst day, I'm better than most people on their best."

"And what about me?" Michel asked.

Sassy shrugged. "You're with me."

Michel smiled. Now it was beginning to feel like old times.

Chapter 43

"Any luck?" Michel asked, setting a large coffee on the corner of Sassy's desk.

"I talked to Bobby Lee Collins's sister," she said, shaking her head with dismay. "It took a while to convince her she couldn't get in trouble for agreeing to harbor a dead fugitive, but she finally admitted that he called her last Wednesday. She said he was heading there, but said she wasn't expecting him until the end of the week."

"So that confirms the sudden change of plans," Michel said.

"She also said he mentioned stopping in Houston and Dallas on the way."

"Then what the hell was he doing way up in Arkansas? That doesn't make any sense."

"He'd already gotten rid of Ellis," Sassy said.

Michel gave her a blank look.

"The fastest route to Dallas is Interstate 10, right through the heart of the Atchafalaya," Sassy said.

"Which would have been a great place to dump the body if they still had it." Michel finished the thought.

"Exactly."

"So now we just have to figure out why they dumped it in Gretna instead," Michel said.

He dropped into his chair and took the lid off his coffee.

"Actually, I think I've figured that part out," Sassy replied.

Michel raised his eyebrows.

"I've only been gone 20 minutes."

"It's not my fault I'm that good," Sassy replied.

She picked up Al Ribodeau's notebook and tossed it across the room. It landed on Michel's desk like a wounded bird.

"You know, I would have gotten up to get it," he said, staring down at it with mock distaste.

"I was looking through it while I was talking to Collins's sister," Sassy said. "Take a look at the last page of notes."

Michel quickly thumbed through it.

"Okay, his files might be meticulous, but his handwriting is atrocious," he said. He turned to the last used page. A notation had been circled and underscored with three question marks. He turned his head from side to side trying to decipher it. "It's either a grocery list, or something about a scanner in the Airstream or Lance." He looked up.

"Bingo," Sassy said. "I checked it out, and the Feds found a portable police scanner in the Lance camper."

"And?"

"And then I checked the police logs," Sassy replied. "A statewide APB for a tan 2006 Airstream Land Yacht with Georgia plates went out just after 11 PM."

"Al probably put it out," Michel replied, shrugging.

Sassy shook her head. "He didn't know the make or model until it was found in the river the next morning. He put out an APB for a Class A recreational vehicle with possible Georgia tags earlier that night, but the second APB was specific. I did a little digging and found it was based on an anonymous call from someone who said they thought they saw a body being loaded in the back."

Michel sat forward in his chair. "It was a setup."

"Sure seems like it," Sassy replied, "but Collins and Bettis must have heard the APB on the scanner, and then gotten rid of the Airstream and Ellis."

"Wow, that's cold," Michel said, then frowned. "But wait, Rhodes and Gaudreau had to know Collins and Bettis would throw them under the bus if they got caught."

"Sure, but who would you believe?" Sassy replied. "A bunch of fugitive meth heads transporting a dead body, or the son of Trish Campbell Rhodes Taylor? Especially since DNA would link Collins and Bettis to the murders of Rachel and Woods."

"I suppose," Michel replied, still not entirely convinced.

"Besides, given Collins's temperament," Sassy went on, building her case, "Rhodes and Gaudreau probably assumed he and Bettis wouldn't live long enough to point fingers if they were stopped by troopers. It could have been Butch and Sundance against the Bolivian army all over again."

"Butch and Sundance with sores and really nasty teeth," Michel said, warming to the theory.

Sassy smiled with self-satisfaction.

"I already ran it by Al's FBI contact. He liked it."

"And what about the Captain?"

Sassy stared at the ceiling, pretending to whistle.

"And what about the Captain?" Michel repeated.

"To quote someone else I know, 'Don't worry, I'll talk to him,'" Sassy said.

Michel gave only a perfunctory fake smile. He was happy to see her so energized and engaged again.

"See that you do," he said, putting the notebook aside.

"So, what about you?" Sassy said. "Any ideas, or am I going to have to solve this all by myself as usual?"

"It must be nice to have such a rich fantasy life," Michel replied, "and yes, I do have an idea. I think it's time we paid another visit to the building and snooped around Gaudreau's apartment. See if we can find a real name for him."

Sassy nodded enthusiastically, pushed back from her desk, and stood up. Michel gave her a concerned look.

"It could wait until tomorrow if you want to rest."

"I think I've still got another hour or two in me," Sassy replied, shaking her head.

"Okay, then let's go," Michel acquiesced.

Blue suddenly jumped up and cocked her head at Michel.

"Should we take her with us?" Sassy asked.

Before Michel could respond, Blue ran into the hallway.

"There's my girl!" Chance's voice came through the doorway.

Blue ran excitedly back into the room, then out again. Chance appeared, carrying a large box. He squatted and dropped it at the foot of the stairs, then turned to Blue.

"Did you miss me?" he asked, scratching her neck.

She responded with a quick nose lick. Chance kissed her head, and looked up.

"Hey," Michel said. "I tried calling you this morning. Did you get my messages?"

"Sorry," Chance replied. "I haven't seen my phone since yesterday. I either packed it or left it at your place."

"I didn't see it anywhere," Michel replied.

"Did you check under the bed?" Sassy chimed in.

Michel and Chance both pointedly ignored her.

"We were just on our way out," Michel said apologetically. "We're going to check out Fierce Gaudreau's apartment."

"That's okay." Chance replied. "I wasn't actually expecting you to be here. I was just dropping stuff off."

"Oh," Michel said, then felt embarrassed, realizing it had sounded both pathetic and accusatory at the same time.

Chance stood, smiled awkwardly at Sassy.

"Ummm, so do you want me to watch Blue while you're gone?" he asked, barely looking back at Michel.

His tone was cordial, but not warm. Michel suspected the offer was more for Blue's benefit than his own.

"That's okay," he said. "I know you're busy."

"I don't mind," Chance shrugged. "I can start unpacking."

Michel nodded, uncertain what to say next.

"Great. Maybe we could have dinner afterward?" he tried.

"I should probably get home and keep packing," Chance replied quickly. "I have a lot more shit than I thought."

"You're sure?" Michel said. "I was going to stop by Jacques-Imo's to talk to Skylar Ellis's friend."

"But you'll be working," Chance said.

"I could call when I've finished talking to her," Michel offered.

"I don't have my phone, remember?" Chance replied.

It was a clear dismissal. Michel studied him for a moment, then nodded.

"Yeah, maybe another time would be better," he said. "If you need to get going, you can just leave Blue here. We should be back in an hour or so. She'll be fine."

*****

"That went well, don't you think?" Michel said as they headed for the car.

"Yeah," Sassy replied. "Not uncomfortable at all."

Chapter 44

"By the way," Michel said, "I spoke to one of the agents who investigated Angel Peterson's disappearance. He said the bus usually stops at a barbecue joint in Tuscaloosa, but it was closed for the holidays."

"That doesn't mean Rhodes or Gaudreau couldn't still have been there," Sassy replied. "They could have followed the bus."

Michel didn't respond. He pulled the truck to the curb, his attention focused farther up the block. Sassy shielded her eyes and squinted through the windshield. The door to Gaudreau's building was open, a nondescript tan sedan parked in front.

"Looks like the other team got here first," Sassy said.

Michel nodded, unconsciously reaching for his cigarettes.

"What do you want to do?" Sassy asked. "Confront them, or pretend we were never here?"

Michel lit a cigarette and absently rubbed his chin with his right thumb. He realized he needed a shave.

"I think we should get out of here before they see us," he said. "We can check it out later."

"Assuming there's anything left to see," Sassy replied.

Michel put the truck in reverse and eased back through the intersection, then turned right on Desire.

"So now what?" Sassy asked.

"Jacques-Imo's?" Michel replied. "I'm buying."

Sassy considered it a moment, then shook her head.

"I think I'll pass. I'm starting to feel a little tired now."

"Geez, I can't even bribe a date today," Michel replied.

Sassy gave him a gentle smile.

"That's fine," he said. "Let's go back to the office so I can get Blue, then I'll take you both home."

Chapter 45

Michel's mouth began to water as soon as he stepped across the threshold. He closed his eyes for a moment and breathed in the rich, spicy aromas.

"I'm sorry, but we won't be open for another half-hour," a cheerful voice cut through the exuberant zydeco music pumping into the narrow room.

Michel opened his eyes to see a small, thick man in a colorful print shirt moving toward him. He looked to be in his late fifties, though his tan face was still smooth, his movements surprisingly quick and compact.

Michel nodded a greeting and flashed his badge. The smile in the man's eyes died.

"Is this about Skylar?" he asked.

Michel nodded again.

"I figured the police would show up sooner or later," the man said. "Why don't we step outside." It almost sounded like a challenge, until he added, "Can I get you a drink?"

"No, thank you," Michel replied.

They walked out to the sidewalk, and the man immediately pulled a cigarette from behind his left ear and lit it. He saw Michel looking curiously at the cigarette behind his other ear.

"It's how I limit myself," the man said. "Two a night. I usually wait until we've turned the first service before I have one, but this seems like a good time to make an exception." He stuck out a plump, furry hand. "Dez Cherry. I'm the manager."

Michel shook the hand and introduced himself.

"Very sad about Skylar," Cherry said. "He was a nice kid."

His voice was soft and honeyed, almost musical.

"Did you know him well personally?" Michel asked, as he took out a cigarette of his own.

"We didn't socialize together, if that's what you mean," Cherry replied.

"That's what I meant," Michel replied. "So you didn't know about his personal life? His relationship with Cam Rhodes?"

"I met Cam a few times," Cherry replied, "and if I had to guess, I'd say things were rocky between them as often as not, but I never asked about it. I try to maintain a professional distance with the staff, expecially the younger ones. They don't do well when the boundaries become blurred."

Given Cherry's natural warmth and affability, Michel suspected it was a philosophy he'd arrived at the hard way.

"I was told that Ellis was close with one of his coworkers," he said.

"Saffron Lewis," Cherry said, nodding deeply.

"Saffron?" Michel repeated, trying not to make a face.

A phlegmy chuckle rumbled up from Cherry's barrel chest.

"That's her 'stage name,'" he said, making air quotes with his stubby fingers. "She's in the drama program at Tulane. Her real name is Sally, but Sally Lewis doesn't much sound like the name of an Academy Award winner, does it? Everyone just calls her Saffy."

Michel smiled reflexively. "Is she around?"

"She's taking some time off," Cherry replied, his tone suddenly more solemn.

"Do you know if she's still in the area?" Michel replied.

"I imagine so," Cherry replied. "I overheard a few of the other girls talking last night. One of them stopped by to see her yesterday afternoon."

"Do you have an address and phone number?" Michel asked.

Cherry smoked his cigarette down to the filter in a single drag, dropped the butt on the ground, and stepped it out.

"After you," he said, opening the door and offering a small, courtly bow.

Michel put his still-unlit cigarette back in the pack, and went inside.

"Sure I can't get you something to drink?" Cherry asked.

Michel's stomach growled. He wished the offer had been for gumbo or red beans and rice. He shook his head.

"I'm fine, thanks."

"Suit yourself," Cherry replied. "I'll be right back."

He glided off, gracefully navigating the narrow gaps between tables, and disappeared through a door near the back. He reappeared almost immediately.

"That was fast," Michel said, then made a show of sniffing the air. "Smells good."

"It is," Cherry replied, his voice less animated than before. "You should come for dinner some time."

He hesitated a moment, then handed Michel a folded piece of paper. His eyes seemed troubled, though he didn't say anything more.

"Thanks," Michel said, tucking the paper into the inner pocket of his jacket. "I appreciate your help."

Cherry nodded, then looked down at the floor and frowned slightly. Michel could see he was debating whether to say something, and waited.

"Just do me a favor," Cherry said finally, looking up. "Take it easy on Saffy. I think she always dreamed that some day Skylar would realize he was in love with her, and they'd live happily ever after. His death has been really tough on her."

Michel smiled reassuringly. So much for professional distance, he thought.

*****

The narrow house was set farther back than its neighbors, and needed a fresh coat of paint badly. Weeds and overgrown shrubs clotted the front yard behind a rusted iron fence. Michel guessed that a long line of students living on tips had called the place home over the years. He dropped his cigarette to the sidewalk and put a hand on the gate, then stopped as he saw the flare of a match in the shadows of the porch.

"Come on in," a girlish voice called out.

Michel opened the gate and crossed to the porch. The sweet and earthy tang of pot smoke wafted out to greet him. He stepped up and saw a chunky prepubescent girl in a school uniform sitting on a glider at the left end, a bong cradled between thick, bare thighs.

"I'm looking for Saffron Lewis," Michel said.

The girl nodded and blew out smoke.

"I'm Saffy," she said. "Dez told me you were coming."

Michel took a few steps closer, and the illusion dissolved. The girl was at least ten years older than she'd first appeared, and the uniform was just a too-short plaid skirt and white button-down shirt that looked as though they'd been pulled from a laundry pile.

"Did he also happen to mention that I'm a cop?" Michel replied, looking down at the bong.

Lewis shrugged.

"So arrest me. You want some?"

Michel walked to a weathered rattan chair to the left of the glider and sat down. It was obvious now that Lewis had been crying recently, and often. Freckles showed through streaks in the heavy foundation and blush on her cheeks, and the thick kohl outlining her eyes had been rubbed and blurred.

"No, thanks," he said. "My name is Michel Doucette. I'm with the New Orleans Police Department."

He flashed his badge. Lewis shook her head.

"No, you're not," she said. "You're a private investigator. Sky showed me your card."

Michel nodded. "But I used to be a homicide detective, and I've been reinstated to investigate Skyler's murder."

"Why?" Lewis asked, her tone almost accusatory.

"Cam Rhodes's mother arranged it," Michel replied.

It wasn't an entirely accurate representation of the facts, but he hoped it might help him gain Lewis' cooperation. She made a loud farting noise with her mouth.

"Yeah, right! She doesn't even care about her own son. Why would she give a shit who killed Sky?"

Michel sat back and took out his cigarettes. Saffron Lewis wasn't at all what he'd imagined from Kenny Dixon's description. He wondered how much latent anger and bitterness Ellis's death had unleashed in her, and how he could work his way around it.

"I'm very sorry about Skylar," he tried.

"Sky!" Lewis shouted. "He liked to be called Sky!"

Michel lit a cigarette and leaned forward. He decided there was no point in trying to win her over.

"Yeah, well he's dead," he said sharply, "and I'm trying to figure out who killed him. You can help me or not. Your choice. If it was my friend, I'd want to help."

He took a long drag and watched Lewis. She stared back coldly for a few seconds, then carefully placed the bong on a milk crate side table. Michel thought she was going to get up and leave, but instead she sat up straighter and smoothed the skirt down over the tops of her thighs. When she looked back at him, her gaze was imploring, almost desperate.

"I'd like to ask you some questions about Sky's relationship with Rhodes," Michel said.

"They were planning to move," Lewis blurted eagerly.

"To where, and when?" Michel asked.

"To Florida. As soon as they could find a place," Lewis replied, almost breathless now.

She was suddenly like a little girl trying to win her daddy's approval. Michel wasn't sure which was more disturbing, the abrupt change, or the fact that it was seemingly triggered by his harshness toward her.

"Why were they moving?" he asked.

"Because Sky was afraid of Fierce Gaudreau," Lewis replied.

"Afraid? Why?" Michel asked.

"Because Gaudreau was obsessed with Cam," Lewis replied, eyes wide, "and because he'd already killed someone else for getting too close to Cam."

"Who?" Michel asked, though he was sure he already knew.

"A boy named Sparkle," Lewis replied. "He disappeared a few months ago. Sky was convinced Gaudreau killed him to get him away from Cam."

"I know about Sparkle," Michel replied distractedly. He wondered if Ellis had really thought Gaudreau killed Sparkle, or if he'd just been trying to point the finger away from Rhodes. "Were Sky and Cam having any problems?" he asked. "I mean other than Gaudreau's obsession?"

Lewis lowered her eyes for a moment and chewed her lower lip. Michel gave her a gently encouraging smile.

"Cam didn't always treat Sky the way he should have," she said finally.

"You mean he was abusive, or he cheated?"

"Both, I guess," Lewis replied, "though they had an open relationship. And Cam wasn't physically abusive. He just wasn't very nice to Sky sometimes. Then he'd apologize, and everything would be okay for a while."

"But lately things were okay?" Michel pressed. "You didn't have the sense that Sky was worried about Cam leaving him?"

Lewis shook her head vigorously. "No, just the opposite. They even pretended to break up and Cam moved out so Sky would be safe until they could leave town. They were going on the trip so they could look for a place."

"Are you sure about that?" Michel asked. "Because Gaudreau went with them."

Doubt clouded Lewis' eyes. "He wasn't supposed to," she said in a small, anxious voice. "That's why they were leaving Friday night. Gaudreau was supposed to be away."

"Do you have any idea why they would have stopped at his place then?" Michel asked.

"I talked to Sky just before they left," Lewis replied. "He said that Cam had left his wallet there." She stared down at her hands, and her lower lip quivered slightly. "I told him he shouldn't go, but he said it would be safe because Gaudreau was visiting his sister for a week. That's what Cam had told him."

It wasn't logical, but Michel sensed she was telling the truth as she knew it.

"Did Sky happen to mention where Gaudreau's sister lives?" he asked. "Or her name?"

Lewis shook her head miserably. "I never asked."

"That's okay," Michel reassured her.

Lewis suddenly looked down at her clothes, and her eyes began to shine. She took a deep breath and swallowed hard. "Sky helped me pick these clothes out," she said, her voice trembling. "I haven't taken them off since he died."

Michel just nodded, unsure how to respond.

"He said...it made me look...like a naughty school girl," Lewis managed between convulsive breaths, "but I know I just look...like someone...who'd have to go to the prom...with her cousin."

She let out a wail and doubled over, sobs wracking her body. Michel patted her back, trying to comfort her. He was sure she had at least a few failed marriages to gay men and several rehab stints in her future. He hoped she was at least talented.

Chapter 46

"Ellis told Lewis that Gaudreau was obsessed with Rhodes, but he and Dixon both told me it was the other way around."

Michel had the phone trapped between his right shoulder and ear, while he unscrewed the cap from the Jack Daniels bottle.

"So which do you think is the truth?" Sassy asked.

"Maybe neither," Michel replied, "but it seems pretty clear Ellis was obsessed with what was happening between them."

"Apparently with good reason," Sassy replied.

Michel dropped ice into a glass, and poured an inch-and-a-half of Jack over it.

"But I wonder whether he really thought Gaudreau killed Sparkle, or if he was just trying to divert suspicion because he knew, or at least suspected, that Rhodes did it," he said.

"There's another possibility," Sassy replied. "Have you ever wondered why Ellis told you about Gaudreau in the first place?"

"Now that you mention it, no," Michel replied. "Why?"

"Because it doesn't make sense," Sassy replied. "You'd think he'd have wanted to keep you as far away from Rhodes's trail as possible. It would have made more sense to come up with some bullshit story to send you off on a wild goose chase."

"True," Michel replied, "but I'm sure he warned Rhodes that I'd be showing up at Gaudreau's."

"But why tell you in the first place? It just complicated things." Sassy paused, then dramatically added, "Unless he thought it would serve a purpose."

"Such as?"

"Such as sending a message to Gaudreau," Sassy replied. "Something along the lines of, 'I know you're trying to steal my man, and if you don't back the fuck off, I'm going to bring a shitload of unwanted attention down on your ass.'"

Michel sipped his drink as he considered it.

"Gaudreau definitely seems to value his privacy," he conceded, "but how does that relate to Sparkle's murder?"

"We don't know that Sparkle's dead," Sassy replied. "For all we know, he met some sugar daddy at the rest stop and moved to Paris. Maybe Ellis just decided to exploit his disappearance by spreading rumors that Gaudreau killed him."

"To what end?" Michel asked.

"You know people can't keep their mouths shut about things like that," Sassy replied. "Pretty soon the cops would come knocking on Gaudreau's door. More unwanted attention."

Michel grunted noncommittally.

"You said yourself that you didn't think Ellis would give Rhodes up easily," Sassy said. "Maybe he wasn't entirely confident that Rhodes would go through with the move, so he decided to give Gaudreau some incentive to get out of the picture on his own."

Michel didn't reply. He took another sip of Jack.

"It's just another theory," Sassy replied, matter-of-factly.

"And it would provide another possible motive for killing Ellis," Michel agreed finally, "but if Ellis was so worried about Gaudreau and Rhodes, why did he let Rhodes stop at Gaudreau's on the way out of town? Even if he thought Gaudreau was gone, he had to know that someone would mention it, and Gaudreau would figure something was up. It was a pretty stupid mistake."

"Fatal," Sassy said, "and I have no idea why."

Michel walked out to the patio and lit a cigarette.

"I still feel like we're missing huge chunks of the puzzle," he said, wearily running his fingers through his hair.

"So what do you want to do next?" Sassy asked.

"Go back to Gaudreau's, I suppose," Michel replied.

"I'll be ready in 10 minutes," Sassy replied.

"I thought you were tired?"

"I was," Sassy replied brightly, "but then I took a nap, had some dinner, and now I'm not so tired. I'm ready." She paused before adding a faux-ingenue, "Unless, you think it would be better to wait until the other team has a chance to go back for whatever they missed the first time."

Michel looked at his watch, then at his nearly full drink.

"Fine," he sighed. "Let's go while they're home having dinner. Like sensible people."

Chapter 47

Pale light shimmered high on the walls on both sides of the street. Below it, dozens of black-clothed, pale-faced teens and twenty-somethings stood holding candles, all facing Fierce Gaudreau's place. The center door was bracketed by two large wreaths of red and black roses, and more roses lay at the base, scattered among full bottles of scotch and rum, more candles, packs of cigarettes, and piles of Mardi Gras beads. Michel pulled to the curb a half block away and turned off the engine and lights. No one seemed to have noticed their arrival yet.

"Looks like a memorial service," Michel said.

"But for whom? Rachel and Woods?"

"I guess we'll find out," Michel said, pushing open his door.

Faint tinny music drifted into the truck. Over mechanical drums and droning synthesizers, a deep voice intoned about emptiness and the inevitability of death.

"Catchy," Sassy said. "Music to slit your wrists to."

Suddenly Kenny Dixon stepped out of the crowd. He was wearing just a leather thong and calf-high Doc Martens boots, and his blond hair had been tinted black and spiked. Heavy mascara ringed his eyes. He raised a bony arm and gave an enthusiastic wave.

"Is that the Dixon kid," Sassy asked, "or have you started dating anorexic 12-year-old leather queens?"

"Funny," Michel replied.

They got out of the truck as Dixon approached.

"What's all this about?" Michel asked.

"It's a vigil for Fierce and Cam," Dixon replied excitedly. His pupils were dilated, his eyes shining.

"A vigil?" Michel replied.

"Yeah, in case they're dead," Dixon replied. "So why are you here?"

It was an oddly abrupt, casual transition.

"We need to search Fierce's room," Michel said.

"He won't like that," Dixon replied.

"I don't think he's going to mind if he's dead," Michel replied, "or if he's in trouble and it helps us find him."

Dixon's eyebrows furrowed, then he nodded slowly.

"That's true, but *they're* still not going to like it," he said, jerking his head toward the would-be mourners.

Michel noticed a few watching them now, with a wariness bordering on hostility.

"You said there's another way in," he said. "Off Piety."

Dixon nodded. Michel looked down at his near-naked body and frowned doubtfully.

"You wouldn't happen to have the key on you someplace, would you?"

"Someplace," Dixon replied coyly, cocking his narrow hips and holding his arms out. "You want to search me?"

Michel just stared back blankly.

"We'll park on N. Rampart and circle around," Sassy said. "Meet us there in 10 minutes."

Dixon dropped his arms and gave a small pout.

"Please," Michel added.

Dixon pretended to weigh it, then smiled brightly.

"Okay."

*****

"Aren't you guys going to get in trouble with the cops for this?" Dixon asked, as he led them up a dark, narrow staircase at the back of the boarded-up market.

"We *are* the cops now," Sassy replied directly behind him.

The tip of her right shoe caught the edge of a stair, and she put a hand on the wall for balance. She quickly pulled it back, hoping that the soft, raised texture was wallpaper and not mold.

"Since when?" Dixon asked.

"Since this morning," Sassy replied.

There was a loud thump.

"Fuck!" Dixon cried.

Michel and Sassy both stopped climbing.

"What's wrong?" Sassy whispered.

"I thought there was one more stair," Dixon replied loudly. "I tripped into the wall."

"Are you okay?" Sassy asked, stifling a laugh.

"Yeah. Ow," Dixon replied dramatically. There was a soft jangle of keys. "So what happened to Detective Ribodeau?"

"He's in the hospital," Sassy replied. "He had a stroke."

"Is he going to be okay?" Dixon asked, with what seemed genuine concern.

"We don't know yet," Sassy replied.

"Bummer," Dixon said. "He seemed like a nice guy."

"He is," Sassy replied.

There was a scraping sound, then the hard click of a bolt being thrown. Dim light crept into the hall as Dixon pushed open an ornately carved black door on the right side of the landing. Now Sassy could see a dark floral pattern on the walls, and another, simpler door on the left.

"What's through there?" she asked.

"The building next door," Dixon replied. "It's basically just a passage to the main building."

He stepped through the open doorway, and bright light suddenly flooded into the stairway.

"Jesus," Sassy exclaimed, quickly following him. "I thought we were trying to be discreet."

"Don't worry," Dixon said, pointing to a heavily draperied window. "They're all boarded up, too."

Sassy looked at the floor-length purple velvet for a moment, then began to take in the rest of the room.

"Wow," she said. "I didn't realize we still had any 19th-century bordellos operating in the city."

"What?" Michel asked, coming in behind her. He stopped short and let out a bark of laughter.

The room spanned almost the entire building. Every inch of floor had been covered by oriental rugs, and every inch of wall either draped with purple velvet or papered with flocked purple and black diamonds. A cluster of gold and black brocaded settees formed a seating area on the right, and a large Regency desk and newer wheeled chair faced the door on the left. The back wall was dominated by a four-poster bed with purple satin canopy and spread, and four burled walnut armoires topped with gold candelabra.

"What's the word I'm trying to think of?" Michel asked.

"Understated elegance?" Sassy offered.

"That's two words," Michel replied, "neither of which quite does it justice." He shook his head, and blew out a loud breath. "Where do we even begin?"

Sassy looked around considerately.

"I'll take the desk. You start with the armoires."

"What about me?" Dixon asked.

Michel nodded at a bookcase behind the seating area.

"Read a book."

*****

"Kenny, does Gaudreau have a computer?" Sassy asked, looking up as she closed the middle drawer of the desk.

Dixon sat cross-legged on the floor in front of one of the settees, a large book open across his thighs, his body hunched over it. He flipped to the next page.

"Kenny!" Sassy said more sharply.

Dixon's head snapped up, and he blinked at her. "Huh?"

"I asked if Gaudreau has a computer," Sassy said.

"Um, yeah," Dixon replied. "It's usually on the desk."

Sassy gave him an annoyed face.

"Is there anything else obviously missing?" she asked.

Dixon laid the book on the floor and stood up. He hugged his arms over his little-boy chest and turned in a slow circle.

"The safe," he said finally, pointing to the corner to the left of the bed.

"He had a safe?" Michel asked, coming into the middle of the room.

Dixon nodded.

"Any idea what he kept in it?" Sassy asked.

"Nothing," Dixon replied. "It wouldn't open."

"You're sure about that?" Michel asked.

Dixon nodded emphatically. "It was already here. He didn't have the combination for it." He looked back at the spot, speculation pinching his face. "I wonder who took it, and how they got it out? The thing must have weighed a ton."

"That should keep the other team busy for a little while," Michel said, smirking.

"What other team?" Dixon asked.

"Long story," Sassy said. She looked back at Michel. "Find anything?"

Michel looked at Dixon.

"Are you sure Gaudreau wasn't having sex?"

Dixon shrugged.

"Yeah, I think so. Why?"

"Because there's a drawer full of sex toys."

"Maybe he uses them on himself," Dixon said.

"Handcuffs?" Michel replied dubiously.

"Don't knock it until you try it," Dixon replied, then dropped back to the floor and picked the book up again.

"Did you find anything else?" Sassy asked.

Michel shook his head.

"Just clothes and dirty magazines. You?"

"Nothing," Sassy replied, rolling back the chair. "Either our friends took all the good stuff, or Gaudreau cleaned the place out before he left. We may as well go home and get some sleep."

She stood and stretched as Michel walked over to the desk. They both looked at Dixon.

"You coming?" Michel asked.

"In a minute," Dixon replied distractedly, flipping to another page.

"What's so interesting?" Sassy asked.

"Photos," Dixon replied. "I think it's his sister's wedding. The flowers alone must have cost like $50,000."

Sassy let out an exasperated groan.

"What?" Dixon asked, looking up.

"You didn't think that might interest us?" Michel asked.

"How would I know?" Dixon replied defensively. "I'm not a cop."

The album was square, the cover elegantly tooled white leather with a black-and-white photo of the bride and groom set in the middle. Underneath, it had been embossed in flowing silver script: *Lily and Andrew, June 23, 2007*

"No last names," Sassy said. "Figures."

She opened to the first page. An inscription had been handwritten on the dove gray lining of the inside cover.

To My Favorite (and Only) Brother — Don't worry, you're not in any of them. Just thought you might like to remember the day.

Love,
Daisy

"Bingo," Michel said.

"She looks a lot like Fierce," Dixon said, pointing to the photo on the opposite page. The bride wore a simple lace and satin sheath with delicate lace capped shoulders. Her dark chestnut hair was pulled back, but she wasn't wearing a veil.

Her make-up was understated. "They have the same eyes and mouth," Dixon said, "but Fierce's hair is almost black, and his face is wider."

Sassy tried to picture it for a few seconds, then turned the page. She and Michel both studied the photos carefully.

"See anything?" Sassy asked after a moment.

Michel shook his head. Sassy turned to the next spread.

"What are you guys looking for?" Dixon asked.

"Anything with a last name on it, or even the name of the church or reception venue," Michel said.

"I didn't see anything like that," Dixon replied. "But why do you need a last name? I already told you it was Pierce."

Michel opened his mouth, then stopped as his eyes suddenly found a familiar face. His heart began beating faster as he studied it to be sure it wasn't just wishful thinking.

"You know what?" he said, trying to keep his tone even. "We should probably just take this with us and look at it more carefully tomorrow."

*****

"Okay, so what didn't you want Dixon to see, and why?" Sassy asked, pulling the passenger door shut.

Michel smiled as he flipped through the album.

"Why is because I'm not sure we can trust him," he said. "Rhodes or Gaudreau may have just told him to play nice and keep an eye on what we're doing. And the what, is this."

He turned on the interior lights, and passed the album.

"Look familiar?" he asked, pointing to a woman in a wide-brimmed cream hat in the background of a reception photo.

Sassy held the album closer to the light. The face was slightly blurred, but unmistakable.

"Trish," she said, looking up with surprise.

Michel nodded.

"I think we know where Bea Bell fits into the picture now."

237

"Gaudreau's mother," Sassy said.

"Unless Trish went to more than one high society wedding last June," Michel said.

"Should we call her and ask?" Sassy asked.

Michel shook his head.

"I don't trust her either," he said. "Besides, it shouldn't be too hard to find out if Bell has a daughter named Lily and a son named Franklin."

Sassy suddenly let out a loud yawn.

"Think it can wait until morning?" she asked hopefully.

Michel nodded.

"Yeah. If Rhodes and Gaudreau are dead, they're not going to get any deader," he said, "and if they're just playing games, another few hours won't make a difference."

"And what if we've been wrong all along and Rhodes really was kidnapped?"

"Then by my calcuations, we still have at least two and a half days until the ransom is due," Michel replied. "In the meantime, I'm tired, I'm hungry, I want a drink, and my dog probably needs to pee."

Chapter 48

"Oh goody," Sassy said, excitedly rubbing her hands together. "More coffee, and just in time."

Michel put the cup on her desk, and raised an eyebrow at the papers scattered across the top of it.

"How long have you been here?" he asked.

Sassy leaned forward and rubbed Blue's neck and face, cooing sweetly. Michel sipped his own coffee while he waited.

"Since just after six," Sassy said finally.

"Why so early?" Michel asked.

Sassy sat up, shrugged, smiled. Blue shook her whole body, then walked to her corner by the window.

"I couldn't sleep," Sassy said. "I guess I was just excited."

"That's good," Michel replied, "but don't overdo it."

He just managed to stop from adding "again."

"Don't worry," Sassy replied. "If I get tired, I'll take a nap."

"You'd better," Michel said, then nodded down at the desk. "So what's all this?"

Sassy held up her left hand while she took a a few gulps of coffee, then put the cup to the side and started sifting through the papers.

"Here we go," she said, pulling a sheet free. "The good news is that Beatrice Bell, born Beatrice Leonora Pierce, has two children: Lily Pierce Bell Weldon, age 28, and Franklin Pierce Bell, age 25."

"What's with rich white women using their maiden names as their kids' first and middle names?" Michel interrupted.

Sassy let out an impatient sigh. "I don't know. You're a rich white woman. You tell me. *Anyway*, as I was saying, she has two kids, and Lily did, in fact, get married in the Hamptons on June 23rd of last year."

"That's great," Michel said, "so what's the bad news?"

"I did a search on Franklin and came up with almost nothing," Sassy replied. "No activity on his credit cards or bank account since he withdrew $20,000 last Wednesday, and no property in his name anywhere."

"What about the sister?" Michel asked. "Do we know where she is?"

Sassy nodded before taking another sip of coffee.

"She lives in Manhattan," she said. "I already called, but she'd left for work, and whoever answered wasn't too keen on giving me a work or cell number. I figured we'd give her a chance to call back first, then try Bea if that doesn't pan out."

"Makes sense," Michel replied. "I suppose we should call the Captain."

"Already done," Sassy said.

"Really?" Michel replied, his eyebrows arching in surprise. "And how'd that go?"

"He seemed...appreciative," Sassy replied, then chuckled. "I'm guessing they opened the safe and found out they'd spent a lot of time and effort for nothing."

"Yay for our team!" Michel said, raising his left hand for a high-five. Sassy look at it and shook her head. He sheepishly lowered it. "So what do we do until Lily calls?"

"We should probably check in with the Taylors just to keep up appearances, then I was thinking about visiting Al."

"Any change?" Michel asked hopefully.

"No, but I like to think he'll still know I'm there," Sassy replied, then shrugged. "Maybe it's just to make me feel better."

"Nothing wrong with that," Michel replied. "Mind if I come with you?"

Chapter 49

The shades were drawn, and the only sound was the steady woosh of the respirator and the low ping of the heart monitor. Butch Ryan sat in a chair at the foot of the bed, his head bent forward, his arms dangling at his sides. He was dressed in jeans, a faded black Harley-Davidson t-shirt, and scuffed brown cowboy boots. A well-thumbed paperback of Zane Grey's *Riders of the Purple Sage* lay face down on his left knee.

"Officer Ryan?" Sassy said quietly.

Ryan's eyes opened, though he remained still for a moment. Then he slowly lifted his head and looked from Sassy to Michel and back, without apparent recognition.

"We met two days ago when Al was here interviewing Jamie-Lynn Dale," Sassy said. "I'm Alexandra Jones, and this is Michel Doucette."

Ryan continued staring at her blankly for another moment, then nodded.

"Oh right. You used to work homicide," he said, sitting up and rolling his shoulders stiffly. He pushed to his feet. "I'll get out of your way. I was about to get some air anyway."

He was out the door before they could respond.

"Chatty fella, ain't he?" Michel said.

Sassy gave him a thin smile. "I have a feeling he sees us as intruders." She nodded toward the window. "We should have brought flowers."

Michel looked at the single wilted lily on the sill. "I'm surprised," he said. "Al seems to have a lot of friends."

"He does," Sassy replied, "but they're probably nervous about coming to visit."

"Why? Cops are in the hospital all the time," Michel replied. "It's no big deal."

"This is different," Sassy said. "When another cop gets shot or killed in the line of duty, everyone understands the narrative. Fallen hero. But something like this makes them uncomfortable because it reminds them they're all going to die one day, and it could be from something as mundane as a stroke or heart attack or cancer. No blaze of glory. No 21-gun salute. Just dead and forgotten."

"Wow," Michel said, shaking his head. "That was dark. You know, if he can hear you, I don't think you're cheering him up."

Sassy looked down at Ribodeau. Despite the tubes snaking into his nose and mouth, he looked more peaceful and relaxed than she'd seen him in years. "Sorry about that, Al," she said.

"So what are we supposed to do?" Michel asked. "When I visited my mother, she was usually awake."

"You can still talk to him," Sassy shrugged.

"About?"

"The case," Sassy said. "Otherwise he's going to be really pissed when he wakes up and doesn't know what's going on."

*****

Ryan was sitting on the same bench where Ribodeau had fallen asleep. A book lay open in his lap, and a cigarette dangled from the left corner of his mouth. When he saw Sassy and Michel approaching, he placed the book on the bench with seeming reluctance. His smile barely moved his mustache.

"Did you have a nice visit?" he asked without warmth.

"Probably about the same as yours," Sassy replied. "How long have you been here?"

"Since about nine," Ryan replied.

"Can we buy you a cup of coffee?" Sassy asked.

Ryan looked at his watch and offered a more pronounced smile that made Michel feel as though they'd just stepped into a trap.

"Coffee?" Ryan said. "It's almost noon, and I'm off-duty." He stood and started toward the sidewalk without waiting for a response, then turned back when he realized he was alone. "Don't worry, I'm sure they have coffee, too," he said.

*****

"So how long have you known Al?" Sassy asked.

Ryan eyed the shot of Jameson and pint of Guiness on the table in front of him, but didn't touch them. He lit a cigarette and blew the smoke at the ceiling.

"We came up together," he said "Graduated from the Academy in the same class, both got assigned to the 8th our rookie years. We've been close since."

"Did you know his ex-wife?" Sassy asked. "Do you know if anyone's told her what happened?"

Ryan gave a rough laugh. "The less that's said about that one, the better. She wasn't cut out to be a cop's wife."

"How's that?" Michel asked.

"High maintenance," Ryan replied. "Expected him home right after his shift every night. And no overtime."

"They were newlyweds," Sassy said. "It's only natural she'd want him around."

Ryan shook his head dismissively. "If she'd had her way, his career would have been over before it got started. You can't expect to be accepted into the fraternity if you don't hang out with the boys. That's when the bonds are formed." He lifted the shot glass. "She finally gave him an ultimatum, and Al chose the job. Smartest move he ever made."

He threw the whiskey back, banged the glass on the table, and immediately nodded to the bartender for another. Then he smiled at Michel and Sassy with satisfaction, and took a sip of

Guinness. He blotted the creamy tan foam from his mustache with his right index finger and thumb.

"I have to say I was a little surprised when he decided to go for his shield, though," he said. "I didn't think he was the type."

"What type is that?" Sassy asked.

Ryan's eyes suddenly grew wary. "The suit-and-tie type," he said. "That's all I meant. I never thought he'd want to leave the streets. No offense intended."

"None taken," Michel said quickly, wanting to keep things light. He had a feeling Ryan could turn nasty in a heartbeat.

Ryan cast an anxious look toward the bar and puffed impatiently on his cigarette. Michel could see his shoulders tensing. Finally the bartender walked over and set two shots on the table. Ryan visibly relaxed.

"That should save me having to come back over again in another minute," the bartender said.

Ryan picked a shot up and downed it defiantly.

"Jesus, take it easy, Butch, why don't you?" the bartender said. "You haven't even had your lunch yet."

"Get bent, for Christ's sake, will you, Sully," Ryan growled. "If I wanted someone to nag me, I would have stayed home with Loraine."

"God forbid," Sully said, flapping his hands at Ryan. "She's a saint to put up with you as much as she does. Every time you walk through the door, I'm surprised she hasn't killed you yet."

He turned and walked back to the bar. Ryan chuckled. Michel suspected variations of the same conversation had been going on for years. Then Ryan's expression suddenly turned somber. He finished his cigarette, lit another, and silently nursed his beer for a minute.

"Poor Al," he said finally, shaking his head. "That's no way for a cop to go out. It should be sudden, not lingering."

"Actually, I think I'd prefer to go peacefully in my sleep while rocking on the front porch on a sunny day," Michel said.

Ryan smiled sourly. It was clear his mood had shifted.

"Obviously you weren't a cop for very long," he said. "We don't get sunny days and rocking chairs in the end. The bad memories just get worse, and we miss the adrenaline more and more until it becomes unbearable. That's why they teach us how to use a gun." He lifted his right hand and mimed firing a bullet into his temple.

Sassy eyed him appraisingly, then shook her head.

"That's pretty cynical," she said, "and don't tell me I wasn't a cop for very long. I got my 20 and then some."

Ryan downed the other shot and shrugged.

"Yeah, well maybe you were just one of those lucky ones," he said bitterly. "Most of us aren't that lucky."

Sassy leaned forward, resting her elbows on the table.

"I'm sure that's comforting for you to believe," she replied. "That I must not have gotten the same raw deal that all the *real cops* get, or else I'd understand. That's crap. You have no idea what I gave up for the job. But we all have a choice of how we deal with it."

"Oh, I get it," Ryan said with a scornful laugh. "You're one of those 'if life gives you lemons make lemonade' types. Well, maybe I don't like lemonade so much."

He picked up his stout and swallowed half of it, then tried to get the bartender's attention. His bloodshot eyes had already lost their focus.

"No, I'm one of those people who believe in taking responsibility for being an asshole," Sassy replied, shaking her head with exaggerated pity. "It always amazes me how many cops like to play victim when it comes to their personal lives."

Ryan's eyes locked back on her. They were wild and angry, but also nervous. Sassy held his gaze for a long moment, then looked pointedly at his wedding ring.

"Tell you what," she said. "Tonight when you get home, instead of spending all your time with Jim Beam or Mr. Jameson, spend a little time with your wife. Maybe even be a little nice to her. Then when you retire, you might actually have something worth living for." She threw a twenty on the table and pushed up out of the booth. "Though frankly, I doubt it."

*****

"And again she comes out swinging," Michel said when they hit the sidewalk.

"Let me put it this way," Sassy said, "after wallowing in it for the last few months, my tolerance for self-pity is at an all-time low."

Michel stopped.

"You want to talk about it?" he asked.

Sassy considered it, then shook her head.

"No, I'm good for the moment. And getting better. You?"

Michel gave her a wry smile.

"Afraid I'm still going to have to get back to you on that."

"Whenever you're ready," Sassy said.

Chapter 50

"Hold on a moment, please, Mrs. Weldon," Sassy said, waving Michel over to her desk. "I'm going to put you on speaker so my partner, Detective Doucette, can hear you, too."

She plugged the speaker's jack into her cell phone as Michel settled on the edge of her desk, then hit the ON button.

"Can you hear me?" she asked.

"Yes." Lily Pierce Bell Weldon's anxious voice filled the small room. "Your message said you were calling about Frankie. Is he all right?"

"So far as we know," Sassy replied, phrasing it carefully, "but another boy we're looking for was last seen with your brother on Friday night, and neither one has been seen since."

"Friday night?" Weldon replied.

"Yes. I'm sorry we didn't call earlier," Sassy replied, "but we didn't know your brother's last name until this morning."

"Have you contacted my parents yet?" Weldon asked, her voice turning cautious.

"Not yet," Sassy replied. "We thought we'd try you first."

"Good," Weldon replied. "It would be better if you didn't."

Sassy and Michel exchanged surprised looks.

"Why's that?" Michel asked.

"Because Frankie doesn't want to have anything to do with them," Weldon replied. "He doesn't even want them knowing where he lives."

"Any particular reason?" Sassy asked.

Weldon's laugh was hard.

"Take your pick. Richard and Bea treated us more like accessories than children. But at least I was an accessory they took out and paraded around occasionally so they could pretend they were proud of me. They preferred to pretend Frankie didn't even exist."

"Why?" Sassy asked.

"Because he was fat," Weldon replied, "and to them, being fat is a sign of inferiority. They think all fat people are either poor, uneducated, or lazy, which is ironic given that neither one of them ever had a real job. They couldn't deal with the fact that their own son was fat, so they ignored him."

"That's horrible," Sassy said.

"Yeah, well there was never any chance they were going to win Parents of the Year," Weldon replied. "Anyway, as soon as Frankie turned 18 and got control of his trust, he left. The only time he's seen my parents since was at my wedding last summer. And I had to beg him to come."

"We saw the photos," Sassy said. "It was lovely."

"I'll let Bea know you thought so," Weldon replied wryly. "It was more her big day than mine. I just had to show up, smile, and say 'I do.'"

There was a long pause. Michel and Sassy heard what sounded like the click of a lighter, followed by a deep exhale.

"But if you didn't already know about the problems between Frankie and our parents," Weldon came back on, "why didn't you call them first?"

Michel held up his hands as if to say, "I'm not touching that one." Sassy narrowed her eyes at him.

"Because your mother is friends with Trish Taylor," she said, "and the missing boy is Mrs. Taylor's son, Campbell."

"So?" Weldeon asked.

"So, we thought it would be better to wait until we know exactly what's going on before we told Mrs. Taylor your brother might be involved," Sassy said.

"And you were afraid Bea would call her," Weldon said.

"Yes," Sassy replied.

There was another pause, then a sigh.

"Frankie's in trouble, isn't he?" Weldon asked.

Her voice was measured, direct.

"We don't know yet," Michel replied.

"But you're homicide detectives," Weldon said, "which means somebody must be dead, right?"

Michel raised questioning eyebrows at Sassy. She shrugged "why not?"

"Campbell Rhodes's boyfriend, Skylar Ellis," Michel said. "He, Rhodes, and your brother left Frankie's place together around nine on Friday night. Ellis's body was found about six hours later. Your brother and Rhodes haven't been seen since."

"So are you saying you think Frankie might have killed this Skylar Ellis, or that he might be dead, too?" Weldon asked.

Her tone was still surprisingly calm.

"As I said before, we have no reason to believe anything's happened to your brother," Sassy said.

"So he's a suspect," Weldon said.

Michel and Sassy braced themselves for an angry outburst, but it didn't come.

"I spoke to him two days ago," Weldon said instead.

"Are you sure about that?" Michel asked.

"Yes, we talk every Sunday," Weldon replied.

"Did he tell you where he was?" Sassy asked.

"Not directly, but he said he'd gone to an exhibit at the New Orleans Museum of Art that afternoon," Weldon replied. "A local artist named Rodrigues. I looked him up because Frankie said he thought I'd like his work."

Michel looked at Sassy and shook his head. He remembered seeing posters for the exhibit. It had closed two weeks earlier.

"How did he sound?" Sassy asked. "Did he seem upset about anything?"

"No, but then he probably wouldn't," Weldon replied. "Not that he's a sociopath, but he's emotionally very guarded. It's almost impossible to tell what he's thinking or feeling. Even for me. I think it was his way of getting back at Bea and Richard. He wouldn't give them the satisfaction of seeing how much they hurt him." She gave a small hum of introspection. "Sometimes I worry that he shuts out all the good stuff, too."

Sassy gave the speaker a sympathetic smile.

"Would you be willing to call him for us?" Sassy asked. "Tell him we'd like to talk to him?"

There was another pause.

"I can't," Weldon replied. "I don't have his number."

"But you said you talk every Sunday," Michel pressed.

"We do, but he always initiates the calls, and his number is blocked. The only way I can contact him is through a post office box."

Weldon's voice conveyed both embarrassment and hurt. Michel thought they sounded genuine.

"I'm sorry," he said. "Has he ever mentioned any friends we might try contacting?"

Weldon let out a plaintive sigh.

"Our relationship isn't like that," she said. "I didn't even know that he knew Campbell Rhodes until you just told me. Sometimes he tells me about things he does, like going to the museum, but I know there's a lot more he doesn't tell me about, including his friends."

"So then what *do* you talk about?" Sassy asked.

"Death," Weldon replied bluntly.

"Excuse me?" Sassy asked.

"My brother is obsessed with death," Weldon replied. "He's had a morbid fear of it since he was a little kid, which he deals with, in part, by constantly talking about it."

"In part?" Michel asked.

"Some asshole shrink had the brilliant idea that the fear would go away if Frankie became de-sensitized to images of death. So first Bea and Richard got him a bunch of obscenely violent video games, then he went through a revolting phase of collecting taxidermy and listening to death metal, then finally it morphed into the whole goth thing."

"So you know about that," Michel said.

"You should have seen what he wore to my wedding," Weldon replied.

"Any idea where the fear came from?" Sassy asked.

"It's definitely justified," Weldon replied. "Our grandfather had a heart attack while he was babysitting Frankie. Frankie was alone with the body for six hours."

"How old was Frankie?" Sassy asked.

"Four."

Sassy flashed back on the day she'd taken soup to Miss Nettles, and shuddered. "The poor kid," she said. "No wonder he was traumatized."

"That's actually why he calls me Daisy," Weldon said. "He didn't know I was named after a flower until Grandpa's friends inundated the house with lilies. Frankie was too young to grasp the whole resurrection thing, so he just figured they were death flowers and wouldn't call me Lily anymore. I suggested Daisy because daisies look happy. In retrospect, I wish I'd come up with something prettier like Rose or Iris, but Daisy stuck. It was just something between us, though. Bea hated it. She said it was undignified." She gave a humorless laugh.

Sassy looked Michel and mouthed, "Anything more?" He drummed his fingers for a few seconds before shaking his head.

"We appreciate your time, Mrs. Weldon," Sassy said, "and if Frankie calls, please ask him to get in touch with us."

"I will," Weldon said, "and I'm sorry I couldn't be more help. I know he didn't kill anyone. He's a little messed up, but he's not a killer."

"I hope you're right," Sassy said. "We'll be in touch as soon as we know anything."

"Thank you," Weldon replied, then paused before adding, "You know, I've always thought it was funny that Frankie moved down there, especially given his obsession with death."

"Why's that?" Michel asked.

"Because Bea's great-grandfather was a mortician in New Orleans. He had a funeral parlor someplace across the river. E.J. Gaudreau & Sons."

*****

"The building was condemned in 1989, but there's no record of it being torn down," Michel said excitedly.

"Who owns it?"

"Apparently no one. The last property tax records are from August of 1976, under the name of B. Gaudreau."

"How far is it from the Domino warehouse?" Sassy asked.

"Maybe a half-mile, give or take. It's by Huey Long Park and the cemetery." He leaned to the side so he could see Sassy around his monitor. "So now for the million-dollar question, do we call DeRoche?"

Sassy hesitated, pursing her lips in deliberation.

"I'm not sure. He'll have to call in the Gretna PD."

"So?

"So if we're wrong, we'll end up looking like assholes on both sides of the river."

"I can live with that," Michel replied. "I hardly ever go over there, anyway. The shopping is terrible."

"But if we're right," Sassy continued, ignoring him, "then Gretna gets the bust, and we get nothing."

"Since when have you been a glory hound?" Michel asked.

"It's not about the glory," Sassy said. "It's about legacy. For both of us."

"The last time I checked, I'm the only one who needs to redeem himself with the department," Michel said. "Twice."

"I know that," Sassy replied, "and that's the point. Last time I was able to go out on my own terms, and that's why I was able to live with it. I don't want to be forced out on someone else's terms this time, and I don't want you to be, either."

"It's not so bad," Michel said with a teasing smile.

"I'm serious," Sassy said.

"So what are you suggesting?" Michel asked.

"Just that we check it out first," Sassy replied. "We can go over there now to get the lay of the land, then wait until it gets dark to see if anyone happens to turn on the lights. That's all."

"And if they do?"

"Then we call DeRoche and he sends in the cavalry, but at least we'll be there for it."

"Fine," Michel said, sighing dramatically, "but if you get me fired again, I'm going to be really pissed."

Chapter 51

"I understand him shutting out his parents, but not his sister," Michel said. "It seems like she really cares about him."

"It's probably fear," Sassy replied.

She took a sip of coffee and made a face. It was tepid and bitter now. She poured the remaining inch out the window.

"Of what?" Michel asked.

"The past."

Michel gave her a blank look.

"He transformed himself from some little fat kid into a god, and some people actually bought it," Sassy said. "But let's face it, no matter how successfully you reinvent yourself to the rest of the world, all it takes is one word from family to bring the illusion crashing down."

"But Lily wouldn't do that to him," Michel argued.

"Not on purpose, I'm sure," Sassy replied, "but she's always going to be an uncomfortable reminder of his past. There's no way around that until he comes to some kind of peace with it. If he controls the interactions, though, he can keep her from intruding into his life beyond his comfort zone." She turned her head and looked out the window for a moment, then turned back. "Still, it's sad. I think she misses him."

Michel suddenly wondered if she was talking just about Franklin and Lily Bell. He tried to read her expression, but couldn't in the fading light.

"I'm sure he misses her, too," he said.

Sassy didn't respond. She turned her back toward the

passenger window, and the funeral parlor beyond. Michel sighed silently and checked his watch. It was 7:44 PM. The sun would set in twenty minutes.

"I'm going to have another cigarette," he said, pushing open the driver's door.

He stepped out and looked over the truck's roof. Across the corner of the park, he could see the raised two-story brick building. The entire ground floor was already in shadow, but the top floor glowed bright orange in the last rays of sun. It looked almost as though it were on fire. Michel lit his cigarette and hoped it wasn't a portent.

*****

They approached on foot, through the park. The sky had been full dark for a half-hour now, and they stayed beyond the reach of the streetlights. They walked fifty feet past the funeral parlor, then cut left and crossed the street. A low, corrugated warehouse spanned almost the entire block. They moved quickly in its shadow to the corner, and stopped.

A narrow driveway separated the two buildings, tufts of weeds dotting the cracked asphalt. Beyond it, a sign rose from what had once been a lawn. The carved gold letters were nearly the same faded black as the background now, but it was still readable. At some point the name had been changed to simply GAUDREAU FUNERAL HOME.

Sassy studied the building.

"Unless the front door's open, it looks like we'll have to go in up there," she said, pointing to the flat roof of a one-story annex at the back. "The shutters down here look like steel. Even if they're not locked, I'm sure they're rusted shut."

Michel blinked at her.

"What do you mean, 'go in?' I thought we were just on a scouting mission to see whether anyone's in there."

Sassy closed her eyes, pressed her fingertips lightly to her

255

temples, and screwed her face up like a five-year-old mimicking intense concentration.

"Gee, I can't tell from out here," she said. "Can you?"

She dropped her hands with a self-satisfied smirk. Michel shook his head.

"I knew you were going to get me fired."

"You mean from your imaginary job?" Sassy asked.

"Good point," Michel said, then frowned. "But how the hell are we going to get up there?"

Sassy jerked a thumb to their right. Under a security light at the back corner of the warehouse, an aluminum ladder lay partially covered by a blue tarp.

"That'll work," Michel said, "but let's check the front door first. Just in case."

*****

"Okay, now I'm really glad we didn't call the Captain first," Michel said, sweeping the beam of his flashlight down the hall toward the stairs. Three decades of dust lay in a smooth, unbroken carpet over the wood.

"Let's check downstairs," Sassy said.

They moved to the stairs and started down, Michel in the lead, testing the integrity of each tread. They reached the middle landing and turned left. The floor just inside the front door had been rubbed almost clean by footsteps. Michel raised the light. A two-by-four braced the door shut. The wood appeared to be new.

"Is this the point where we call the Captain?" he asked quietly, flipping the safety off his pistol.

"I think it's a little late for that," Sassy replied. "We haven't exactly been quiet."

She took a step forward, but Michel put a hand on her right shoulder. She turned and gave him a questioning look. He nodded down at her waist. She sighed and unholstered her gun.

They continued down to the entryway. Footprints led in and out of the three open doorways off the hall, though most ran between the front door and another at the far end of the hall. Michel gestured to the doorway on the right. Sassy nodded and moved in behind his left shoulder. On a silent count of three, they both stepped inside.

*****

Michel closed the door of the small bathroom under the stairs, and turned to the final door at the end of the hall. It looked like an ordinary two-panel door, though considerably wider. Michel lay the palm of his left hand on it, below a tarnished brass plate reading PRIVATE.

"What's with all the steel?" he whispered. "I wasn't aware body snatching was such a big problem."

"It wasn't around here," Sassy whispered back, "but it was up north, culminating in riots in New York. This place was probably built during the height of the hysteria."

"And you would know that why?" Michel asked, giving her a mystified look.

Sassy shrugged.

"I've had a lot of time to watch the History Channel lately."

"Well, if this one's locked, we're screwed," Michel said.

He brought his gun and flashlight up as Sassy turned the knob. She pushed, and the door swung silently open.

Chapter 52

Michel stepped through the doorway and took position on the left. Sassy followed immediately and stepped right. They quickly checked the corners of the room, then moved apart, slowly sweeping the room with their flashlights, guns extended in front of them.

An air mattress, open sleeping bag, and pillow lay against the right wall, next to another steel door. Sassy noted that the door was bolted from the inside. She knelt down and pressed her left hand to the pillow. It was cool, but she thought she smelled fresh cigarette smoke. She stood and moved toward another door on the back wall.

Michel circled behind an embalming table in the center of the room. He squatted down and ran his light under it, then turned to the left wall. A deep stainless steel counter ran the width, metal cabinets above and below. He opened the first high cabinet. It had been stocked with scotch and cartons of Camel cigarettes. He opened the lower. It was stacked top to bottom with rolls of toilet paper. He left the doors open, and continued down the line.

Someone was planning to stick around for a while, he thought.

*****

"At least they're tidy," Sassy said, looking at the two garbage bags in the middle of the otherwise-empty garage.

"Unless those are filled with body parts," Michel said.

"That would still count as tidy," Sassy said.

She opened the closest bag and briefly poked around inside it with her flashlight. She gave the other a kick.

"No bodies, but someone's got a serious caffeine and nicotine addiction."

They ran their flashlights over the walls and ceiling, then stepped back into the embalming room.

"That just leaves the cooler," Sassy said.

Now that the adrenaline of their initial discovery had worn off, she was fading quickly.

"What if old man Gaudreau forgot to clean it out before he left?" Michel asked, wrinkling his nose.

Sassy aimed her flashlight at the scarred white door in the center of the back wall.

"It could be worse," she said with a tired smirk. "We haven't found out where they've been going the bathroom yet."

"That's just nasty," Michel said.

Sassy stood to the right of the door, not even bothering to bring her gun up. Michel removed the locking pin and pulled the latch. As the heavy door opened, a noxious wave of filth and decay hit them.

"Fuck!" Michel gagged, falling back a few steps.

He pulled his t-shirt up over his mouth and nose, and threw his body against the door.

"No wait!" Sassy yelled, stepping forward and blocking it with her left shoulder.

"What?" Michel asked. He swallowed hard and took quick breaths through his mouth. He was sure he could taste the putrid air.

Sassy pushed the door open wider, and stepped cautiously inside. In the beam of her flashlight, Michel could see a body lying in a fetal position, facing the rear wall. It was nude, except for a thick leather belt around the waist. What appeared to be dried feces caked the buttocks and backs of the thighs.

Sassy jammed her pistol into her holster and knelt beside the body. She could see it was a young male now. She touched the side of his neck.

"He's still alive," she said. "Help me get him out of here."

"We shouldn't move him," Michel said.

"I know that," Sassy said impatiently, "but we're not going to do him much good if we pass out."

She gently rolled the boy onto his back. A red ball gag had been strapped into his mouth, and wide leather cuffs held his wrists tight to metal clips on the sides of the belt.

Michel played his flashlight quickly around the embalming room, then holstered his gun and stepped reluctantly into the cooler. He tucked his flashlight under his left armpit, and slipped his hands under the boy's shoulder blades.

"Let's put him on the mattress," Sassy said, as they carried the boy through the door.

She kicked it shut behind her.

"It's Rhodes," Michel said, studying the boy's face in the bouncing beams of their flashlights.

"Are you sure?" Sassy asked.

"Not 100 percent," Michel replied, "but yeah."

"So much for our fake kidnapping theory," Sassy said.

"But why would Bell do it?" Michel replied. "His sister confirmed he doesn't need the money."

"From the looks of it, maybe he just wanted Rhodes to suffer before he killed him," Sassy grunted back.

They laid Rhodes carefully on the mattress. Sassy unclipped his hands from the belt and pulled the sleeping bag over his legs and torso. His chest was crusted with dried blood, dozens of small wounds dotting the skin underneath.

"No signal," Michel said, holding his cell phone up toward the ceiling. "Let me try yours."

Sassy pulled her phone from her jacket and handed it to him. He lifted it and walked in a tight circle.

"Still nothing," he said. "Must be all the steel."

"Try upstairs," Sassy said. "And hurry. His breathing is really shallow."

Michel sprinted out of the room and down the hall. As he turned for the stairs, he suddenly stopped, his conscious mind finally registering the rolls of toilet paper on the floor in front of the corner cabinet. His heart stuttered as he looked back toward the embalming room. The door silently closed.

Chapter 53

Sassy felt the air move before she heard the lock turn. She went for her gun, but stopped as the overhead lights blinded her.

"Please don't," an anxious voice said.

Sassy squinted, shielding her eyes with her right hand, and turned her head toward the door. A gaunt young man wearing baggy black jeans and an oversized black t-shirt stood in front of it, a small revolver extended toward her with shaky arms. Sassy's eyes dropped to the gun for a split second. It looked old, and she doubted he could get off a steady shot, but she slowly raised both hands.

"Frankie?" she said.

Though his face was shadowed by long black bangs, the resemblance to his sister was unmistakable. Franklin Pierce Bell blinked at her uncertainly, then took a step forward.

"Don't call me that," he said without conviction. "Only my sister calls me that."

"And you call her Daisy," Sassy said, nodding.

"Daisy." Bell repeated, blinking quickly several times. "You talked to Daisy." It was a statement.

"She's worried about you," Sassy said.

"Why did you talk to her?" Bell asked, his voice half-whine, half-accusation.

"We were afraid you might be in trouble," Sassy replied evenly, pivoting on her knees to face him.

Bell's eyes turned wounded.

"Did she tell you where to find me?"

"Did she know?" Sassy asked, smiling sympathetically.

Bell appeared to give it serious thought for a moment.

"No," he said, his tone almost remorseful. "She never knows."

"It's not too late to change that," Sassy said.

Bell didn't respond, but he lowered the gun a few inches. Sassy nodded down at Rhodes.

"I'd like to take the gag off him and give him some water," she said. "If that's all right."

The gun immediately came back up.

"No!" Bell cried, more pleading than demanding.

He looked wildly around the room for a moment, then his eyes fell back on Sassy. He seemed almost surprised she was still there. Sassy tried to reconcile the impressions she'd been given by Rachel Davis and Lily Weldon with the person in front of her. Killing Skylar Ellis had clearly unhinged him in a way that killing Angel Peterson apparently hadn't.

"Just go," he said abruptly.

"I'm afraid it's too late for that," Sassy replied. "More police are already on their way." A muted bang on the door caused Bell to flinch. Sassy wondered if Michel could hear them. "But it's not too late for all of us to get out of here alive," she added.

She watched for a reaction, but Bell's bloodshot eyes just darted nervously behind her, as though he expected Rhodes to suddenly spring up and come after him.

"Frankie, let me help you," she said more forcefully.

He gave her a fleeting glance, then looked back at Rhodes, and his hands began to tremble. Sassy prayed the gun wouldn't go off. She knew she needed to focus his attention on her.

"So tell me something, Frankie," she said loudly, her voice reverberating off the tile walls and floor. "What scares you?"

Bell's head snapped toward her. The directness of his gaze told her she'd finally cut through the noise in his head. She lifted her eyebrows challengingly.

"You tell me first," he replied, his voice suddenly calm and curious, the tone smooth and deeper.

He tilted his head and gave a teasing smile. Sassy realized she was finally seeing Fierce Gaudreau.

"I'm afraid you're going to throw your life away," she said tentatively, "and I'm afraid that Daisy is going to spend the rest of her life missing you."

The disappointment in Bell's eyes indicated it wasn't what he'd wanted.

"And at the moment," she added, "I'm afraid that you're going to put a bullet in me, and I'm going to be rolling around on the floor in pain until you decide to give yourself up, or the police bust through that door."

She could see she'd hit the mark this time. Bell's eyes narrowed quizzically.

"You're not afraid of dying?" he asked.

There was no hint of skepticism, only cautious excitement. Sassy shook her head.

"Been there, done that."

"You've been dead?" Bell asked, barely more than a whisper.

He watched Sassy as though she were something rare and beautiful. She found his intensity both unsettling and oddly seductive, and remembered what Rachel had said about feeling like the most important person in the world with him.

"More or less," she said. "A long time ago."

"What happened?" Bell asked.

He lowered the gun and took a few steps closer.

"Is it all right if I sit down?" Sassy asked.

Bell nodded eagerly. Sassy sat back onto the edge of the mattress, and rubbed her knees.

"I was shot trying to rescue a little girl who'd been kidnapped," she said.

"Did you save her?" Bell asked.

Sassy looked down at the dusty tile for a moment. She felt an unexpected rush of emotion.

"No," she said, "and I lost my baby, too."

She hadn't intended to say it, but it had felt oddly cathartic.

She wondered briefly if Bell was using some form of hypnosis on her, then looked up and saw genuine empathy in his eyes.

"I'm so sorry," he said.

"Thank you," Sassy said, wiping a tear from her right eye.

Bell squatted so they were at the same eye level, the gun dangling between his legs.

"If you don't want to talk about this, I'll understand," he said carefully, "but you're sick, aren't you?"

Sassy considered how to answer. She took a deep breath.

"I finished treatment for cervical cancer a few weeks ago," she said, "and everything looks fine, but I won't know for sure for a few months. If then."

Bell nodded thoughtfully.

"Did it scare you?" he asked. "Being sick?"

Sassy let out a barely audible laugh. It was something she hadn't been willing to discuss with Pearl or Michel or Russ, but now she wanted to talk about it with a stranger. She nodded.

"But you said you're not afraid of dying," Bell replied.

Sassy nodded again.

"What I meant is that I'm not afraid of death," she said, "because I know what that feels like, and there was nothing scary or painful about it. It was just...nothing."

Bell looked momentarily troubled, then curious again.

"Then what were you afraid of?" he asked.

Sassy felt her emotions welling to the surface again, and took a deep, wet breath.

"Of the pain," she said slowly, "and uncertainty." She paused to take another breath, then wiped at the tears flowing down her cheeks. "And wondering whether I was going to die alone in a pool of my own piss, shit, and vomit."

A sob ripped through her chest, and she let out a sound like a wounded animal. Her shoulders and chest began heaving. Bell sat down quietly and averted his eyes.

Chapter 54

"Thank you," Sassy said, dabbing her eyes with the right cuff of her shirt.

"For what?" Bell asked.

"For letting me get that off my chest." Sassy sighed and offered an embarrassed smile. "Obviously I've been needing to for a while."

"So why didn't you?" Bell asked.

It came across as academic rather than prurient, but Sassy shook her head.

"Long story," she said. "Maybe if we get out of here, I'll share it with you some day, but right now we need to focus on what's happening in this room."

Bell gave a small frown.

"So where do we go from here, Frankie?" Sassy asked.

Bell shrugged.

"You're going to have to do better than that," Sassy said.

"Why is it up to me?" Bell asked, his tone suddenly sharper. "We both have guns."

He smiled, though Sassy didn't see any warmth or humor in it. She realized she was losing him again.

"Yes, we do," she said evenly, "but I don't think you want to go there. I know I don't."

"You think you know me?" Bell asked with a taunting smile. "Cam thought so, too, but look what happened."

Sassy took a steadying breath.

"What *did* happen, Frankie?" she asked.

The antagonism in Bell's eyes faded instantly, and he looked anxiously at Rhodes again. Sassy felt suddenly uneasy, and looked over her shoulder. Rhodes's face was still slack, the position of his body unchanged.

"Tell me, Frankie," she pressed, turning back.

Bell looked down at the floor.

"I heard what you said when you were carrying him," he said. "I wasn't trying to punish him."

He sounded wounded, and his eyes searched Sassy's face as though desperate for a sign that she believed him.

"So then what happened?" she asked. "Why didn't you just kill him like Skylar Ellis?"

"I tried," Bell replied quietly, "but I couldn't."

Sassy tried to read his tone. She noticed a slight tremor beginning in his hands again.

"Because you love him?" she asked.

Bell didn't respond for a long moment, then shook his head.

"No," he said. "I just couldn't."

This time his tone was unmistakable, resignation and regret. Sassy looked down at Rhodes, and felt a chill as she realized the wounds in his chest were the same as those described in the coroner's report on Ellis.

"Frankie, you didn't kill anyone, did you?" she asked, looking back at Bell.

For a few seconds he didn't respond, though the trembling of his hands grew more pronounced. Finally he gave an almost-imperceptible shake of his head. Sassy looked back at Rhodes, then at Bell.

"Why did you lock him up, Frankie?" she asked.

Bell's eyes filled with tears and his narrow shoulders began quivering beneath his oversized shirt.

"Because he told me he'd kill Daisy if I didn't kill Skylar," he replied. "I had to stop him."

Sassy didn't feel the pistol being slipped from her holster as she pushed forward.

"I'm so sorry, Frankie," she said, getting slowly to her feet.

Bell slumped forward as the tears overcame him, and lay the revolver on the floor. Sassy walked over and picked it up, then gently stroked his hair for a moment.

"It's going to be okay, Frankie," she said. "You were just trying to protect Daisy."

She turned for the door, then froze as she heard a pistol being racked. For a split second, she was aware only of her own ragged breathing, then reflex took over and the ravages of time and sickness suddenly fell away. She brought Bell's revolver up as she spun toward Cam Rhodes, then smoothly squeezed the trigger. The hammer clicked on an empty chamber.

A moment later, a deafening roar ripped through the room, and a 9mm slug tore into Franklin Bell's chest. Sassy was only dimly aware of more muffled gunshots to her right.

*****

Michel fired another shot at the lock, stepped forward, and aimed a hard kick just to the left of the knob. As the door burst open, a bullet whizzed past him, lodging in the wall to his right. He dropped into a crouch and fired two shots. The first was high, but the second hit Campbell Rhodes in the throat. He fell back against the mattress, but tried to lift Sassy's gun again. Michel fired one more time.

Chapter 55

Distant sirens cut through the silence. Michel sat against the wall to the left of the doorway, his head back, eyes closed, an unlit cigarette pressed between his lips. Sassy cradled Bell's head in her lap. The floor was slick with blood.

"I'm sorry, Frankie," she said. "It was my fault."

Bell tried to shake his head, but managed only a feeble wobble. He ran a dry tongue over dryer lips.

"No, it wasn't," he rasped.

Sassy gently touched his cheek. It was cold.

"Save your breath," she said. "The ambulance will be here soon. We can talk later."

Bell gave her a knowing smile.

"It's okay. I'm not afraid, anymore," he whispered. "It doesn't hurt now."

He closed his eyes and smiled peacefully.

"You're going to be all right," Sassy lied, then felt tears welling up, and shook her head in frustration. "Why didn't you just go to the police?" she said quietly to herself.

Though she wasn't expecting an answer, Bell's eyes suddenly fluttered opened.

"Because they didn't stop him before," he said.

Sassy looked down at him with confusion.

"Who didn't stop him?" she asked.

"The police in Boston," Bell said, his voice so faint Sassy could barely hear him, "when he killed his friend Damian. He said his mother wouldn't let them."

Chapter 56

"Are you okay?" Sassy asked.

They sat in a windowless office within the squat Gretna Police Department complex, waiting to give their statements.

"I don't know," Michel replied, staring down at the empty styrofoam cup in his hands. "It doesn't feel real yet."

"I'm sorry," Sassy replied.

"It wasn't your fault," Michel said.

"Of course it was," Sassy replied. "I basically handed him my gun. I should have been paying attention."

"Come on, Sas," Michel replied. "He looked about three breaths past dead. There was no way to know he was just playing possum."

"Still," Sassy said, "I should have secured my gun when I holstered it. That's Cop 101. And I should have listened to you and called the Captain as soon as we knew about the funeral parlor. It was my fault we were in there at all."

Michel let out an exaggerated sigh.

"Yeah, and it was my fault because I'm the one who took the case in the first place, and it was Smith & Wesson's fault because they made the gun, and it was Trish's fault because she raised a fucked-up kid, blah blah blah." He paused and gave her an expectant look. "I thought you were done with self-pity."

"I meant the old self-pity," Sassy replied with a tired but appreciative smile. "This is new self-pity. And I'm with you on that part about Trish. I hope she pays for it."

"She already has," Michel replied. "She lost her son."

Sassy looked as though she were going to argue, then gave a solemn nod. "I suppose she has, but if she helped cover up the fact that he killed Damian Pope, she's going to pay more."

"It's going to be tough to prove," Michel replied. "Let's face it, the only evidence we have is a cryptic statement from a dead kid who seemed none too emotionally stable at the time."

"At the very least, I hope the Boston cops open up an investigation," Sassy replied. "Pope's parents deserve to know the truth."

"I'm sure they will," Michel replied, not at all confident it was true. "So are you done with the guilt and self-pity now?"

"Not by a long shot," Sassy replied, looking down at her hands. Her expression grew pained. "The truth is that it's not just guilt," she said. "I also feel humiliated."

"Humiliated? Why?"

"Because there's no fool like an old fool. Just because I was feeling better and managed to knock a little rust off, suddenly I was thinking I was *Cleopatra* Jones." She shook her head. "But I don't belong in that world anymore. I'm a liability."

Michel knew there was no appropriate response, and waited for her to continue. After a minute, she sighed and gave him a self-conscious smile.

"I'm sorry," she said. "I didn't mean to drop that on you. I know you have your own issues to deal with right now."

"It's okay," Michel replied. "My issues aren't going anywhere. Go ahead. Talk."

Sassy shook her head. "Not now. There's a lot to talk about, but it can all wait until tomorrow. It's going to be a long night."

Michel was reluctant to let the moment go, but nodded. "Which reminds me, I'd better call Chance and ask if he'd be willing to look after Blue."

"You sure you want to do that?" Sassy asked.

"Yeah," Michel replied. "He's obviously got some issue with me right now, but he still seems okay with Blue."

271

Chapter 57

Michel yawned and glanced at his watch without registering the time for the third time since he'd dropped Sassy at home. As he fumbled with his keys, the front door opened.

"Hey," Chance said uneasily. He'd given up on sleep just after midnight, and had spent the last two hours smoking on the patio, his mind racing, his mood alternating between anger, worry, and sullen resentment. Now, as he saw Michel's face, he settled back on worry. "Is Sassy okay?"

Michel just nodded and stepped into the hallway. Blue stood at the far end. Her eyes were anxious, her movements tentative. Michel squatted and held his arms out. After a few seconds, she came to him.

"Are you okay?" Chance asked.

Michel didn't respond, but leaned down to kiss Blue's head. She pressed into his chest as he gently stroked her sides. Chance suddenly felt intrusive, and unnerved by the silence.

"I should go," he said.

For a moment the words hung there, then Michel looked over his shoulder. "I was kind of hoping you'd stay," he said. "If you don't mind."

"Sure," Chance replied uncertainly. He tried to read Michel's expression, but couldn't.

Michel turned back to Blue and rubbed her neck for a few seconds, then kissed her head again and pushed to his feet.

"I really need a drink," he said.

*****

272

Michel handed Chance a glass, then settled into his usual chair, laying his cigarettes and lighter on the side table. "Thanks for looking after Blue," he said. "I was worried you might not get my message."

Chance's averted eyes made it clear he'd missed Michel's call intentionally. He took a quick sip of his drink, then asked, "So what's wrong?"

Michel fell silent again, his attention fixed on the fountain for a long moment, then the corners of his mouth pulled down and he looked at Chance.

"I killed Cam Rhodes tonight," he said.

"Fuck," Chance replied in a stunned whisper. "Are you okay?"

Michel shrugged and looked down at the table. Again his expression was unreadable.

"It's okay if you don't want to talk about it," Chance said, though he wasn't sure he meant it.

Michel shook his head. "It's not that I don't want to. It's just that I'm not sure what to say." He paused, tasted his drink, lit a cigarette. He watched the smoke drift up and away for a few seconds, then looked back at Chance. "With Joshua Clement, it was different. I went there planning to kill him, then couldn't go through with it. This was so...unexpected. So sudden. I didn't even have a chance to think about it. It was just reflex, but now Rhodes is dead."

"I'm sorry," Chance said.

"It's just so strange," Michel continued. "When I woke up yesterday morning, I'd never have imagined I'd end the day by killing someone, but now it's always going to be part of me. I can't undo it. I'm always going to remember that moment I pulled the trigger."

"I still dream about trying to shoot Clement sometimes," Chance said, with a sympathetic nod, "and each time I pull the trigger, I feel the exact same overwhelming rush of remorse, then relief that the gun didn't go off."

"Why didn't you ever tell me that before?" Michel asked.

273

"You haven't exactly been big on talking and sharing since Joel died," Chance said, realizing too late how bitter he'd sounded.

"What?" Michel asked.

"Never mind," Chance replied.

"No, tell me," Michel pressed, though he felt suddenly apprehensive. "What did you mean?"

Chance cocked a dubious eyebrow at him.

"Do you really want to go there right now?"

"Go where?"

Chance searched Michel's face, trying to decide if he was being purposefully obtuse, or genuinely didn't understand. Michel stared back blankly.

"What do you think happened between us?" Chance asked.

"You mean when we first had sex, or since then?"

"I mean before that," Chance replied. "Since Joel died. Why do you think we really drifted apart?"

"You said it yourself," Michel replied weakly. "Neither one of us was able to talk about him."

"And that's how you remember it?"

Michel shrugged.

"I only said that because I thought you were finally ready, and I wanted to make it easier for you," Chance said. "I was being nice. I never had a problem talking about Joel. You had a problem listening to me. Remember?"

"That's not true," Michel replied immediately, defensively.

"No?" Chance replied. "Every time I tried, you shut me down. You'd either pretend you didn't hear me, or suddenly change the subject. And then you pretty much shut me out entirely except for our nice safe dinners where you knew I couldn't bring him up."

Michel's mouth worked for a few seconds before he finally managed, "That's not why I took you out. I thought you'd appreciate a break from fast food and takeout."

It was a lie he'd told himself so often that it had begun to feel like truth.

"That's bullshit, and you know it," Chance replied angrily.

Michel shook his head, more trying to clear it than in disagreement. His heart was racing, and he struggled to focus as emotions he'd kept in check for so long threatened to break free.

"You're the one who moved on with his life and decided there wasn't room for me anymore," he blurted angrily, the words coming out before he'd consciously thought them.

Chance threw an ugly smirk. "And let me guess," he said. "Sassy abandoned you when she married Russ, you had no choice about rejoining the police, and you had to be wherever you were tonight with a gun?"

Michel's jaw tightened, but he didn't reply.

"It must be nice to live in a world where you don't have to take responsibility for anything that happens," Chance said. "Where you're always the helpless victim of circumstances."

"You should know," Michel spit back.

Chance stood and started toward the door, then suddenly whirled back around.

"Yeah, I do know," he shouted, "but guess what? I moved on from that, too." He picked up his glass and drained it, then banged it down on the table, causing Blue to take refuge on the far side of the fountain. "God, I feel like such a fucking idiot," he said. "I actually believed you when you said you wanted to talk about him, and then it took me almost a week to realize that all we did was get drunk and screw. And then I let you use me so you could go play cop."

He closed his eyes and took a few deep breaths.

"Yeah, I moved on," he said, fixing Michel with a steady gaze, "because I was tired of being a victim every time something shitty happened. But I never pushed you out of my life. I just got tired of trying to keep you in it. It was just too painful."

Michel's brow puckered.

"Painful?" he repeated.

"You've been stuck in the same fucking loop since Joel died," Chance said. "You get up every morning and go through the motions, but other than work, you don't have anything. The only emotional connection you have left is with Blue. You pushed the rest of us away." He shook his head sadly. "Sassy deserves a lot of credit for trying as long as she did. If she hadn't gotten sick, she probably never would have stopped."

"What did you say about Sas...?" Michel began, but trailed off as the shock of memory hit. It wasn't of a specific time or place, but a familiar feeling, a quick gut punch of fear and confusion.

"I kept waiting, thinking that someday you'd be ready," Chance went on, though Michel only half-heard the words over the loud buzzing in his head, "but it never happened. You just shut yourself off more and more, and I finally gave up."

Michel took quick, shallow breaths, trying to fight back a swell of nausea. Chilled sweat slicked his skin.

"Why can't you just talk to me about him?" Chance pleaded, his voice breaking. "Why is that so hard?"

The noise in Michel's head suddenly stopped, and he began to cry.

Chapter 58

Michel wiped his eyes and nose with the bottom of his shirt, and let out a long ragged breath.

"Are you okay?" Chance asked.

Michel turned to him and nodded. "Though I have a much more vivid understanding of the phrase 'cry your guts out' now." He took a short sip of his drink and fished out a cigarette. "I'm sorry," he said.

"It's not like you haven't had to watch me cry before," Chance replied.

"No, I mean about the last two years," Michel said. "You were right. About everything."

Chance searched his face.

"Are you saying that just to shut me up, or because you really mean it?" he asked.

"Because I mean it," Michel replied. "I think I just had one of those 'moments of clarity' that alcoholics talk about, except it didn't have anything to do with drinking."

"Do you want to talk about it?" Chance asked.

Michel nodded, then smiled tiredly.

"That was a trick question, wasn't it?"

"A little bit," Chance replied.

"I'm not sure where to begin," Michel said. He pressed the cigarette between his lips, but just stared straight ahead for a few seconds before snatching it back out. "Do you remember the weeks after he died?" he asked. "When we both came back to the city?"

"Sort of," Chance replied. "A lot of that time is still kind of a blur, like it was just a bad dream."

"For me, too," Michel said, "but one thing I remember clearly is that I wanted to talk about Joel with you. That was why I came back when you did. Sassy said that you and I were the only ones who could really understand what the other was feeling, and I wanted to be there for you."

"So what happened?" Chance asked.

Michel shrugged, then shook his head.

"No, that's not true. I do know. I was afraid."

"Of losing it in front of me?"

"Of not losing it," Michel replied.

Chance raised a questioning eyebrow.

"The other night was the first time I've been able to cry since he died," Michel replied.

"I'm sorry," Chance replied reflexively.

"It's not your fault that I'm emotionally constipated," Michel said, "but it wasn't until we both got back and I saw you again that I realized it, and it scared me because I thought there was something wrong with me, and that you'd think it was because I didn't really love him."

"I never would have thought that," Chance said.

"Why not?" Michel replied softly. "I began to wonder myself. It took a long time before I stopped feeling guilty about that."

He lit the cigarette and passed it to Chance, then lit another for himself.

"I guess it makes sense," Chance said. "In a really fucked-up sort of way. But for two years?"

"Well, there might have been some seething resentment, too," Michel replied with an embarrassed smile.

"Are you being serious?" Chance asked.

"Festering might be more accurate," Michel replied dryly.

Chance blinked with surprise. "But why?"

"I already told you," Michel replied. "You moved on without me. You and Sassy, both."

278

"Yeah, but..."

"I know, I know." Michel cut him off. "I'm not saying it was justified. I'm just saying that's what I felt. Or at least what I think I felt. I'm still trying to work that all out. Right now all I know is that I threw myself a big pity party and forgot to leave for two years." He paused and took another drag on his cigarette. "Somewhere along the line I created this comfortable fantasy that I was the victim."

"You just described at least half of my life," Chance replied with a wry smile.

"But the sad part is that I actually started to believe it," Michel said.

"So did I," Chance replied. "Life is a lot simpler when you don't have to take responsibility for it."

They lapsed into quiet contemplation for a minute, then Chance leaned forward in his chair.

"Do you want to talk about him now?" he asked.

Michel felt the familiar tightening in his shoulders and chest, but forced himself to relax.

"Yeah, but I don't know what to say," he replied. "I've never known what to say when someone dies." He paused and looked at his glass. "I miss him. Every day." He shrugged to himself. "But how many times can I say that?"

"What do you think about when you think of him?" Chance asked.

Michel closed his eyes and let the feelings wash over him.

"The man he might have been, and how things might have been for us if he'd lived," he said.

"So tell me about that," Chance said.

"That seems kind of weird given the situation," Michel said.

"I don't mind," Chance replied.

Chapter 59

Michel reached out and touched the other side of the bed. The sheets were cool. He lay still for a moment, listening to the quiet, then opened his eyes. Pale light filtered in around the edges of the window shades. He rolled his head to the left and looked at the nightstand clock. It was almost 10 AM.

Wow, he thought, sitting up. He yawned and stretched, scanning the bedroom floor for Chance's clothes. Though he still felt physically and emotionally drained, he also felt surprisingly relaxed. He pushed to his feet and shuffled to the bathroom.

Thank God I feel better than I look, he thought, as he flipped on the light and blinked at himself in the mirror.

He emptied his bladder, splashed water on his face, and walked to the kitchen. A note lay in front of the coffeemaker.

I decided to stop using you as an excuse for not packing (I had a "moment of clarity" last night, too). Call me later. Dinner, maybe? By the way, I kidnapped Blue. Your cell phone's been blowing up all morning, so I figured you were going to have a busy day.

— Chance

Michel gave a tired smile. He felt the coffee pot and decided it was still warm enough, then poured himself a mug and headed for the patio. It was the first time he'd been completely alone in the house since Blue had come to live with him, and the stillness was both relaxing and slightly disconcerting.

He unlocked the door and stepped outside. The air was still surprisingly cool and fresh against his bare skin. He grabbed his phone and cigarettes from the table, and sat on the edge of the fountain. As he checked the call log, he pulled a cigarette from the pack and lit it. There'd been one call from Sassy, and four from Carl DeRoche, the first at 7:15 AM.

He hit speed-dial for Sassy, but the call went straight to voicemail. He flipped the phone shut without leaving a message. The world could wait, he decided, as he sipped his coffee. He wasn't ready to give up the moment yet.

Chapter 60

"You look like hell," Carl DeRoche said.

"Rough night," Michel replied.

"And morning?" DeRoche replied.

"Morning was okay," Michel said. "Once I finally woke up."

DeRoche gave a vague smile, then nodded to one of the chairs on the other side of his desk. Michel dropped into it.

"I owe you and Sassy an apology," DeRoche began right away. "You should never have been put in that position."

"It was our choice," Michel replied. "Or mine, anyway."

"But you didn't have all the facts," DeRoche said.

Michel gave him a questioning look.

"You were reinstated because that's what Trish Taylor requested, but a friend in Internal Affairs told me they'd set up a parallel investigation of their own," DeRoche said.

"Internal Affairs? That doesn't make any sense," Michel replied. "Why would they get involved?"

"The new Deputy Superintendent came up through IA," DeRoche explained. "He put a few of his old team members on it. It was strictly off-the-record."

"So if something got fucked up, Sassy and I would be the ones with our asses in the fire," Michel finished the thought.

DeRoche shrugged. "That would be my guess. I'm sorry. I should have let you know what was going on."

"Well, at least it's nice to know the other team wasn't working for you," Michel said, then cocked an eyebrown. "So where do we stand now that I killed Rhodes?"

"Under other circumstances, I'm sure we'd all be feeling pretty crispy by now, but as soon as word got out that Trish might have covered up Damian Pope's murder, her 'friends' started distancing themselves."

"You think she might face charges?" Michel asked, surprised.

"Doubtful." DeRoche shook his head. "Pope was killed in Massachusetts, and she's still got plenty of juice up there."

"But what about Angel Peterson's murder?" Michel asked.

"There's no evidence she knew about it," DeRoche replied.

Given what he'd learned about Rhodes's compulsion to share with his mother, Michel doubted that was the case, but knew there'd be no way to prove it unless Trish came clean.

"So it's all over?" he asked.

"It appears that way," DeRoche replied.

Michel frowned. "It's too bad we'll never know exactly what happened," he said.

"Actually we already know quite a bit," DeRoche said. "Or at least Bell's version of it. He wrote it all down in a notebook we found under the mattress at the funeral parlor."

Michel straightened in his chair. "And?"

"He and Rhodes had a pretty twisted relationship," DeRoche said. "Rhodes found out that Bell had a fear of death, and offered to 'cure him' by teaching him to control it."

"Through killing?"

DeRoche nodded. "And in exchange, Bell fulfilled Rhodes's craving for discipline."

Michel raised his eyebrows. "You mean sexually?"

"Yes and no," DeRoche replied. "According to Bell, there was no sex, but Rhodes got off on being restrained and punished. Bell just played along."

Michel nodded. Though it was an unexpected twist, it fit what they knew about Bell, and cast Rhodes's attempts to provoke his mother in a disturbing new light. He wondered whether any lives would have been saved if Trish had just spanked Rhodes as a kid.

"Angel Peterson's murder was essentially a test run," DeRoche continued. "Rhodes did the killing while Bell watched, then they both buried the body in the DeSoto National Forest."

"Any idea where?" Michel asked.

"Unfortunately, no, but we've alerted the authorities in Mississippi, and they're going to do a search."

Michel nodded. "And what happened with Ellis?"

"He was supposed to be Bell's kill, but Bell couldn't go through with it," DeRoche replied. "He tried to stab him a dozen or so times, but just punctured the skin. Finally Rhodes got angry and finished Ellis off himself. That's when the relationship ruptured."

"Because Rhodes threatened to kill Bell's sister," Michel said.

"And because Bell found out about Rachel Davis' and Jesse Woods' murders," DeRoche said. "That was never part of the plan. Bell paid Bobby Lee Collins and Clay Bettis to dispose of Ellis's body, but they decided to rape the Davis girl on their own." He grimaced. "She apparently wouldn't beg the way they wanted, so things escalated and they killed her. They were bragging about it when they showed up at the funeral parlor to pick up Ellis's body."

"Jesus," Michel said, shaking his head sadly.

"Bell snapped after they left," DeRoche continued. "He beat Rhodes unconscious and locked him up, then called the State Police with a tip about the body in the Airstream."

Though they'd gotten the basic relationship between Rhodes and Bell completely wrong, Michel realized he and Sassy had fit most of the individual pieces together correctly. He tried to remember if there were any other loose ends.

"What about the ransom note?" he asked finally.

"Rhodes just wanted to fuck with his mother," DeRoche replied. "Get her worrying about the Bea Bell connection. He sent the package to a friend in Atlanta last Wednesday, with instructions to overnight it to Boston on Saturday. Obviously he wasn't expecting his mother to be here."

Michel murmured agreement. "Sassy thought he might have underestimated how much Trish cared about him," he said, "but I think Bell just fucked up the plans. If he hadn't called the State Police, Ellis's body would be somewhere between here and Tulsa right now, and Trish would still be in Boston thinking Rhodes was just playing games." He gave a wry, tired smile, then stood and pulled the black leather badge holder from inside his jacket. "I believe this belongs to you," he said, tossing it on the desk.

DeRoche stared at it for a moment, then motioned Michel back into the chair.

Chapter 61

Michel pulled to the curb in front of his house and turned off the engine, but didn't get out. He was still trying to absorb his conversation with DeRoche. He lit a cigarette and put his head back, absently watching the smoke curl up and flatten into a haze across the truck's ceiling.

A sharp rap on the passenger door startled him, and he jerked his head so quickly that he felt momentarily dizzy. He stared open-mouthed at the face framed in the open window for several seconds before realizing it belonged to Trish Taylor. He reached slowly toward his belt, then remembered his gun was in the lockbox inside the house.

"If I were planning to kill you, I wouldn't have bothered to knock," Trish said brusquely, opening the door.

She stepped up on the running board and slid onto the bench seat. Michel noticed she was wearing well-worn Levis, as though she'd planned to spend the afternoon in a pickup truck. She yanked the door shut, lit a cigarette, and took off her sunglasses. Her eyes were swollen and red, but focused.

"I'm sorry," Michel said, unsure what else to say.

Trish studied his face for a few seconds, then nodded. "I think you really mean that," she said, "though I don't know why. From what the police told me, you didn't have much choice. In any case, I didn't come here looking for an apology."

Michel tried to read her tone, but couldn't.

"If you don't want an apology and you're not going to shoot me, then why *are* you here, Mrs. Taylor?" he asked.

"I think you can call me Trish now, don't you?" Trish replied. "And I'll call you Michel."

Michel nodded uneasily.

"As for why I'm here," Trish went on, "because you strike me as a man who takes his work personally, Michel."

Michel nodded again, wondering where she was headed.

"Some people might find that an admirable trait," Trish continued. "I find it to be tiresome. People who take their work personally tend to be zealous. They won't let things go, and they worry about trivial matters like compromising their integrity."

"I think you've spent a little too much time around politics," Michel replied dryly.

Trish gave him a patronizing smile. "Compromise is what makes the world go around, cupcake," she said.

"So is that why you're here?" Michel asked. "You're hoping for some kind of compromise? Maybe convince me to walk away now instead of trying to prove that you covered up Damian Pope's and Angel Peterson's murders?"

Trish didn't respond. Michel gave her a thin smile.

"Well, I hate to disappoint you, Trish," he said, "but I honestly don't give a shit about you anymore. I've already moved on."

Trish flinched slightly, but her expression remained placid.

"For how long?" she asked. "A week? A month?"

Michel knew she was probably right, but wouldn't give her the satisfaction of admitting it.

"So what are you offering me?" he asked. "A bribe?" He shook his head. "I don't need your money."

"I'm aware of that," Trish replied, "and I'm not offering a bribe. I'm offering you the truth."

Michel let out a harsh laugh.

"The truth? Why would I believe anything you tell me now? You've been lying to me since we met."

"What do you have to lose?" Trish shrugged. "Listen to what I have to say, then decide for yourself if it's the truth."

Though he didn't trust her, Michel was intrigued. He decided to test her right away.

"Did you know Cam killed Damian Pope?" he asked.

"Yes," Trish replied without hesitation.

"When?" Michel asked.

"I suspected it wasn't a suicide right away," Trish replied, "but Cam didn't tell me he killed Damian until a few weeks later, when we were on the Cape."

"Why did you suspect it wasn't suicide?" Michel asked.

"Because Damian wasn't the type to kill himself," Trish replied. "He embraced life. He was ambitious and curious and engaged. He wasn't just passing time."

Michel furrowed his brow, wondering if the last comment had been directed at him.

"It sounds like you actually liked him," he said, "but your husband told me you didn't trust him."

"I adored Damian," Trish said. "Everyone who met him did. He was very special. But I worried because I knew Cam was in love, and I was afraid how he'd react when he realized Damian would never love him back in the same way."

"Because Damian was straight," Michel said.

"It certainly seemed that way to me," Trish replied, "and Scott thought so, too."

Michel nodded.

"Why didn't you go to the police when you found out what had happened?" he asked.

"Cam may have been a monster," Trish replied, "but he was still my son, and I loved him. I thought that if I got him help, he'd be able to control his impulses again."

"Again?"

Trish quickly lowered her eyes. Michel wondered if it was just for effect.

"There were some problems when he was younger," she said after a long pause, but didn't elaborate.

Michel decided it didn't matter.

"So what kind of help did you get him after he killed Damian?" he asked.

"I committed him to a psychiatric hospital for evaluation," Trish replied with a matter-of-fact smile.

Michel remembered the story Scott Taylor had given about the cause of the rift between his wife and stepson.

"So then it wasn't actually rehab?" he asked.

Trish shook her head.

"How did you manage to keep that from your husband?" Michel asked.

He saw a flicker of irritation in Trish's eyes.

"You and Scott seem to have chatted quite a bit," she said.

"Just once," Michel said. "He was trying to convince me that you're not a cold-hearted bitch."

He gave an insincere smile to indicate it hadn't worked.

"The hospital offers a variety of in-patient programs," Trish said. "It wasn't very difficult to hide the truth from Scott. Or from the papers." She took a drag on her cigarette, and exhaled into a tired sigh. "I was hoping that the doctors would realize Cam was unstable, but they decided he was just suffering from depression, gave him some new drugs, and sent him home."

"And you let them?" Michel exclaimed.

"What choice did I have?" Trish asked. "The only way I could keep him committed was to tell the truth about what he'd done, and I couldn't do that."

"For his sake or yours?" Michel asked.

"Both, I suppose," Trish replied, "but also for Scott. We'd already discussed the possibility of running for office, and I knew what the scandal would do. I wanted to protect him."

"So much for that," Michel replied.

"We'll see," Trish replied opaquely.

Michel arched his eyebrows, but Trish seemed not to notice.

"For a few years, things were fine," she went on. "It was almost as if the whole thing never happened, and I thought that maybe the drugs were actually helping him."

"Until he killed Angel Peterson," Michel said.

"I didn't know who the boy was, but yes, Cam emailed me a picture." Trish wrapped her arms across her chest, as though she'd just felt a chill wind. "I called and tried to convince him to come home, but he wouldn't. He told me the feeling had passed again, and promised it was over. I believed...or convinced myself...that everything was going to be okay, at least for a while. I thought I had time to figure out how to deal with him. Then he disappeared."

Michel realized that with anyone else he might feel some degree of sympathy, but for Trish he felt only contempt.

"So you hired me," he said.

"I was hoping you'd be able to find him before he did anything else," Trish said with a nod.

"And if I had?"

"I'd made arrangements," Trish replied. "He would have been in a safe place."

Michel decided not to push for details.

"Why me?" he asked instead.

Trish hesitated for just a split second before answering.

"Because I was told you were competent, and based on my research, it seemed you'd be well-suited to the job."

"Because I'm gay?"

"And because of what happened to your boyfriend," Trish replied. "I assumed you'd jump at the chance to try to save another poor unfortunate boy."

Michel felt blood pounding in his temples, but fought to keep his expression neutral.

"I said I'd tell you the truth," Trish said. She took a last drag on cigarette and threw it out the window, then pulled an envelope from her purse and laid in on the seat between them. "Unfortunately, you weren't quite as easy to manipulate as I'd hoped, and Cam moved more quickly that I'd expected."

Michel stared at the envelope for a few seconds as he tried to get his anger under control.

"I thought you said you weren't going to bribe me," he said finally.

"It's not a bribe," Trish replied. "It's payment."

"Most clients wait until I bill them," Michel said curtly.

"I don't believe in leaving debts unsettled," Trish replied.

She cracked the door open, and twisted toward it.

"Why did you tell me all this?" Michel asked abruptly.

Trish paused and looked back over her shoulder, then shrugged. "You can't prove any of it, and at least a dozen witnesses will swear this conversation couldn't have taken place because I never left the hotel this afternoon."

"But you said it yourself," Michel said. "I take my job personally. Why risk it? You don't strike me as the guilty conscience type, so what in it for you?"

For a moment Trish's expression was flat, then she fluttered her lashes and smiled with curdled sweetness.

"Because I'm told that every cop has one case they can't forget," she almost purred. "One that haunts them for the rest of their lives because they know they failed. I want to make sure this is *that* case for you. I want to make sure you know that I covered up Damian's murder, and that four innocent people died as a result, and that there's nothing you can do about it."

Michel was stunned speechless.

"You killed my son, Michel," Trish continued coolly, though hatred flashed in her eyes, "and whether it was justified or not, I'll never forgive you for that."

She stepped out of the truck and brushed the creases from the front of her jeans.

"By the way, I'm checking myself into rehab," she said, her tone suddenly chatty and relaxed, as though the previous few seconds hadn't happened. "According to unnamed sources, I've fallen off the wagon. In fact, it seems that I've been secretly drinking for several years."

She opened her purse, took out another Marlboro 100, and lit it with her thin silver lighter.

"Poor Scott had no idea, of course," she continued, "but after what happened with Cam, I've suffered a complete breakdown and he's discovered the truth. He'll still have to pull out of the Senate race, but I'll grant him a divorce in a few months, then he can start fresh. It will be a great way to build sympathy for him."

*****

Michel finished his third cigarette, and stubbed it out in the truck's ashtray. His mind was still spinning, but he felt calmer. He took out his phone and dialed Carl DeRoche.

Chapter 62

"It was like she came to pick a scab I didn't even know I had yet," Michel said.

"I would have slapped her," Sassy replied.

Michel chuckled, sipped iced tea. The late afternoon sun felt good on his face.

"Amazingly, she kind of crystalized things for me," he said.

"How so?"

Michel lit a cigarette and blew the smoke away from Sassy.

"The Captain offered to reinstate me permanently this morning," he said.

Sassy didn't even try to hide her disapproval.

"So when do you start?"

"I don't," Michel replied. "I called right after Trish left and turned him down."

Sassy cocked the bare trace of an eyebrow.

"Why?"

"Like I said, she kind of crystallized things for me," Michel replied. "I mean, she and Butch Ryan were right. For too many cops, the end is just about regrets and reliving failures. They spend so much of their lives dealing with pain that it becomes part of them. It was worse when we were on the force, but even now, nobody hires me because something good is happening. It's because they think they're being cheated on, or someone's missing, or they're being blackmailed. Why would I want to wallow in that for the rest of my life?"

"Because it's an obsession?" Sassy replied.

"Right," Michel said. "An obsession that will turn me into a bitter piece of shit like Ryan, or leave me with no one to take care of me like Al." He shook his head. "I don't need it."

Sassy pursed her lips and studied his face.

"Amen to that," she said finally, "but do you really think you can walk away from it?"

"Yeah, I really do," Michel replied. "At least for now. Maybe someday I'll feel the need to play hero again, but right now, I just want some peace."

"So you're going to become one of those ladies who lunch?" Sassy asked.

"I don't know about that," Michel replied. "I was thinking I might just become one of those queens who works out."

Sassy looked him up and down.

"I'm not seeing it," she said.

"Yeah, probably not," Michel agreed, "but maybe I'll try doing a sit-up in between cocktails. The point is, I can do whatever I want now."

"You always could," Sassy replied.

Michel shook his head.

"I wasn't ready. In a lot of ways."

Sassy nodded thoughtfully.

"So where do things stand with Chance now?" she asked.

"We had a long talk last night," Michel said.

"And?"

"And I'm sorry," Michel said.

"For what?" Sassy asked.

"For blaming you for everything that's happened between us," Michel replied. "I realize it wasn't you. I kept trying to push you away, and you finally let me go when you got too sick to hold on anymore."

Sassy gave him a gentle smile, then frowned.

"Yes and no," she said.

Michel's brow creased.

"That was how it began," Sassy said, "but once I let you go,

I realized it was easier not having you there, so I kept you away, and then I began to push Russ and Corey and Pearl away, too."

"But why?" Michel asked.

"Because you were the ones I knew it would be hardest to leave, and I thought it would make it less painful when it was time to say goodbye. It was sort of a preemptive strike."

Michel regarded her skeptically for a moment, then let out a brittle laugh.

"Since when do you steal from my playbook?" he asked. "That's the sort of dumb shit I pull, cutting myself off from anything good so it won't hurt as much when it's gone."

"I didn't say it was a smart idea," Sassy replied dryly, "but it made sense at the time."

Michel immediately recognized the irony that he and Sassy had both cut themselves off from the people they loved most in misguided attempts at self-protection.

"But what about Chance?" he asked. "I know you were still talking with him. And Al and the Captain."

Sassy nodded.

"Al and the Captain are friends, but they're not family, and Chance was different. Talking with him never made me sad."

Michel felt a small twinge of both jealousy and guilt, but pushed it back.

"There's something I want to ask you," he said instead.

Sassy's eyes grew wary, but she nodded for him to continue.

"I heard what you said to Frankie Bell," Michel said, "about the uncertainty, and dying in your own piss, shit, and vomit, but I still don't understand why getting sick was so much more terrifying than being shot or stabbed. You've been a lot closer to dying before."

"For one thing, bullet and stab wounds don't come back," Sassy joked. "Once you survive them the first time, you're pretty much in the clear." Then her expression turned serious, and she studied her hands for a moment before continuing. "I guess because I didn't have a chance to be scared when those things happened. At least not the same way." She considered it, then nodded to herself. "Hell, I wasn't even conscious after MacDonald shot me, and only woke up long enough to shoot the fucker when Drew Clement gutted me."

"But what about Joshua Clement?" Michel asked. "He had you tied up for two days. You knew he might kill you."

"Yeah, but it was out of my hands, and I knew that whatever happened, that would be it. He'd let me go, or he'd kill me, and that would be the end," Sassy said, then smiled ruefully. "Of course I wasn't counting on him shooting me in the leg and setting the house on fire, but when it happened, there was no time to be scared. I just knew that if I wanted to survive, I had to drag my fat ass down those stairs."

Michel nodded, then frowned.

"That's the part that's the hardest for me to understand," he said. "You've always dragged yourself down the stairs, or woken up in time to kill the bad guy, or just picked yourself up and moved on with your life. You've never just given up before."

Sassy straightened in her chair, and her body stiffened.

"It sounds like Mr. Turner's been telling tales out of school," she said.

"He wasn't telling tales," Michel said evenly. "He stopped by because he thought your panic attack might have been caused by something that happened while we were together. He was just being a responsible and caring husband."

Sassy looked only slightly mollified.

"So is it true?" Michel asked. "Did you really give up?"

Sassy stared at him without blinking for a long time, then gave a slight nod.

"For a few days."

"Why?" Michel asked.

Sassy looked at Blue lying in the shade in by the fountain. A quick, wistful smile played across her lips, then she let out a profound sigh.

"Because the cancer was different. It was my own body

turning against me," she said, her voice softer, almost meditative. "I've seen what that's like, and it still scares the shit out of me." She sipped her iced tea, then quietly added, "And it was different because there was...*is*...no guarantee that it won't come back."

"And there are guarantees that you won't get hit by a truck tomorrow, either," Michel said.

"Thanks a lot," Sassy said.

"Hey, you're the one who's always telling me to stop waiting for guarantees," Michel replied. "Besides, there's something to be said for the whole 'Rage, rage against the dying of the light' thing. That's the Sassy I've always known."

Sassy smiled.

"Don't you worry," she said. "Sassy's definitely got her rage back. If they didn't get all of it, or it comes back, I'll be kicking some cancer ass. I'll be like Xena, Cancer Warrior Princess."

Michel gave her a deadpan look.

"And still you say you're not a lesbian." He reached out and squeezed her hand. "Good. Now that I've got you back, I'm not going to let you go again."

"Just like I expected," Sassy said, shaking her head in mock exasperation. "Taking over my whole life again."

"Just a little corner," Michel replied.

They were both quiet for a few minutes, then Sassy gasped.

"What?" Michel said anxiously.

"If you're retiring, we can close the office," Sassy said, her eyes wide as though she'd just had a startling revelation.

She watched for the flicker of panic in Michel's eyes, then laughed.

"Okay, we can leave it open for a few months until you get used to the idea," she said, "but I'm taking your keys. I don't want you being like one of those crazy moths that keeps flitting back to the lightbulb until it finally fries his ass."

Chapter 63

Sassy sat waiting in the living room. She heard heavy footsteps coming fast down the stairs, and pushed to her feet.

"Corey!" she yelled.

Corey stopped halfway to the front door, but didn't turn.

"Where are you going?" Sassy asked.

"Out," Corey muttered.

"That remains to be seen," Sassy replied. "Get in here."

Corey hesitated a moment, then sighed elaborately and turned around. He took three grudging steps forward.

"What?"

"Empty your pockets," Sassy said.

"What?" Corey repeated, this time in disbelief.

"You heard me. Empty them," Sassy said.

Corey sighed again, but dug into his front pockets. He pulled out a few crumpled bills, some coins, and a Chapstick. He held them out for a few seconds, then flipped his hands. The coins and Chapsticks bounced and chattered on the hard wood floor.

"Now the back pockets," Sassy said, not missing a beat.

Corey made a show of checking both pockets, then came out with just a wallet in his right hand. Again, he dropped it to the floor. Sassy fought the urge to slap him.

"And now the cigarettes," she said calmly.

"I don't have any cigarettes," Corey replied.

"Boy, do not make me throw your narrow ass against the wall and frisk you," Sassy said, taking a step closer.

Corey's face immediately went blank, though his eyes still blazed as they locked on a spot somewhere above Sassy's head. It was the same look of wounded dignity that Sassy had seen from hundreds of young black men she'd arrested over the years, and it broke her heart that Corey had already learned it, and that she was the cause of it now.

She took a silent deep breath, and held out her right hand. Corey continued staring straight ahead for almost a minute, then his eyes flicked down. He reached under his oversized white t-shirt and pulled a pack of Marlboro Reds from the waistband of his shorts. He placed them in Sassy's hand.

"Thank you," she said, feeling both relief and sadness.

She put the pack in her pocket and waited until Corey looked up at her again.

"If I ever see you with another cigarette, or smell smoke on you again," she said, "there are going to be consequences."

"What are you going to do? Tell Dad?" Corey asked, the challenge still not entirely gone from his voice.

"I don't need to tell your father," Sassy replied evenly. "This is my house, too, and as long as you're living here, you're going to follow both our rules. And you're going to start showing me some respect."

She looked at him expectantly. He shrugged.

"I'm sorry," Sassy said. "I didn't hear that."

"Yes, ma'am," Corey replied in a tight voice, his lips barely moving. "Is that all?"

Sassy studied his face for a moment, then shook her head. She took a step forward and wrapped her arms around him. His body stiffened.

"I'm sorry I got sick," Sassy said quietly, "and I'm sorry if you thought I didn't love you anymore, because I do love you. As much as if I'd given birth to you. It's just that I was scared, and I didn't know what to do. I'm not used to being scared, you understand?"

Corey's body relaxed a little.

"I can't promise you that it's all over," Sassy continued, "but I promise I'm not going away easily, no matter what happens. I want to stick around so I can get all up in your business for a long time. Long enough to see you with pain-in-the-ass kids of your own. Okay?"

Corey didn't reply, but his arms came up and gently hugged Sassy back. Sassy closed her eyes and smiled. She knew it was only a temporary reprieve at best, but wanted to enjoy the moment. Finally she let go and took a step back.

"Good, now get out of my house," she blustered. "I'm tired of always having children underfoot. I can't even get any peace."

Corey let out a surprisingly childlike giggle. He stooped to pick up his things, and stuffed them back in his pockets.

"And don't even think about being late for dinner," Sassy said, following him to the door. "And you need to find a job for the summer."

"Yes, ma'am," Corey replied with just a trace of an eyeroll.

Sassy watched him go down the walk, then shut the door and turned toward the kitchen.

"How long have you been lurking in there?" she asked.

Russ Turner stepped into the doorway.

"What gave me away?"

"I could smell the cookies on your breath," Sassy said.

"Long enough," Turner said, with a chuckle. He cocked an eyebrow. "You know that wasn't the last of it, right?"

"I'd be disappointed if he gave up on being a teenager that easily," Sassy replied, with a resigned grimace. "I just want to make sure he hates me for the right reasons. And that he knows I won't put up with any more shit."

"Sounds like I've got my Sassy back," Turner laughed.

"Which means you better not step out of line, either, old man," Sassy teased.

"Yes, ma'am," Turner replied. He kissed Sassy, then fixed her with a mock reproachful look. "But you *were* going to tell me about those cigarettes, right?"

"Of course," Sassy said, smiling sweetly. "Right after you told me about your conversation with Michel last Friday."

Chapter 64

Chance walked out onto the patio. Michel was sitting in his usual chair, smoking, a glass of Jack Daniels cradled in his right hand. Blue dozed a few feet to his right.

"What are you doing?" Chance asked.

"Just having a good sit," Michel replied.

Chance wrinkled his nose.

"Want to join me?" Michel asked.

Chance gave him a dubious look, but took the other chair. His eyes roamed the patio restlessly for a minute before settling back on Michel.

"So what's this good sit all about?" he asked.

"Just a chance to relax and reflect," Michel said.

"And we're doing this why?" Chance asked, making a face.

Michel considered it a moment, then laughed.

"Tradition?" he tried.

"Gee, and all those times Joel called you a freak, I thought he meant in the bedroom," Chance said.

"I can only imagine your disappointment," Michel replied.

Chance gave a small, grudging smile. He lit a cigarette, sipped his drink, and looked up into the night sky.

"Do you think he'd be okay with this?" he asked suddenly. "Whatever *this* is."

"I think so," Michel said. "I hope so. He loved us both. I think he'd want us to be happy."

"So does that mean you're happy?" Chance asked, cutting a cautious sideways glance.

"Yeah, I am," Michel replied without hesitating. "What about you?"

Chance stared down at the flagstones for a few seconds, then nodded.

"Oddly enough, yeah."

"I'm underwhelmed by your enthusiasm," Michel said.

"That's not what I meant," Chance said. "I just never expected it to happen, you know?"

"Yeah, me neither," Michel said.

He almost added, "but I'm glad it did," then realized that wasn't right. Though he was grateful for another chance, he still wished every day that Joel were still alive.

"I'm going up to Bayou Proche to visit my father at the end of August," he said. "You want to come up for a few days before school begins?"

"With or without pants?" Chance asked.

"Probably a little of both."

"I don't know," Chance said with mock seriousness. "That's a big step. Inviting me home to meet your father?"

"It's not home, and it's just a vacation," Michel replied. "It's not like I'm asking you to marry me."

"Good thing," Chance replied, "because I'm way too young to get married."

Michel fluttered his eyelashes as though momentarily stunned, then began laughing.

"Right, but *I'm* the one who's disconnected from reality," he said.

Epilogue

February 2009

Michel placed two red roses on the oak casket, and turned away. He didn't want to see the body lowered into the ground.

Most of the mourners were still gathered in small clusters near the cars, chatting in hushed, respectful tones. Butch Ryan held ostentatiously somber court to a small group of men in full dress uniform, nearer to the grave. Michel skirted them, offering just a cursory nod to Ryan, and scanned the far side of the roadway. He spotted Chance standing with Russ Turner in the shade of a cottonwood tree.

"I didn't expect to see you here today," he said, as he walked up and shook Turner's hand.

"I came to pay Sassy's respects to Al," Turner replied.

"I placed a rose on the coffin for her," Michel replied.

"She'll appreciate that," Turner said.

"So how is she?" Michel asked.

"A little better today," Turner replied. "She slept though the night, and was able to eat a little breakfast."

Michel's throat tightened, but he swallowed and took a deep breath against it.

"And what about emotionally?" he asked.

"Good," Turner replied, the naked optimism in his smile reassuring Michel more than the word.

"Do you think it would be okay if we stopped over?" Michel asked. "Just for a few minutes?"

A shadow crossed Turner's face, then he seemed to catch himself, and nodded enthusiastically.

"I'm sure she'd like that a lot," he said.

Made in the USA
Las Vegas, NV
19 December 2020

14161513R00182